Praise for
Gillian Roberts and
her Amanda Pepper mysteries!

Caught Dead in Philadelphia
"Roberts provides a story that quickly engages the reader. . . .Her writing sparkles with warmth and humor."
—*The Virginian-Pilot & the Ledger-Star*

Philly Stakes
"Entertaining . . . Amanda never loses her sense of humor, and her upbeat narration gives the story its breezy verve."
—*San Francisco Chronicle*

I'd Rather Be in Philadelphia
"Literate, amusing and surprising, while at the same time spinning a crack whodunit puzzle."
—*Chicago Sun-Times*

With Friends Like These . . .

Gillian Roberts

BALLANTINE BOOKS • NEW YORK

Copyright © 1993 by Judith Greber

All rights reserved under International and Pan-American Copyright Conventions. Published in the United States of America by Ballantine Books, a division of Random House, Inc., New York, and simultaneously in Canada by Random House of Canada Limited, Toronto.

Library of Congress Catalog Card Number: 92-97480

ISBN 0-345-37784-2

Manufactured in the United States of America

First Hardcover Edition: August 1993
First Mass Market Edition: September 1994

10 9 8 7 6 5 4 3 2 1

For Jean Naggar
—volumes of affection and
appreciation

One

It was a dark and stormy night. Honestly. Earlier, it had been a dim and stormy day. Demonstrating no originality, March had indeed come in like a lion—a wet, angry one who blew ill winds every which way.

And here I was, not home cuddling by the fire with whatever was available—a man, a cat, a book—but driving in the rain with my mother, wearing my sister's panty hose and fulfilling social obligations that were not mine.

I clutched the steering wheel and thought about the difficulty of raising parents, particularly mine, particularly today.

My father had overreacted, overprotected, and overparented me into this pickle. Generally speaking, my father is so quiet that any woman near him (namely my mother) gets the urge to scream, simply to compensate for the sound deficit. His favorite way of interacting with the women of his family is from behind the shelter of his newspaper.

All the same, this afternoon some late blooming swashbuckler hormone kicked into his system and he suffered an attack of galloping, completely unnecessary heroism. As a result he lost his mobility and I lost my Sunday night.

* * *

WE HAD ALL BEEN IN MY SISTER'S LIVING ROOM, ENDURING THE sometimes elusive pleasures of a Long Parental Visit. Bea and Gilbert Pepper, a.k.a. Mom and Dad, had arrived four days earlier. Since then I'd been puzzling how to once and for all establish the concept that I was not willing to be a child for as long as Gilbert and Bea were willing to be parents—i.e., forever, i.e., right now.

It was hard pondering this delicate issue or anything else in the din of family. Everyone—except my father—talked at once, and the chatter was compounded by background music: my niece Karen's recording of Mother Goose done rap style. I remembered how unfond I had once been of the endless, enclosed hours of Sundays, and I remembered why.

I allocated twenty more minutes to this visit, by which time my exit wouldn't seem abrupt or overeager. The good thing about teaching English is that the bad thing about teaching English—endless papers to mark—provides a perpetual excuse to split.

Once I knew there was a definite reprieve ahead, I relaxed and tuned back into the conversation.

"I do hope the messenger delivered the gift in time," my mother was saying. "I've never done this before." She had read, in *People* magazine, of tributes arriving via messenger, and had decided that was the appropriate style when gifting a Somebody. Apparently, the host of the party she was attending tonight fit that category. "And not too soon," she continued. "What if it arrives before Lyle gets there? Would the hotel accept it?"

Everybody murmured reassurances, just as everybody had fifteen minutes earlier, the last time she'd worried over the matter. Only Karen, dancing to her barked-out rhymes, seemed unconcerned.

My Floridian parents had braved the last gasps of a Philadelphia winter to attend the fiftieth birthday party of a man they said was an old friend, but whose name I'd never heard. I don't keep close tabs on my parents' social life, but the invitation confused me, particularly since the birthday boy had sent them their airline tickets and was treating

~~them~~—~~and~~ all his other out-of-town ~~guests~~—to rooms at the small hotel where the party would be held.

I was amazed by this stranger's largesse, so that now, when the conversation again veered toward the party, I poked around for more information. "Mom," I said, "explain why I've never heard of Lyle Zacharias."

"I told you," my mother said. "We've been out of touch for a long time."

About then my niece yelped. That's all it was, a minor blip, a five-year-old's reaction to bumping an unimportant body part on the coffee table.

But my father must have heard something primitive, a summons. He levitated, saying "Whooah!" or "Oh, woe!" and frantically, as if Karen were sinking into quicksand with only her teensy nose still poking out, he attempted to swing—without benefit of a vine—across the room to rescue his granddamsel in distress.

There were suddenly a lot of other sounds, too. Karen's infant brother, Alexander, keened. Their mother, my sister Beth, said, "Dad?" My mother said, "Gilbert! What on earth are you—" and even I stood and cried, futilely, "Watch out!" Only Karen, her bump forgotten, said nothing whatsoever. She was too busy boogying again.

Meanwhile, half of my father landed on one of her former musical selections and, almost immediately, his swash buckled. Down onto a pink plastic record went his right foot, skating straight ahead. His left foot, however, stayed put, pending further instructions. The rest of him flailed and looked bewildered, like a cartoon character running on air over a chasm.

The family attempted a save, but by then he'd achieved a split Baryshnikov would envy. He made another, sadder and less heroic "Whooah" and collapsed, the rug-skating leg tilting where it should not.

IT'S AMAZING HOW MUCH TIME AND PLASTER TAPE AND MEDI-cal staff it takes to set a fracture. As wet gray day slid into wetter, darker night, we hobbled back to Beth's house. The party my parents had flown hither to attend loomed.

My mother bit her lower lip and looked like the frantic heroine of a silent film. My father grinned wickedly. His painkillered pupils were pinwheels. A whole new Daddy on dope. I told him he'd look sexy on crutches at the party.

My practical sister—who, being married, had a permanent companion, and who was therefore in no danger of being deputized as Mom's date—reacted immediately. "That little hotel might not have an elevator, Mandy! After all, it used to be a boardinghouse. How would Daddy get to his room?"

"We could call and find out." I was snappish, but only because I knew what was coming. I tried to stop it, but it was as effective as putting a hand up to stop a boulder rolling downhill. "And if there's no elevator, Mom and Dad can come back here tonight."

"Gilbert," my mother said. "Lyle wants you, not me, at his party. He wasn't part of my family."

Did that mean, then, that this Lyle person, this Somebody, was a secret part of my father's family? The black sheep? That sounded almost interesting. "Who *is* this man?" I asked again.

My father beamed. Sedated, he was more placidly impervious to female noises than ever. I couldn't believe my mother wanted to be accompanied by a space cadet, but the need for an escort has made lots of women drop their standards.

"He's a producer." My mother tossed the words my way. An answer, I realized. Lyle the mystery man was a producer.

My mother's attention was again wholly on my father. "Gilbert?" His answer was the downward flutter of his eyelids.

"Broadway?" The word *producer* is so mysterious. What does it mean? What does one do? If it's real, why isn't there a college major called Producing?

"Television." My mother woefully considered her comatose husband.

"What kind of—"

"The Second Generation." Beth looked sheepish. "It's on

every afternoon. Something to do while I'm feeding the baby."

My mother eyed her older daughter with concern.

"Don't worry," Beth said. "Dr. Spock does not object to watching soaps while nursing."

I could almost see my mother scan the Dr. Spock data base in her brain. He'd been her guru, and the final authority during our growing years, and she still idolized him. But we weren't talking about pediatricians. We were talking about producers, and I steered my mother back to the topic.

"Years ago, Lyle had a show on Broadway," she said. "A great big hit. Then it became a TV series, and that's how he got into the field." She turned back to my father, who was awake, but just barely. "We really have to go. Everybody will be there," she said. "And I've already made all those tarts and messengered them."

That was it, I was sure. She'd done a jet-set thing as per *People* magazine, and she wanted—and deserved—the acclaim for both her baking and her au courant presentation. Tarts seemed poor reasons for dragging a semiconscious man on crutches to a party, but as I knew who his stand-in was likely to be, I said nothing.

"The queen of hearts, she made some tarts," Karen chanted. There were collective frowns as we were reminded of her nursery rhyme collection, and in fact, of the infamous pink record that had resulted in this impasse. Karen didn't notice. "All on a summer's day!" she continued. "The knave of hearts, he stole—"

"How can we accept plane tickets from the man and then not go to his party?" my mother asked.

"I didn't ask him to invite me." My father spoke slowly. "You're the one who insisted we accept, even though you didn't like him, either, after. . . ."

"You're too harsh," my mother said. "Be tolerant. Think about how much he's suffered. He's reaching out to us now."

She didn't deny my father's accusation that she disliked Lyle Zacharias. But her overabundant supply of guilt and do-goodness would demand that she celebrate the birth of a man she wasn't fond of, if she thought he'd suffered in some way.

"You go," my father urged.

"Alone?" My mother's jaw dangled. No date for a party?

I deliberately ignored the wide-eyed flares my sister was hurling in my direction. She escalated to a *psst* that I was forced to acknowledge. Behind my mother's back she mouthed, silently, a question. It didn't take long to decipher it, although I wished I hadn't.

She had pantomimed, "Do you have a date tonight?"

I didn't. I was supposed to. We had planned to go to the movies, like normal people. And afterward we were going to buy hoagies stuffed to the brim with saturated animal fats. And after that, who knew?

However, normal people aren't homicide cops, and neither are the folk who keep homicide cops busy. This morning, just before I toodled out to the suburbs for Sunday brunch, C. K. Mackenzie had called in his regrets. Our date was off because it was his turn on the wheel to be assigned, and a fingerless corpse had been found on a brick-littered lot up in The Badlands near Germantown Avenue. Recently, the city has tried quashing drug dealers by demolishing their lairs. The de-digitized corpse had been left on the rubble of a former crack house. Mackenzie would undoubtedly work well past a normal shift.

Philadelphia does not give its police compensatory time off. Instead it pays overtime, which is no time at all. This policy enlarges wallets, shrinks social lives, and allows significant others to experience only the *others* part. After nearly a year of nearly knowing Mackenzie, I was still much fonder of him than of his job, and I still didn't know what to do about it, since the two appeared only in combination.

But the point was, I didn't have what anyone might call a date tonight. As if she had overheard my brain synapses, my mother turned. "Mandy!" she said with an air of discovery. Sometimes I look at my mother and see myself, gently distorted as in, perhaps, a kindly fun-house mirror. She is smaller, rounder, her features not truly mine, but definitely their source. We both have precisely the same auburn hue on our heads, although now hers is mostly chemical. She achieved the match by holding up swatches of my hair—my head still attached—to every box of chestnut, auburn, brown, and red dye in the pharmacy.

Unassisted nature made our eyes the same confused green, which a seriously yuppified acquaintance described as the color of overhandled money. But whatever their tint, there is a horrific optimistic innocence in my mother's eyes that I hope is missing in mine.

"No," I said firmly. "I have things I absolutely must—tomorrow is a workday and I have papers and—"

"It'll be fun."

"Not for me. I'll drive you there, I'll pick you up, but I really don't want to go to—"

"A once in a lifetime chance."

"For what, Mom? Please."

"Show people. Household names."

In my household the names were Amanda and Macavity Pepper, and I already knew them. I shook my head. I'm adulation-challenged. I lack the celebrity-gawking gene, the part of the DNA that makes people line sidewalks and stage doors in hopes of glimpsing a famous face. I don't even understand the urge. And even if I were into such behavior, in this case the household name produced a soap opera I'd never seen. The potential thrill quotient was absent.

"Just for dinner," my mother said. "Okay? We won't even stay late. Who knows? Maybe you'll even meet somebody. Those actors can be very handsome, you know."

I envisioned my mother scanning the room for potential son-in-laws, then climbing on a chair and auctioning off her single daughter-overstock to the highest bidder. The closer I crept to thirty-one—and I was now only days away—the more panic-stricken she became. "Please, Mom!" A whine I thought I'd outgrown along with my training bra was back in my voice. I reminded myself that I was a mature woman with a mind and life of my own.

My mother raised her eyebrows. "I only meant you might meet a man who spends his time with people who

are still alive, unlike your policeman friend." She laughed
warmly, maternally, slyly.

Like I said, she was getting desperate. "I don't know
Lyle Zacharias," I said. "I never heard of him before today.
Whatever your ties to him might be, he's not connected to
me in any—"

"Cindy was Lyle Zacharias's first wife."

I looked at my sister. She looked at me. We both looked
at my mother. My father, on the other hand, looked away.

"Who," Beth and I said in unison, "is Cindy?"

"Cindy." My mother spoke loudly, as if our incompre-
hension was a hearing problem. "Of course you've heard of
her. She was your father's foster sister."

Repetition of the name made it seem dimly familiar, part
of ancient hazy childhood impressions, but nothing more.

"You even met her. They lived in New York and we
didn't see them much, but you did meet her."

"You've never talked about her," I said with awe. Bea
Pepper, the Scheherazade of family gossip, she who trolled
all lines for a nibble twenty-four hours a day, the village
chronicler of Philadelphia, had remained silent about a foster sister of her husband's?

"I'm sure we were invited tonight because we'd be the
only people there who knew Cindy and that time in his life.
A tragic time." She sighed and stopped looming over my
father and, instead, sank onto Beth's chintz-covered love
seat. "Right, Gilbert?" My father appeared to be visiting
outer space, and to be having a good time there.

My mother put her hands up. "He doesn't like to talk
about it." Whenever she is truly upset with my father, she
speaks of him only in pronouns. "Lyle kept a gun in his
house. For protection. They lived in New York, after all.
We told him it was a bad idea, dangerous. Then one day—
it's so horrible—Cindy's little girl found it and killed her
mother with it."

"Accidentally." My father's blissful obliviousness had
been replaced by a perturbed expression. Cindy was making it through the drug barrier. "They have laws some
places for that now. He'd go to jail nowadays for leaving a

gun where a three-year-old child could find it." He shook his head, still appalled.

"When did all of this happen?" Beth asked.

My mother began her infamous circular computations. "Let's see, it was just after Uncle Lewis's seventy-fifth birthday, so when would that be? He and Aunt Gloria had a big anniversary party—their silver—the same day as your first birthday, Mandy, and I remember he married late in life, he was a famous bachelor around town, which means that by then he must have been—"

"For heaven's sake!" my father said. "Cindy died nearly twenty years ago."

When I was ten or eleven. How could I have missed an accidental homicide in my own family? What else could have occupied my attention back then when puberty hadn't even kicked in? Beth looked equally baffled.

"Well, it happened in New York in their home," my mother said. "You barely knew her, anyway. She never lived near us. Besides, you were away at the shore at the time, visiting Grandma. What was the point of going out of our way to tell you terrible news about somebody you didn't even know? Parents are supposed to protect their children from bad things when they can. That's what we did."

I appreciated the sentiment, but I nonetheless felt uncomfortable. Family secrets jutted like hard-edged foreign objects under the smooth skin of our lives.

"What happened to his little girl?" Beth asked softly.

"Betsy?" my mother said. "She wasn't Lyle's, biologically. Cindy was one of those flower children. And then she became one of those flower mothers. The flower father was nowhere to be found."

My father looked away from us, as if he still found Cindy's history embarrassing.

"Did he keep her—the little girl—Betsy, after . . ." Beth's voice dribbled off.

My mother shook her head. "He was all to pieces, beside himself. Hattie, Lyle's aunt, who raised him, took the baby.

Lyle couldn't be around her. Your father and I talked about adopting her."

"Look," my father said, cutting to the chase, "the . . . um, natural father was back from Vietnam by then, and when he found out what had happened, he took Betsy. He wouldn't speak to the family after that."

My mother stood up. "And we weren't so much better. Never really tried to see Lyle after that, poor man."

"He should have kept the baby. Besides, he did fine without us." My father sounded uncharacteristically hostile.

"I hope nobody ever told that little girl what she'd done," Beth said, provoking a long, heavy silence.

My mother finally broke it with a pragmatic return to the issue at hand. "I still think it would be wrong to stay away from his party. He wants so much to make peace finally. Did you see the invitation, girls?" She walked to the hall table and rummaged in her pocketbook, returning with a large, cream square.

At first glance it looked quite standard. Heavy stock with bold engraving. It might have been a wedding invitation, except that it was so verbose, like nothing I'd ever seen before.

Most of life moves double-time, too quickly to see each individual frame or even to make sense of it. But the half-century marker is a time to pause, take stock and seriously consider the course. I'm very excited about my next fifty years as I switch from one rodent image (the rat race) to another (the country mouse).

But now, before I move on, I want to believe that you—and I—*can* go home again. Please join me back where my voyage began, to celebrate the points along the way where our lives touched. You are a part of my story, and I of yours, and the only birthday present I want is a chance to see my life in front of me, whole, in your faces, to heal what needs healing and to drink a toast to auld lang syne.

Beth let go of her half of the invitation. "Forgive me, but I think it's weird," she said. "Slightly creepy. Inappropriate.

Sounds like he has a lot of enemies, for one thing. And then—oh, maybe he just needed an editor, a more careful choice of words. But the way he said it—seeing his life before him—that's not a birthday wish, that's what's supposed to happen to a dying man."

It wasn't like my sister to be morbid, so her words struck with extra impact. Which is not to say they deterred my mother.

"You'll go with me, won't you? It could be awkward," she said to me, "without your father there. It's important."

And because of the need in my mother's eyes, the image of a long-dead flower child and the odd wording of an invitation, I wound up borrowing panty hose and a cocktail dress from my sister and going to a party for a man I didn't know.

And that, in turn, meant that later in the evening I was there to witness it when, just as Beth had suggested, Lyle Zacharias got his wish and saw his life pass before his eyes. Exactly the way a dying man is supposed to.

Two

BASED ON MY DEEP PREJUDICE ABOUT THE GLITZ SET, I WOULD have expected Lyle Zacharias to hold his gala at the Museum of Art—after he had it refurbished to his taste, of course. Certainly something splashier than a former boardinghouse turned into a small hotel in a not superglamorous neighborhood—even if the small hotel had been written up in travel magazines as a place to be.

If I had to go to the party, I wanted it to be more spectacular, even vulgar, so I could sneer. "Why The Boarding House?" I asked as we drove.

"He grew up in Queen Village, across the street from it," my mother answered. "That's where Hattie lived and raised him. And if I recall correctly, when she was a young woman, she lived in the real boardinghouse itself for a while. Or if not that one, another one. Of course, back then we didn't call it Queen Village, just part of South Philly, and it was pretty hardscrabble."

So Lyle's desire to go home again was not pure metaphor. This was half party, half pilgrimage.

The windshield wipers swept back and forth, clearing brief glimpses of street scenes between blurred and aqueous blindness. Driving was difficult and unpleasant and I felt very much the martyr.

I drove past the edges of Society Hill and crossed South

Street, its mix of chic and funk on and off visible, like wet strobe lights.

"Did I really see *that*?" The wipers had cleared a view of a pink awning that stood out even in the rain and dark. "A store called Condom Nation?" My mother's voice squeaked just a bit.

"Clever wordplay, huh?"

"I try to be modern and up-to-date, but honestly . . ." She seemed relieved when the brick row houses became more modest and the stores less outrageous. Even here, however, there were signs of creeping gentrification in the scaffolding around buildings and the flower boxes that matched brightly painted window frames and front doors.

My mother sat low, huddling inside her ancient Persian lamb, as if afraid someone might spot her. She was horrified about wearing fur, but refused to buy a replacement because she had no need of a winter coat in Florida. Beth and I reminded her that lambs were not on the endangered list, but in truth, the particular lamb whose curls my mother wore had most definitely been endangered while becoming a coat, so that argument seemed weak.

Thoughts of the sacrificial lamb made me think again of my father's surprising revelations: a foster sister, a baby, and a terrible accident. The radio played a suitably melancholy song as background to my mulling.

And then an announcer, sounding self-important and solemn, replaced the music. My mother automatically upped the volume. She had become a weather junkie since moving to Boca Raton, and was transfixed by meteorological excesses. Obviously, retired life in Florida didn't offer a whole lot of excitement. "Forty below in Fargo!" she'd exclaim. "I can't believe it! Why, at home it's probably seventy-five or eighty."

It was always seventy-five or eighty at home, even when it was actually a hundred and twelve or in the midst of a hurricane. I guess it meant she was a happy transplant, but I found it hard to take.

"Flash floods from Paoli north," the announcer said, even before getting to world news. My mother rolled her eyes and tsked. Only now with the weatherman's statistical reassurance could she truly believe in the torrential rain pelting the car. She sighed with pleasure. "I'll bet it's hot and sunny at home."

"It's not sunny at night. Even in Florida."

She changed the subject. "I feel bad that I'm not using the room Lyle rented. I hate to waste things." The radio duly reported news of revolt, bloodshed, and inhumanity. My mother turned down the volume.

I had agreed to be my mother's date. I had agreed to wear my sister's black and white beaded dress after I'd tried the excuse that nothing I owned suited champagne and caviar. I had tolerated being allowed back in my house only long enough to feed Macavity, check my silent answering machine, and retrieve my lipstick and black silk shoes. But I drew the line at lingering at the event one minute longer than I had to, and that definitely included sleeping over. The Boarding House's rooms were for Lyle Zacharias's out-of-town guests. I fit neither category. Nonetheless, my mother was disappointed. I suggested, as tactfully as I could, that she was behaving rather cavalierly about my injured father.

"You wouldn't want to leave Dad alone all night, would you?" That was a better argument than the real one, which was that I wanted to be home. There was always the chance that Mackenzie and his pals would find either the killer or the dead man's fingers and call it a night.

"I promised to bring him whatever's delicious. Remind me, okay?" My mother babbled, girlishly excited by the evening, or by being on the town without her husband. "I hope he still likes tarts."

"Daddy? He loves your—"

"Lyle. Years ago, he said they were his idea of heaven, and the only snake in Paradise was sharing them. So I wrote 'No Sharing This Time' on the tag. You think he'll get it? Still remember?"

I hoped so. I also hoped he was so ecstatic about Bea Pepper's tarts that he failed to notice that her daughter had arrived uninvited and empty-handed.

"Otherwise," my mother continued, "what could a person like me give a man like him? Dad thought of it, actually. He said my tarts were one thing Lyle couldn't buy with all his success. I made lemon and cherry-almond and hazelnut-cream and peach-pistachio. Fifty. One for each year. But now I'm wondering: what if he's developed a cholesterol problem, or a weight problem?"

My mother was debating herself and did not require input. The good news was that the hotel was a matter of minutes away, so her festering could not go on indefinitely.

"I'm afraid I packed them too tightly. They're probably all crumbled. If that messenger drove as wildly as some I've seen . . . I put cardboard between the layers, but . . ."

The radio announcer spluttered something about a traffic jam due to a three-alarm fire. It didn't seem possible that anything could burn in this downpour, but weather was my mother's specialty, not mine. I listened carefully, wanting to detour around it, if necessary.

"And what about the tin?" my mother asked her invisible auditor. "Did it seem sick? I thought it was funny in the store, but now . . ."

The tin the messenger had delivered was enormous and black, with silver lettering on its side that said OVER THE HILL. Its main failing was its clichéd predictability, but I didn't tell her that. I was too busy listening. It seemed the fire was just outside the city, in Cheltenham. No problem. And then the location registered.

"The Cavanaugh Hotel had a second life and became something of a local landmark during Prohibition, and will be remembered for . . ."

"Oh, no!" I said. "The hotel!"

"Here? We're there?" my mother asked.

I shook my head. The Cavanaugh Hotel was where Philly Prep was holding its Senior Prom at the very end of May. *Had* been going to hold. Could you rebuild a massive Victorian in seven weeks?

I knew the answer without asking. I also knew the amount of trouble we were going to have finding an alternate site. Poor kids. Between weddings, graduation parties, and proms, nothing suitable would be left to rent.

"You're right! We *are* here!" my mother said with audible delight. And we were, to my surprise. There was even a parking spot not too far from the entry to The Boarding House.

I imagined the building without green awnings and planter boxes filled with forced azalea bushes. I pictured men in handlebar mustaches and muddy boots, and stenographers wearing shields to protect the cuffs of their shirtwaists. Lyle's parents, perhaps, along with his aunt Hattie, who, my mother had explained, had raised him after her brother and his wife both died.

There had been an awful lot of loss in Lyle Zacharias's life, and I could understand my parents' decision to accept his invitation despite their sad associations with the man.

THE ECONOMICS OF BOTH THE BOARDING HOUSE'S GUESTS AND its decor had been upped several social stratifications since its original days. As soon as we opened the door, the sounds of people celebrating their enormous good fortune in having been born themselves flooded us. They were not immediately visible. Instead, we faced a bald and jovial man who sat at a minuscule mahogany desk which constituted the reception area. My mother launched into a lengthy overexplanation of why she wasn't going to sleep in her room. The man at the desk didn't care, but he let her anxious apologies run their course, and then he handed her an enormous brass tag and said to feel free. Whatever. He smiled ever more broadly.

In the parlor to our right, the cheery group burst into laughter, then someone made a toast to Lyle and to birthdays in general. "What, after all, is the alternative?" I heard. The decor, although of a long-ago style, was polished and glowing: dark woods, inlaid or waxed tabletops, garnet velvet upholstery, and richly patterned carpets.

The guests, however, were exceptionally *now*, giving off so much self-assured heat that I knew without looking that all their teeth had been fixed to perfection, their hair lovingly arranged, their bodies toned, their wardrobes brilliantly conceived. I was also sure without checking that these were the TV outlanders from the Big Apple, and I immediately became a proper hick and felt inferior and defensive.

"Look!" my mother whispered. "That one, there, by the fireplace. That's Dr. Sazarac."

"Your doctor's here?"

Her laugh was incredulous. "Not my doctor! He's the doctor on *Second Generation.*"

He was fiftyish and pink-skinned, properly topped with silver hair. Give me a break.

My mother plunged a lamb-covered elbow into my side. "His real name is McCoy. Shepard, but they call him The Real."

"Who *was* the Real McCoy?" I asked.

She waved away my question. "He's single again," she hissed. "I read about his divorce in *Parade* magazine."

"He'd make a better date for you than for me!" Except, of course, she was married and I was not, and that was the sum of it to her.

A woman with a full-length mink coat and none of my mother's fur qualms swept into the vestibule along with a blast of cold air.

Like peasants, my mother and I automatically stepped back, allowing the grande dame free passage. My mother mouthed the woman's name in my direction. I didn't catch it, and I didn't care. Another character from *Second Generation.* "Why don't we get rid of our coats and join the other guests?" I quietly suggested. "Let's at least use our room as a closet."

She looked troubled. "Mother," I whispered. The fur lady, whose perfumed aura was nearly as dense as her mink, registered. "Stop gaping. You're Lyle's guest as much as she is."

"I know I am. What are you talking about?"

"You look so worried, I thought . . . if it's not that, then what's bothering you?"

"My tarts. Where do you think they are?"

I looked to the concierge, but he had bustled off with the mink lady. There did not seem to be a table, as for a wedding, with gifts on it. The out-of-towners making merry in the living room had probably left their offerings upstairs, and in-towners were arriving slowly.

"What if they never got here?" she whispered. "What if they're in a warm place? There's whipped cream on some of them. If they sit out for too long in a heated . . . How could I have let your father talk me into such a troublesome gift?"

My mother's competence had dissolved in the presence of semicelebrities. I half expected her to get the vapors, or to curtsy for the TV contingent. I shook my head and guided her around and behind the staircase. Somewhere there had to be a kitchen, and I was willing to bet Mrs. Pepper's tarts were in that same somewhere.

We went through open double doors that led into a bright and modern, mildly chaotic kitchen. A young and harried-looking man scooped frilly lettuce—a small mountain of it—into enormous plastic containers. "Oh, God!" he kept saying. Then, with a wave to us, he left the room.

There was evidence of prior chopping, peeling, and slicing all over the counters, but only one other worker visible; a pudgy figure in white bent over the sink.

The Boarding House had opened for business only a short while ago, and despite rave reviews for the rooms and the restaurant, Lyle's party was probably the biggest crowd and challenge of the hotel's short career. The fragrance of tension was almost as strong as the more delicate aromas filling the room.

My mother knocked on the door frame. The figure at the sink didn't budge.

My mother moved closer. "Excuse me," she trilled like dowagers in Thirties movies. "Hate to bother you, but—"

The dishwasher remained with back to us, but turned off the water. I heard humming and a shh-bump beat, which I traced to small earphones attached to a yellow Walkman sitting on the windowsill.

"—I had a large tin messengered here today—" my mother continued.

"Can't hear you," I said.

My mother opened a few throttles in her throat. "I wonder," she bellowed, "whether they arrived and whether they're being refrigerated and—"

"Mom, don't shout! There are earplugs in—"

Of course my mother didn't hear me. She was shouting too loudly. "Some of them have *cream*," she bellowed. "They could go *bad*!"

Smack in the middle of this last nonexchange, the person at the sink chose to remove the plugs and turn around. She—because it was now clear the round figure was female and not a man with glandular problems—opened her eyes and mouth extra wide, and screamed.

I couldn't blame her, really. There was a strange woman shouting at her, after all.

She put a hand to her chest. Below the turquoise bandanna tied around her hair, her skin looked blanched with fear, and a spray of freckles on her cheeks stood out like gold sequins.

"Why are you screaming?" My mother sounded truly baffled by the girl's excesses.

The young woman closed her mouth and swallowed whatever noisemaking might have been left. "Sorry," she said, which seemed pretty inappropriate to me since she had done nothing but be frightened. Further proof of my mother's powers.

"I was saying that I messengered a tin today. For Mr. Zacharias. But—"

The kitchen door swung again and a voice demanded information even before its owner was fully in the room. "Whatever is going on here? We have *guests*! What kind of place is this? Who screamed? Who are all of you? Why aren't you wearing aprons?" This was barked out in the surprisingly strong voice of a woman who looked as if her face had been cross-hatched before it was put in to rise. Small eyes under baggy, crepey overhangs inspected the three of us. "Well?" she demanded. "Answer me."

"Sorry, ma'am," the dishwasher said. "I screamed because I was startled."

The old woman hmmphed, as if that were a suspect alibi. "Who are you?" she asked.

"Lizzie, ma'am."

We were in a time warp, back to The Boarding House's roots by way of Dickens. The steamy kitchen, the imperious old woman, and Lizzie, the cowering kitchenmaid. Surely, a little lame boy in a cap would soon hobble in.

"You work here?" the old woman asked.

"Yes'm. Catering. Food preparation." Her turquoise bandanna slipped forward, down onto her forehead, and she pulled it off. Frizzy carrot-colored hair sprang free.

"What about you?" The old woman now faced me, hooded eyes like a bird of prey's. "Where's your apron? What's your name?"

"My—I—" I sounded just like Lizzie. "Pepper. Mandy. I don't work here, I'm one of the . . ." But I wasn't really one of the guests. I spluttered a few more words but my mouth couldn't work properly while my mind was stuck on the really relevant issue: was I so inappropriately dressed that I looked like a waitress or the kitchen staff instead of a partygoer?

"Sorry for the noise," my mother told the old woman. "Hope it didn't upset anybody out there, but it was all my fault. I scared her. Not on purpose, of course."

"I know you," the old woman told my mother. She cranked her head in my direction, like a wrinkled hawk, then swiveled it back to my mother. "You a Pepper, too? I once knew a family of Peppers. Way back."

"Aunt Hattie," my mother said. "I should have recognized you. Mandy, this is Lyle's aunt, Hattie Zacharias." I smiled and shook her hand. It was dry and brittle, all bird bones.

Aunt Hattie redirected her glare at Lizzie. "You another of them? Another Pepper? You look familiar, too." She squinted and turned her head to view Lizzie sideways.

Lizzie shook her head. "My name's Chapman," she said. "My dad and I own this place. I'm the one who talked with you on the phone, Miss Zacharias. About the reservations and menu and all." She grinned, showing broad teeth with a wide gap between the front two.

"I was trying to find out about the tarts I sent over. I baked fifty of them for Lyle," my mother told Aunt Hattie, who nodded, as if that degree of homage were only to be expected. "Couldn't think of what else he could possibly want or need." She laughed nervously, still worried about her gift. "They probably need to be refrig—" At what seemed the same moment, we all saw the enormous tin with its funereal silver on black Over the Hill motto and we gravitated toward it.

On top, a taped-on oversized tag, said: FOR LYLE'S OLD TASTEBUDS ONLY. NO SHARING THIS TIME.

My mother carefully lifted the lid to inspect the contents. "Oh, dear," she said.

"Something's gone bad?"

"That messenger must have jostled it. Some of the edges are cracked." She tsked and shook her head and pursed her mouth, waiting.

"They're beautiful, Mom."

"Better than anybody in my class at culinary school could have done," Lizzie said. "They look ready for a photo spread." My mother was visibly heartened by praise from a professional.

"Do you think they should go into the—"

"There's really no room just now," Lizzie said. "Later, for sure, after dinner. Meanwhile, if you'd like, I can put them outside. There's a small overhang and I think the tin would stay dry, although the rain's awfully strong."

"Flash floods in Paoli," my mother said. "We'd better keep it inside."

"You here, Aunt Hat?" Once again the voice preceded the actual entry. Maybe it was a genetic trait in that family.

The tall man who entered was nothing at all like what I'd expected. I'd anticipated a similarity with his friends in the front parlor, an effortless slickness. Styled hair, silk suit.

But what I saw was a man who looked as if he'd been working hard to smooth down his rough edges. Lyle Zacharias was completely bald, which made his black, piercing eyes beneath heavy brows even more compelling. His smile was charming, complicated, and half hidden in a thick beard. He looked as if his dark hair had fallen down inside his skull and was exiting via his chin.

He didn't belong with his friends in the front parlor. He didn't belong anywhere I could think of.

A pirate, I decided. A pirate pretending to be one of us. I was sure that when he undressed at night, he put on the eyepatch and the peg leg.

I felt queasy—repelled and attracted and, for the first time, not sorry I'd wound up here . . . at the pirate's party.

Three

"WHOOPS," LYLE SAID UPON SEEING OUR LITTLE GROUP. "Didn't mean to interrupt. Just looking for—oh, there you are." He raised his hand in greeting to his aunt.

Lizzie was truly weird when it came to authority figures. The second Lyle appeared, she relapsed into her obsequious servant mode, backing away as if to make herself invisible. She looked even more Dickensian and wretched than she had with Hattie—almost disoriented by a groveling fear. Perhaps we were too much for her, barging in, interrupting her schedule, but how odd for someone in the hotel business. Of course, cooks are probably unused to an audience.

"We must be in your way," I said. "Maybe we should . . ."

She didn't seem to hear. She continued to stare at Lyle Zacharias with an expression of frozen panic.

"My birthday boy!" Hattie said.

"Lyle," my mother said softly. "You haven't changed a bit in twenty years."

He winked at my mother. "Going bald in my twenties helped a lot. I looked old when I wasn't, and that's the bad news. But then I looked the same way forever. And that's supposed to be the good news."

"I guess you don't remember me," my mother said.

"But I do. Give me a second. Never forget a face—it's just the name that's slipped . . . old age, you know."

I steeled myself for a rash of geriatric jokes.

"Oh, Lyle," my mother said. "You really are just the same." I was sure he didn't recognize her, but she eternally believes the best—thereby fitting the definition of bleeding heart do-gooder and sucker. Now she believed Lyle, and the idea that she was memorable was audibly thrilling her. You could hear the smile cradling her words, her joy in not being forgotten.

"Okay," Lyle said. "I've got it." He lifted his hand to his eye, index finger pointed in the manner of a gun. "Your name is—"

Lizzie inhaled forcibly. The sound was a combination sob and gasp.

Lyle looked at her quizzically, as did my mother and I. "Is something wrong?" I asked stupidly. Of course something was out of kilter, even if it was no more than a breathing difficulty or a serious tic.

But she was less sure than I. "I don't know," she whispered. "I don't know why, but I—I—" She sounded scared, and near tears, and her eyes remained wide and wild. She made a soft moan.

This was more than overawe of authority or a minor physiological problem. Something was profoundly awry. Something was also profoundly touching about her confusion and vulnerability. She reminded me of the adolescents I teach—seemed one of them, in fact, even though she had probably been out of high school for half a decade or more.

Lyle didn't seem to notice the cook's confusion. His concentration was focused on my mother. And then he pointed his index finger again and said, "Bea Pepper, as I live and breathe!"

I had been wrong about him, unduly suspicious and cynical. The old pirate actually remembered my mother.

Bea gurgled and babbled and launched into a long tale about my father's accident, which, of course, highlighted my uninvited, second-string status. I tried to melt into the black and white floor tiles, although our host immediately made hospitable sounds. "Of *course* any daughter of yours is welcome here! Don't be *silly*." He was so effusive, I was sure he was faking the emotion.

My mother pulled over a wire-backed chair and sat down next to the black and silver tin, gesturing to everybody to find seats, but no one else was as much of a settle-in-the-kitchen kind of partier as she. "I baked you tarts, Lyle," she said. "Fifty of them. All different flavors, all special, the way you used to like them."

"Now, Bea," he said, "that's not fair! I'm an old man now! I have to count calories and fat grams. I have to practice Olympic level self-control, and now—my favorite food in the world, Bea's tarts—how could you do this to me?" His tone and expression belied his words. He smiled broadly, white teeth dramatic against his black beard. "Tell me you aren't tempting me with the one with the macadamias and peaches."

My mother's expression was the very definition of bliss. Even I was impressed by his memory—or by his taste buds.

"I certainly am." My mother's voice was love-struck. "But I never thought you'd remember."

"Unfortunately for my waistline, I remember it all too well."

"You'll only turn fifty once. Enjoy yourself, and don't you give them away to anybody." My mother sounded flirtatious. Maybe that's why my father disliked Lyle Zacharias. "In fact, why don't you sample one now, while nobody's watching?" She grabbed a wooden spoon from a large crockery container and used its handle to push a bit of whipped cream off a tart. "Look at that—I found it right away," she said. "I remember putting it in and thinking this was your very favorite. Peach and macadamia. Try it." She found a clear glass plate and put the tart on it and then, for good measure, added a second, and held the dish out to Lyle.

He shook his head. "Not a chance tonight. I'm really counting calories, aren't I, Aunt Hattie?"

Hattie viewed him as if he were a work of art. "When

Lyle says something, believe him. I always do, because he always really means it," she said. "Since he was a child."

"Have to lose a couple or ten pounds," he said. "Tonight—a little birthday cake, for sentiment's sake, but that's all."

Hattie seemed inappropriately proud of him for this self-control. My mother stared at the glass plate with the tarts. I knew she was silently deciding whether to be happy about Lyle's praise or depressed about his diet.

While she pondered, the swinging doors opened with less fanfare than they had before. This time the newcomer checked out the room before speaking.

She looked like a woman who enjoyed entrances and made sure her audience shared the thrill. She was voluptuous, barely covered with something sequined, and she had a perfect-featured, vacant face, like the *Draw Me* girls who used to be inside match covers. I think I'm being objective and not speaking out of jealousy. I honestly think so, even though her body was as symmetrical and perfect as her face, only more clever-looking. I put her age at mid-twenties.

"Lyle," she said, in a little-girl whine. "There you are. It's just so *annoying*, Lyle."

"What's up, Tiff?" He didn't rush to her side, although surely most men would have.

"It's not a suite. It's not even an inside room, and I can't be a hostess *and* negotiate with the staff here. I can't even find the staff." She stuck out her bottom lip in a pout. It was a facial expression seldom seen past the age of two. Somebody must have told her she looked cute when she was angry. Actually, she did, so who cared about age-appropriate behavior?

"Don't worry about it," Lyle said. "Any room will be fine."

"But it's your party," Hattie said. "You deserve what you wanted."

"I knew we shouldn't have it at a rinky-dink place like this," Tiff said. "Didn't I say so?"

"Indeed you did. Countless times." Lyle wore a patient,

semi-amused smile, giving the impression he was quite used to small tempests and riffs. Maybe she had the nickname because she was always involved in a tiff.

"Nostalgia!" Tiff exclaimed. "Ye gads! What's so great about nostalgia? I looked across the street at where you lived. It was a great place to *leave*, if you want to know the truth. Why you wanted to come back beats me."

"My wife, Tiffany," Lyle said with great calm. "Tiffany, this is Bea Pepper, a friend from a time when I was your age. And her daughter, Amanda."

Lizzie didn't count and wasn't counted. Kitchen help, scullery maid, no more. Maybe all of us had slid back to other times, other systems.

"Pleased to meet you," Tiffany said. But her eyes flicked over our faces with subminimal interest, and moved on until they noticed a tall copper stock pot. "You know what? Maybe I'd have fun in a store like this. Kitchen stuff. Lots of copper."

Hattie Zacharias rolled her eyes. "It's easier when you know how to cook." Her voice was low, but audible.

"A fun place," Tiffany said. "You know, guest chefs, demos . . . Either that or an exercise salon—upscale, kicky, don't you think? But something. Something stimulating before I just go . . ."

I wondered why she had chosen this time and this kitchen to request career counseling. I suspected that when and if neurons triggered within Tiffany's brain, Tiffany's mouth reported the results, no matter how irrelevant or inappropriate.

"I'll take care of the room," Hattie told her. "Don't worry about it anymore. Don't worry about future jobs or hobbies, either. Why don't you go back to being a hostess instead?"

Tiffany shrugged, but it wasn't the sort of inconsequential action I might have performed. It was a pneumatic rise and fall of perfectly sculpted shoulders which also managed to heighten awareness of her cleavage. Quite involved and amazing. "I forgot to tell you." Her voice was flat now. "Reed's here."

"I'll be right along," Lyle said. "He'll need attention. It's rough being fourteen at a fifty-year-old's birthday." He stood up and moved closer to her.

"He doesn't *belong* at a grown-up party. It's too"—she searched for a word—"grown up for a kid."

"He's my son! Surely, you—"

"Really, Lyle." Once again she sounded like an aggrieved infant. "I've got my hands full with the real guests. *Please* don't ask me to babysit, too. Besides, his mother is with him. Surprise, surprise."

He spoke to her quietly and, he probably thought, privately; but my mother and I and even Aunt Hattie were all openly eavesdropping. "You must have known I'd invite her," he told his wife. "For Reed, and also because she's a part of my life."

"Nostalgia again!" Tiffany snapped. Then, seemingly self-conscious for the first time, she lowered her voice. But by now every cilia in my ear was on red alert, stretched for maximum listening power. "All this looking back—this crummy hotel, this insane idea about quitting your job and New York and my whole life—I think you're going crazy! It's like the magazines say, the men go through a mid-life crazies! But why should I have to—"

"Tiff," he said, softly. "Let up. Go on out and have fun. You love parties, and this will be a good one."

Tiffany switched gears with a blink of her lush eyelashes. "She's impossible," Tiffany hissed. "And she hates me and poisons him against me and she doesn't discipline him at all."

"Please. Not tonight. Not here."

His baby-wife stared at him with her vacant turquoise eyes. Then she reached some decision, executed another of those incredible slow-motion shrugs, turned, and slithered out of the room.

It didn't sound as if picking wives was one of Lyle's talents. His choice of trophy wife put him very low on the Mandy scale. Look at a man's woman, and you look at his soul, and sometimes, to your embarrassment, at his secret needs and preferences.

But I'm not jealous. Honestly.

The cook worried me. All through Tiffany's scatter-brained and mean-spirited visit, Lizzie had stared at Lyle and my mother with the abstracted intensity of someone having a seizure.

She was still staring now, after Tiffany's departure, while Lyle and my mother resumed tart talk. My mother catalogued the varieties in the tin. Lyle chuckled and said he would have a vicarious eating thrill. She described the strawberry-kirsch tart. He made low, sexy sounds of appreciation. I felt unutterably depressed. Another unsolicited, hazard-free, sensation-free sensual experience. After safe sex, safe eating.

I went over to Lizzie. "Are you all right?" I asked.

The girl had difficulty pulling her attention back to me and my question. Finally, as if coming out of a trance, she answered. "Feel . . . bad." Her voice had changed, been stretched too tight and was unnaturally high and thin.

"Like what?" I whispered. I wondered if she had a medical or emotional condition, if she was in any danger.

"Like . . . in my head . . . things clicking and falling apart."

"Maybe you should sit down. Have you eaten?" I didn't think there was a set treatment protocol for things clicking and falling apart in the head, but food always seems a happy panacea. I spotted a tall container of breadsticks and extracted two—one for me and one for her. She shook her head.

"Dieting," she said.

"What is this, a fad?" Food asceticism, the one religion we can all believe in. But what were we supposed to do, imitate my mother and Lyle and talk food? Discuss breadsticks? "Diet tomorrow," I said, pushing the food into her hand.

Lizzie tried for a smile. "So hard to lose weight around here . . . always tempted . . ."

"I'll bet you're dizzy from not eating," I said.

Aunt Hattie's baggy face came near for a moment. "She all right?" she asked me. "You all right, girl?"

"Lizzie," I said. Bad enough they didn't introduce her, but they could try to remember her name.

Lizzie nodded. I tapped the breadstick in her hand, and she looked at it like a zombie, and held it like a wand. "Got so scared all of a sudden," she said, her free hand to her chest. Her tempo had slowed and her voice was returning to a deeper register. "Heart pounding. Why? And so sad." And indeed she was blinking back the start of tears.

Hattie looked at her, then at me, and then chose to withdraw from whatever problem the kitchen help had.

"Has this ever happened before?" I asked.

Lizzie shook her head, vigorously, perhaps trying to dislodge those falling, clicking entities inside. She took a jagged breath. "Sorry," she whispered, but she still sounded like someone on the verge of a major crying jag. "Feel like a baby!"

Over on the other side of the kitchen, the vicarious eaters seemed sated. "Like that song in *Annie*," Lyle said. "Tomorrow. The tarts will come out—tomorrow, but I can't touch them until then. And don't worry about my sharing them. Tiff never *ever* breaks her diet. I'll ration myself. One a day, like an incredibly delicious vitamin pill. I'll cut back on the cottage cheese, to save calories." He grinned. "But now, time to get back to my other guests. Won't you join me, Bea? Aunt Hattie?"

I didn't mind being excluded, or forgotten. Not horribly, at least.

"I'd better see to Reed," Hattie said. "And that room business."

He nodded. "And Sybil." His expression hardened.

"If only she liked me, I'd help with her, too," Hattie said. "Speak of the devil."

The kitchen doors had opened once again and two people entered. One was the young man who'd been relocating lettuce when I came in, and the other was a stern-faced woman with dark hair slicked straight back into a flamenco dancer's chignon.

Wife Number Two. And who would be behind Door Three?

"Sybil?" Lyle said. "You okay?"

"I didn't think you'd be in here," she said. "I always check the kitchen. After all, I have a son to take care of."

"Reed," Lyle said in a gentle voice, as if speaking with a madwoman. "I know his name. He's my son, too."

"Then you also know that he has allergies," she said. "Sensitivities." Her glance darted over each of our faces, inventorying every detail of the room. "If I don't make sure nothing's going to harm him, who will?"

"I have him on my list, ma'am," Lizzie said. "Reed Zacharias. No pomegranates, radicchio, or duck. We're not serving any of those things."

"Those aren't allergies, Sybil," Lyle said. "Those are preferences. The boy's fine and I wish you'd stop—"

Sybil nodded briskly at Lizzie. "Good," she said. "He gets sick at the thought of pomegranates." She turned and left without another word.

"Sometimes I think she's crazy," Hattie said.

"And sometimes I know it," Lyle completed the old joke.

"I told her we weren't using pomegranates when she phoned up," Lizzie said.

"I'll go fix what can be fixed," Hattie said. "I'll get you a suite for tonight."

Lyle leaned over and kissed her right below the hairline. "Bless you. For this and for all the other times you've taken such good care of me."

Hattie seemed to blush between the wrinkles. She waved him away. "Try to keep your wives out of the kitchen," she said. "Tiff's been in and out, driving this poor girl crazy. I swear, sometimes she's like a *child*."

Lyle shrugged, as if the peccadillos of wives were no real bother, then nodded his head in a near bow. "Well, now—although I am enjoying myself enormously here, I am being a most inconsiderate host. I dragged some of these people—some of them only semiwillingly, I'm sure—hundreds . . . thousands . . . of miles so I could see them again. So the least I could and should do is just that. See them. Come with me, Bea?"

"Just as soon as I make sure the tarts are in a safe place," my mother said, waving him off to his guests.

"Thank you again and again," he said. "It really matters to me, really touches me, that you came." He bent to kiss my mother's cheek, then left the kitchen.

Lizzie lost it again and whimpered. I coughed, in some instinctive attempt to shield her.

Hattie glared at her. "Are you sure you're all right? You're behaving quite oddly. Should you be handling food? I don't want anybody catching whatever you've got."

Lizzie paled, stood, and smoothed the front of her apron. "Fine," she said. "I'm sorry. I'm not ill, just . . . I felt . . . faint. Suddenly faint. Never felt that way before."

"Well, make sure it doesn't happen again. Staring the way you did at my Lyle is bad manners. After all, even though I was the one who spoke with you and made the arrangements, it was completely Lyle's idea to come here. I tried to talk him out of it, in fact, but he was stuck on going back to the old neighborhood and completing some cycle in his mind. The point is, he's who you have to thank for this business, and he's an influential man. He could tell other people about this place. Recommend it, but he probably won't if you keep that habit of gaping. It looks rude."

Frankly, I thought there was major rudeness going on aside from Lizzie's staring.

"Sorry," Lizzie mumbled once more. "It won't happen again. I promise."

"Now you know I only told you that for your own good, don't you?" Hattie said.

Why is everything offered under the label of For Your Own Good always such a bitter pill? And usually only for the good of the mean-spirited person administering the rule or punishment or advice?

"Now," Hattie said, "I must do something about my nephew's room. Didn't you say you and your father owned this place? My Lyle wanted a suite. He didn't get one. Can you take care of it?"

Lizzie looked around the kitchen as if estimating what

was left to do before dinner. Some of her gears still weren't meshing. "My father could help, maybe."

"Fine. I take it he's that man out front near the door."

Lizzie shook her head. "That man's been filling in. He's more of our handyman and bellboy. My dad just got back from a trip this morning and he's kind of jet-lagged, but ask the man at the desk for Roy. That's my dad."

"Lyle and his wife can have my room," my mother said. "We aren't staying over."

Hattie shook her head. "That isn't the point. He wanted a suite and he deserves one, and that nitwit wife of his won't exert herself, so I will. We have the whole hotel, so nobody is going to mind switching rooms with the guest of honor. I'll go find Roy Chapman and take care of it."

"Beecher," Lizzie said. "Roy Beecher. I was married for a while. Kept the name."

Hattie seemed to doubt Lizzie's marital history. She tilted her head and eyed Lizzie with her bird-of-prey cold eye. "So your name is Chapman, but your maiden name was Beecher?"

"That's right," my mother said sweetly, as if Hattie had just mastered a difficult concept.

Hattie held her head straight, flappy-skinned chins wobbling, thin though she was. And then, biting on her lower lip, she nodded and left.

"Well, well." My mother patted the lid of the tart tin and hoisted her Persian lamb on her hip. "If Lyle's not taking our room, let's use it and get rid of our coats. It's time to really be at this party."

Party. I'd forgotten all about that.

Four

IT WAS AN INTERESTING COCKTAIL HOUR. HOURS. NOT INTER-
esting as in captivating, but interesting as in clinically odd
and as a study of how slowly time can creep along. The
players were divided, visibly, between Lyle's past and
Lyle's present. In the past contingent there were several earnest, average-looking souls like my mother and a distant
relative of Hattie's who could have passed for Santa after
Weight Watchers. Those people drank moderately, referred
to Lyle's medium as *the tube*, attempted to mingle, and
were generally somewhat more interesting than their clothing, which was not true of the Lyle-now folks.

Their gelatinous egos spread and pushed for maximum
space and reduced all language, no matter what words were
used, to "Me!"—and they characterized their profession as
the industry.

Lyle Zacharias himself, however, oozed charm that
sometimes was convincing, and regaled his guests with an-
ecdotes about themselves, seeming to remember and cher-
ish every moment he had spent in their company. He had
a different and flattering story for everyone. I know, because I tracked him, like a paparazzo without a camera.

His non–show biz guests entered The Boarding House
timidly and deferentially, but Lyle had a radar that alerted

him when people were in the foyer, and he'd put them at
their ease and make sure they became part of the group.

"Everybody," he said, for example, "this is Richard
Quinn." He had his arm around a lanky, weathered man.
"Quinn is my former roommate, partner, and more or less
my current father-in-law. Met in college then joined forces
in a grungy office off an alleyway. I was supposed to write
and direct, and Quinn was going to produce. That lasted
until Quinn got tired of starving and went off to better
things. Played a string of villains on TV. Recognize him?
The bad guy."

Richard Quinn's features were ascetic rather than villain-
ous, although I could see how, with the shift of a few facial
muscles, he could be menacing. At the moment, he smiled
rather shyly and said, "Been a while since I acted."

I knew my mother was doing an intake evaluation on the
man. I wasn't her daughter for nothing. Besides, I, too, had
made note that he had entered solo, that Lyle hadn't asked
after any missing wife or longtime companion, that he was
probably straight because he was Lyle's father-in-law—a
plus, despite the fact that he'd named his baby Tiffany—
and that the man had cheekbones you could use as
Rollerblades. Of course, having been Lyle's college roommate, Quinn was twenty years my senior and we were
generationally incompatible. I've tried it once and there was
some hope for the relationship until I confessed that yes, I
too remembered exactly where I'd been when Kennedy was
assassinated. I'd been at the pediatrician's, getting my
whooping cough booster shot, and my mother had been so
upset, she'd forgotten to produce the promised lollipop re-
ward for bravery.

Therefore, my evaluation of Richard Quinn was strictly
force of habit. I thought.

"This is Reed, everybody," Lyle said a while later. Lord
knew where the boy had slurked until this moment, since
Tiffany had unhappily announced his presence earlier. He
looked like the kind of kid who would have brought along
an enormous stash of comic books and who would have
found a secret place to read them.

But I liked that his father's graciousness extended to children. Not everybody's does. Unfortunately, Lyle's warmth hadn't been inherited by his son, who was seriously sullen. "Reed has agreed to be bored to death at an old man's birthday party, and I want to thank him publicly. It means a whole lot to me."

Lyle hugged his stiff and unbending son. Reed was in some very late larval stage. Soft and puffy, his head pushed forward pugnaciously, his eyes canvassed the room systematically, almost automatically and with no recognition. Until, that is, he spotted stepmama Tiffany, over in a corner yukking it up with TV's own Dr. Sazarac, and gave her as evil an eye—as evil two eyes—as I've seen.

His anger looked chronic, deep, and familiar. I teach at a school where lots of lost and furious children of privilege wind up. I'd seen that face many times.

"And over there's his gracious mother and chauffeur," Lyle said, one hand still on his son's shoulder. "Sybil is undoubtedly the reason Reed's turning out so well."

I wondered if there was intentional irony in that statement. Maybe not. This was very much a let-bygones-be-bygones evening. Very sophisticated, indeed. Lyle's stock escalated for complimenting his sour ex, who looked as hostile and unyielding as she had in the kitchen. She stood against the far wall, holding a drink, establishing her distance from and possible contempt for all of us and our party.

"Sybil's owner of a thriving landscape business," Lyle told the rest of us. "Built it from the ground up, as they say. Sybil doesn't have a green thumb; she has a green hand. Knows *every*thing about anything that grows."

Sybil acknowledged his greetings with a quick nod. Her features were handsome, if sharp, and she did nothing to soften her appearance. She wore a high-collared black dress and no jewelry or makeup, and the starkness of her costume combined with her severe hairstyle made her look like a mourner and a shockingly dramatic contrast to her glittery successor.

I couldn't get over Tiffany. It had to be embarrassing to be such a blatant pneumatic, giggling stereotype, especially an anachronistic one, but then, what can be expected of girls named after retail stores? She was a commercial production—name by jewelers, body by Barbie. Her spangles barely met the definition of minimal coverage, so essence of Tiffany was everywhere, and in motion. She was extravagant with body language—fond of expansive hand movements, torso tilts, leg crosses—and semiverbal communication: giggles, exclamations, and coos. She was also in a much better mood than she'd been in, in the kitchen.

Not a man there, including both father and son Zacharias, could take his eyes off her for very long.

I could, however. As the hours dragged on, I became less and less captivated with party-watching. Finally, bored to the eyebrows, I fell back on tradition and excused myself to powder my nose. Maybe there'd be a new, Tiffanyized nose, etcetera, in the mirror.

Up in the room, I powdered an all-too-familiar face. At least my disappointment was witnessed only by my mother's Persian lamb and my down coat, both tossed on the bed along with our purses.

Reluctantly en route back to the festivities, I decided to kill more time by checking on the cook. She'd had the opportunity to recover, to be by herself, and to eat something and raise her blood sugar, a folk cure that sometimes actually worked.

Lizzie was flushed from bending over a sauce pot. "I'm so sorry," she said. "I felt like a jerk, but I couldn't help myself. It was so . . ." And then the new calm was gone. Her wire whisk stopped moving. The muscles around her eyes tensed and she looked frightened and dislocated.

"Lizzie?"

She shook her head. "Even thinking about that feeling, about how I felt, and I start to feel it all over again." She cleared her throat, shook her head, and turned around. "How's the food so far? Is everything okay?"

"I came in to compliment the chef. The crab puffs were superb. And I like the waiters, too. They don't interrupt conversations."

Her golden freckles stood out against her blush. "Mr.

McCoy came in and told me he liked the crab puffs, too,"
she whispered. "You know him—he's Dr. Sazarac on *Second Generation*."

I was beginning to understand what people who weren't
teaching or going to school did with their afternoons.

"Actually, lots of guests came in. I was surprised and
very flattered. People are so nice. Of course, some just
wanted to see the kitchen, or to be sure I knew about their
special menus. I showed them the list—I have it all written
down."

I saw what she gestured toward, a roster of all the invit-
ees, with notes next to perhaps a third of the names, including the no-radicchio-for-Reed nonsense. *Sybil Z.—no meat.
Fish okay. Richard Quinn—low cholesterol.* It depressed
me that he had gone from being a professional villain to a
man with a mundane health problem. My father had requested low sodium. I'd probably get his salt-free meal.

"But most people just said hi, and commented on the
food or the building and the rooms," Lizzie said.

"You're an excellent cook."

Lizzie made a rueful face. "All my life, food's been the
good news and the bad news. Well, for a while, once, other
substances were the worse news. But food . . . that's why
I'm on a major, major diet. Once and for all, I want to
prove I can do it."

"You look perfectly fine to me." She did, but I felt
creepy as soon as the words were out of my mouth. It's a
line best spoken by old relatives and people with no standards whatsoever, and never, ever, has it comforted a woman
who's convinced that she's fat.

"Fifteen pounds," Lizzie said. "Not one delicious thing
till then."

"Not even while you were making that?" A froth of
white and dark chocolate curls enclosed an enormous fluff
of birthday cake. "Didn't you at least lick the spoon? Eat
all the broken pieces of chocolate? I could never resist."

She smiled. I left her, justifiably proud of her moral su-
periority and handiwork, and I made my way back to the
front parlor, where Tiffany was still center stage.

I wondered whether somewhere in America less upscale offspring were named after, say, Wal-Mart. Who would baby Walmart grow up to be?

With astoundingly accurate timing, my answer—the spirit of the low-end mall—walked in. Walmartine's borscht-colored hair clashed with her vermilion evening pajamas, their satin straining over her hips. Her face was heavy with makeup, all smearing or melting. I couldn't decide whether she was trying too hard or not trying at all.

Her companion looked familiar to me. I had seen that slight figure before. It had been lost inside an ill-fitting jacket that time, too, but I couldn't place him. "My best friends in high school," Lyle told the group. "Wiley and Janine. The Wileys, nowadays. Back when it was Janine Riley, the three of us were inseparable. The W.R.L.'s we called ourselves—even had jackets with the initials sewn on them. Wiley, Riley, and Lyle—sounds good together, doesn't it? Nearly makes a poem." He hugged each of them. They remained where they were at the entrance to the living room.

"It's been so long," Lyle said to the couple. "Can't tell you how surprised I was," he said, now addressing his other guests. "I called our alma mater for help tracking these two, and I was told that Wiley was right there—as a teacher now."

A teacher. That's how I must know him.

Wiley smiled uncertainly. His wife's blue-coated eyelids drooped and she squinted, as if Lyle had said something suspicious. I tried to imagine those three as a trio, and all I came up with was Lyle as the energy the other two used for fuel. And it looked like W. and R. had permanently stalled once L. moved on.

I watched as he maneuvered them into the party—or gave it an honest try. They were not greeted with open arms.

"I'm really sorry about your father's accident," Lyle said to me once W. and R. were semilaunched. "He's a good man and he was part of a time of my life that was . . . bittersweet. However, I'm glad your mother conned you into coming, or I might never have met you. Tell me more about your work. I'm not familiar with Philly Prep. . . ."

I had watched him do the same intensely interested number with everyone. I knew that was his shtick. But that did not diminish the power of that fierce attention. If only Freud were still around to whine about what women wanted, Lyle could answer him. So could any woman.

Attention. Undivided. It was that simple, that attractive, and that unusual.

Lyle was a master of it. His undiluted concentration gave you—well, why be coy—gave *me* the giddy sense that my life was now as exciting as his, as much fun. That I *mattered* in some brand new way.

I found myself glancing at Tiffany with honest envy, and not of her long, long legs.

The mix of people, no longer strangers, hummed and became a real party in the afterglow of Lyle's industrial-strength attention. All except for Sybil, the unapproachable, who huddled with her son Reed, and except for Wiley and Janine, the unassimilated lumps who recognized me as another outsider and pounced.

"You know these people?" Janine asked as soon as we'd swapped names. I explained as how I knew no one except my mother.

Janine had donned hot pink harlequin glasses which kept slipping down her nose. She pushed them back up and looked balefully at her husband. "Neither do we," she said. "Don't even really know Lyle anymore, either. Haven't seen him in years. Maybe twenty." She inhaled and looked at me as pointedly as one can through tilted, sliding harlequin specs.

"Yes," I said. "He mentioned that it's been a long time."

She harrumphed, as if she had her own special meaning for the words *long time* and she wasn't going to share it, either.

"Come out on a night like this . . ." she said in her oh-I-could-tell-you-things way.

She was obviously hell-bent on having a bad time. I considered another nose-powdering escape. But before I could take a step, her husband leaned myopically close to me. "Don't I know you?" he asked.

"I teach, too," I said. "At Philly Prep. English."

"General Science. Biology. South Philly High."

No curriculum overlap. He was part of the public school system, I was with an independent school. How did I know him?

Janine looked at me sideways, eyes slitted. I felt on trial.

I suddenly had it. "You're the school paper's advisor, right? We met at Junior Journalist Day last year." He nodded, but tentatively, as if he were only pretending to actually remember me.

"We had lunch," I added. No recognition. A sinking depression on my part. How could someone so forgettable forget me? "Going again this year—this week?" I asked.

Janine swiveled her head and stared at her husband, who nodded again.

"Good!" I don't know why I said that, and so emphatically. Perhaps because Mrs. Wiley was behaving as if I were talking in code, cover for a sinister message.

"Can I get you a drink, Janine?" Wiley said. "And you, too, Miss . . ."

"Mandy Pepper." I had said my name no more than seven minutes earlier. I had become instantaneously forgettable. Maybe his wife wore bilious makeup and garish colors just to make an impression on him.

"How about if I get both of you ladies a drink?" he said.

"No, thanks." I was already near champagne capacity for a designated driver.

"I shouldn't have come," Janine whined as soon as her husband was in retreat. "Just look at me. I'm falling apart."

I murmured some noise of polite demur. She didn't appear to be falling apart. She looked like a rock-solid mass that couldn't be toppled. Her body was all function, no form, a utilitarian block of flesh separating her head from her feet.

"I don't feel well," she said. "Certainly not well enough

to go out on one of the worst nights of the year for some party for Lyle Zacharias of all people."

"Oh, my." I tried to sound sympathetic and interested while I searched for a decent exit line. I always attract the kind of person everyone else shuns, but I think I'm better off not finding out why.

"Haven't seen him since . . ." She released a harsh noise I was sure she thought was a laugh. "Right after *Ace of Hearts* opened, remember? His big break. Hah!"

Some friend. No wonder they hadn't seen Lyle in years. Obviously couldn't stand his success. But all I said was, "I wasn't too aware of what was happening on the stage twenty years ago." Didn't I look too young to remember?

"I have sciatica," Janine announced without benefit of a logical transition. "The nerve running down the back of this leg?" She waited until I watched her finger trace her pain route from her left buttock over the back of her thigh. "I try to make the best of it, try to stay sunny, but it kills me, you know? And aggravation makes it worse, like tonight." She tilted her head and waited, as if she'd just thrown down a challenge.

"Coming here has made your leg hurt?" Why did I ask? What did she want, a purple heart for party attendance?

"You got it!" She bobbled her head until beet-blood hair strands jiggled. Then she put a hand on her lower back and sighed in sympathy with her own suffering. "I told Wiley I didn't want to come. Why should I aggravate my back just so Lyle Zacharias can flaunt how far up the ladder he's climbed? My sinuses are starting up, too."

"Maybe you should find a chair. I'll find one for you." I'd build one for her. Anything to get her off her sciatic nerve and my back. Surely it was long past time for dinner. Isn't it supposed to be a—single—cocktail hour?

"How long have you known my husband?" Janine asked.

"What?" My mind was on food, not spouses.

"My husband. How long?"

"I don't really know him at all. Only met at the—"

"How long?"

"I met him last year, I think."

She sniffed and seemed ready for a new complaint, but just as I approached despair, I saw my mother, radar in action, scanning. I knew that when she found me talking to a person no one could consider marriage material, she'd save me. She has never understood that the knight in shining armor, not the maiden's mother, is supposed to rescue the maiden. In the Bea Pepper version, the mother forges and polishes the suit of armor and goes out to find the knight. Still, this once, I was happy about her misplaced protectiveness.

But it turned out I was only a way station on her quest. She was actually matching up Hattie, or trying to, if she could find her. "There's this darling gentleman," she said. "I've seen him on TV. I think on a Hallmark commercial. He's eager to meet her."

"Does he know that, Mother?" I asked as sweetly as I could.

She did not deign to respond.

I introduced her to the listless Janine, who shook her head. "I didn't see Hattie Zacharias," Janine said. "I'd still recognize the old—"

"She went home for a nap," my mother said. "Her apartment's only a few minutes away and she thought it'd be easier to sleep there. But she should have gotten back by now. We're going to eat any minute, and I wanted her to meet Gregor before then. He's a widower, you know, and quite charming."

"Gregor can meet Hattie after dinner," I said, but my mother's face had brightened and she waved energetically. "There she is!"

Even after a nap Hattie looked like one of those baggy Tibetan dogs. "I feel much better," she said as she approached us. "Ready to dance the whole night long!" The pouches and creases of her face rearranged themselves as she arched her eyebrows. "I can, you know, and I intend to!" Then she squinted, as she had this afternoon, this time in the direction of Janine, who had resumed her belligerent silence. "I know you, don't I?" Hattie said.

"I'm Janine."

"Yes. High school. Quite a tomboy, weren't you? Married the Wiley boy, didn't you?"

"You have an amazing memory!" my mother said.

"Yes," Hattie said with no self-consciousness. "Good with names and faces. Good with other things, too. Just got back from Costa Rica, Guatemala, and Panama."

"My!" My mother is a world-class appreciator. "How exciting!"

Hattie nodded. "Lyle's birthday gift to me. Wants me to settle down in my rocking chair, but not yet, I say. Next year I want to go to Galapagos. Central America was splendid. Before I went, I memorized the list of flora and fauna we could expect to find. Everybody else was thirty-forty years younger, but I was the one who knew. They were quite amazed. I don't forget much."

Well, so she wasn't modest. But she was certainly sharp.

"I think it's because I never married," Hattie said. "Didn't waste energy on some man who'd want all my attention and would drain off my energy. All I had to concentrate on was dear, dear Lyle."

"Yes!" Janine was suddenly activated. "I get such headaches from my husband's demands that I think I'm about to—"

We never did find out what neurological damage her husband's existence had done her, because we were saved by the bell—the dinner one in this case, waved delicately, like a tinkling handkerchief, by our golden hostess, Tiffany.

In the light of what followed, we should all have skipped the meal and stuck with Janine's migraines.

Five

AT THE ENTRANCE TO THE HOTEL DINING ROOM, WE PICKED UP place cards with table numbers. "I'm at five," Janine said.

To my great relief, I wasn't.

I was, however, Sybil Zacharias's tablemate. She bumped into me as I pulled out my chair. I thought she might have had too much to drink already. " 'Scuse," she said. "Oh, it's you! Somebody said you teach at Philly Prep."

I nodded.

"Trying to get my son in. Can you help me pull strings?"

As long as those strings were attached to an ATM machine, she'd have no problem. "I'm sure you won't need them," I said, "but if I can help . . ."

"I can't believe I'm networking with Lyle's friend!"

"I'm not," I said, but that sounded wrong, and I gave it up. Sybil nodded and lurched off.

The room was relatively intimate, and our crowd of fifty or so filled it to capacity. Five rounds, each seating ten, encircled a small center table with only four seats. Only two were currently occupied. Hattie sat at one like the dowager queen, her bright pebble eyes gleaming and her wrinkles taking on happy configurations. Next to her, Reed Zacharias looked made of denser material than human flesh and seemed to wish he were anywhere but here.

"You see that woman over at that table?" my mother

whispered as she settled in next to me. "With the canary hair? Her husband left her for an *older* woman, can you imagine? Humiliated, poor dear. And that man there? Just out of the hospital for a duodenal ulcer. Thinks his son, who's in a drug program, caused it."

The woman is a magnet for personal revelations. Within seconds of meeting her, absolute strangers download their secrets. She should have been a spy—or a talk show hostess.

The seating strategy appeared to be one celebrity per table. Anna Pacocci, the Golden-Throated Czech, was surrounded by less recognizable faces at the next table. According to my mother, the former diva's throat had become a slightly less precious metal, and nowadays she played a political refugee on *Second Generation*. Pacocci looked bored with her role as table ornament for the little people, and called out to Rhoda Roundtree, the Brit TV gossip seated one over in the ring of tables. I listened intently for Eurotrash gossip, bulletins from the arts, or whatever bons mots semifamous people swapped with one another.

"Did you haff ze crab things?" she asked. Rhoda pursed her mouth. "So-so," she said. "I've had better."

Didn't they once call people like that the Smart Set?

Our table's designated celebrity turned out to be none other than my mother's idol, pretend-doc Sazarac, Shep McCoy himself. He stood to my right and extended his hand directly in front of my face to my mother, at my left. "Bea," he said. "How lovely to share a table with you. And this, I take it, is the glorious daughter you talked about?"

I didn't know with whom to be angrier—my mother for the daughter-peddling, or McCoy, who behaved as if I, glorious or not, were autistic, paralyzed, or comatose. I considered biting his wrist as it passed by my face.

"And would she mind, do you think, if I were her dinner companion?" It wasn't asked as a question, even of my mother. It was meant as humor, as ridiculously funny, for who wouldn't want the Real McCoy as her tablemate? He seated himself to my right. "Lovely," he said. "And what do you call yourself?"

"I have actually never had cause to call my own self," I said. "I'm always already there, you see." My mother kicked me under the table.

Shepard McCoy blinked several times. When he spoke again, he detoured around me, to my mother. "You know," he said—I had become a backdrop he leaned across—"I was once in a play based on this exact situation."

"You mean a self-important older man—" My mother nicked my anklebone this time, but Shepard hadn't heard me. He was a performer, not a listener, and sound waves operated in only one direction. Besides, I really hadn't said it all that loudly.

"A group of people assemble at a wedding, so that's a little different, but not that much, right? And we're with this table of people who didn't know each other before they sat down." He patted my shoulder, then squeezed it. A fleeting gesture. Innocuous, perhaps, and definitely meaningless, but I moved as far to the left as I could without falling off my chair or into my mother's lap.

"And what happened?" my mother asked after just enough of a bump of time to let me know I should have asked the question, made the effort. Old not-with-my-daughter-unless-you're-marrying-her Mama hadn't noticed the business with the shoulder, or she had written it off as theatrical and therefore excusable.

Shep McCoy shook his silver-topped head. "Alas, it closed after five nights, you know, although my performance was favorably singled out by the *Times*. 'Captures every nuance' they said."

Somebody should tell the man real people do not say *alas*.

"I meant what happened to the characters in the play," my mother said mildly.

Shepard looked blank. "You mean the *other* characters?"

My mother nodded encouragement. "And yours, too, of course."

"Actually, nothing much. We talked back and forth.

Things like 'and how are you related to the groom?' Or, perhaps, 'how are you related to the bride?' I'm a little rusty about it by now, you know. I've played so many roles. But I think it turned out everybody was connected in their past. Oh, yes, and somebody died at the table. Not my character, of course. I don't do corpses. But the death— heart attack, as I recall—stirred matters up."

I was surprised that play had lasted a full five performances.

"Well," my mother said overbrightly, "and how *is* everyone here related to the groom? To Lyle, of course, I mean."

She addressed her words to the table at large, extending her arms like an orchestra conductor to include everyone, make them work together in concert. By now all the chairs were filled. Our group consisted of two young women in black New York regalia—"Film students," my mother whispered; an older woman with great cheekbones above high-necked silk ruffles; a young, tall, and rather goofy-looking fellow who, I believe, was a lighting technician with eyes only for his wife, an equally tall woman who could have been attractive if she weren't so coy and simpering. On one side of the loving couple was Lyle's somber second wife, Sybil, and completing the group, on their other side, the good-looking former bad guy, Richard Quinn. I sighed. There, but for the luck of seating, had gone a much more intriguing dinner companion than Shep. Quinn was still a little old for me—a lot old for me, actually—but then so was his lookalike, Clint Eastwood, and I'd have ogled him, too.

"I'll go first," the older woman said in a thin, high voice. "My name is Priscilla Lemoyes and I was Lyle's high school teacher. English and drama, and I'm just so proud of him! I always favored the late bloomers. Never seemed particularly interested in much, but I always knew there was something special about him. 'I believe in you, Lyle Zacharias,' I always said. 'Reach for the stars.' So I wasn't surprised his senior year when he wrote the hit of the school. And years later, when he polished up that high school skit and it became *Ace of Hearts*, he sent me a ticket to opening night. He never forgot me."

I wondered if I'd live long enough to be told I'd played a significant role in a student's destiny. My pupils are not only late, but seriously detained bloomers. Century plants, perhaps.

Thinking about them reminded me of their promless condition. Poor kids. Booking the hotel had been the one high school assignment they'd handled with efficiency. I wondered if they already knew that their site was a charcoal memory.

Shepard McCoy was staring at me with moony-stupid eyes. At least he now kept his hands to himself, so he was more embarrassing than annoying. I looked away, down, at my watch. I was ready to call it a night and get on with my life, but it was only eight-fifteen. One dinner and at least two hours to go.

My mother eyed me. She'd tried to instill better manners than I was showing. In honor of her, I produced table talk. "You must know the Wileys, then, as well," I said to the sweet old schoolteacher. "Janine and . . ." I couldn't remember her husband's first name.

"There was a boy named Wiley," Priscilla Lemoyes said. "Jerry? No—Terry. Quiet. Never had Lyle's sparkle, but a nice enough boy."

"I was in the TV series that spun off *Ace of Hearts*, you know," Shepard McCoy said with a half cough/half laugh meant to convey modesty while he nonetheless tooted his horn. "Played Wilfred, a rather oafish fellow, remember him?" He laughed again, hail fellow well met. "Casting against type, of course. Challenging. Critics loved me, but TV is devastating." He lifted my hand and placed it on his, as if he were about to propose marriage. I repossessed my hand.

"That's where I met Lyle," he continued. "Nobody else could have convinced me to stay in the medium. I'm a stage actor, you know. I always say, my hair was black until I met Lyle Zacharias. *People* magazine played up that remark, you know."

Every time he said *you know*, my fillings ached. He assumed that the minutiae of his life was part of the core of common culture—and God help us all, was it? I gave him my blankest expression, a face I hoped said, "I have zero knowledge of your career and who did you say you were again?" but his ego was made of kryptonite. If only we could divide and redistribute it, there'd be no more talk about our kids not having self-esteem, and there'd still be plenty left over for McCoy himself.

"Are you all waiting for me?" Sybil Zacharias said abruptly. "Is it my turn now? I, for one, am related to the groom only through past mistakes. Reed opted to accept his father's invitation, and he can't drive yet, so I'm here as his chauffeur and . . . guardian, that's all." She swigged at her drink.

Priscilla Lemoyes looked at her with the expression of revulsion that must have greeted that other party poop, the witch at Sleeping Beauty's christening.

"As far as I'm concerned," Sybil continued, "Lyle's sole justification for existence is Reed. And, having spawned, I wish he'd be like a salmon and die."

The ruffled ex-schoolteacher gasped. "This is his party!" she hissed. "We're his guests!"

"You're horrified, aren't you?" Sybil said to the table at large. "I'm not following the rules, being polite, playing his game. Instead, I'm being honest. Much more so than a lot of others I could name in this room or at this table."

Richard Quinn stared at Sybil intently, with just a glint of his bad-guy persona showing through. The lighting expert whispered to his wife. Lyle's former teacher took a series of deep breaths. Shepard McCoy, apparently oblivious to nuance or even a club over the head—if it wasn't *his* head—turned around to sign an autograph for someone who identified herself as a longtime admirer.

"My turn now? Well, I'm a real fan of Mr. Zacharias," one of the two girls in black said with breathy urgency. "I know him through film school, but I've also been his critter consultant, and let me tell you, you get to know a man's soul in my line of work."

Dare I ask? I dared.

"I help people achieve greater intimacy with their animal companions," she answered, eyes wide open and desperately sincere.

Please, I thought, don't let this turn out to be X-rated.

"I have this gift." She lowered her eyes, modestly. "I communicate telepathically with animals. I've been teaching Mr. Zacharias how to do it, too, and his relationship with Pompom is *much* fuller and stronger now. Really incredible."

Sybil Zacharias ordered another drink and gave the girl a look that would have withered anyone less spiritually evolved.

"And I also think Mr. Zacharias is *marvelous*," her companion said. "I'm just *crazy* for him. He came to our film class about a year ago and he was so funny, and smart, and quick. He told us we're the future—and God, can you believe he included us tonight? We both just want to grow up and *be* him!" Her psychic buddy nodded. Presumably, so did Pompom, telepathically, somewhere.

"Wait till you *are* him," Sybil grumbled. "Wait till you're competition." She sipped at her freshened drink then spoke, pronouncing each word carefully: "Everybody gets excited about Lyle at first. But it's a short honeymoon. Lyle's a man with no old friends."

"Nonsense! Look around this room!" Priscilla huffed. "I myself am an old friend!"

Sybil shrugged. "I won't comment on the room at large. But as for you, with all due apologies, you were never in the game, never an equal, just one of his cheerleaders, so you were never in his way and never a threat."

Nobody else was rude enough to point out that perhaps her status as the ex-wife, plainer and two decades older than her replacement, made her less than an objective observer.

Even my mother seemed stymied by the prospect of navigating back to the easy currents of table talk. We might have sunk into permanent silence had not smattered applause provided diversion. Priscilla Lemoyes was the first at our table to catch on. She pushed back her chair and stood and cheered as the birthday boy and his little woman entered the room. Somebody with a squeaky voice started "Happy Birthday to You." Lyle's face reddened above the beard as he said, "No, no, please," until the squeaky voice stopped and our host and hostess settled at the small table where Hattie and Reed were already seated.

Step-grandmother, stepson, stepmother, stepwife. The prefix-rich new nuclear family.

The second his father was seated, Reed turned to Hattie, spoke briefly and urgently, and then switched chairs with her so that he was no longer next to Tiffany. Of course, as he must have realized, there was no real escape at a small round table for four. He had to be beside or across from her. He compensated by angling his chair so that he only half faced the table, then turned and very blatantly gave the thumbs-up signal in our direction.

Sybil could barely contain her smirk.

Back at the small center table, Lyle reached over and took the thumbs-up hand and spoke to his son in a low voice. After that, Reed resumed his vegetative state and sat with the roaring impassivity only an adolescent can truly master.

Sybil looked satisfied. Through her child, she'd scored a pathetic and mean-spirited triumph. I wondered how much more she planned to spoil Lyle's party.

The lighting man said it was his turn to explain under what circumstances he'd met Lyle, although his tedious account of how, as an apprentice, he'd worked on a short-lived nature series, seemed to have nothing to do with anyone in the room. His wife nodded and simpered. The interminable tale droned on until our first course was delivered with panache by a white-gloved waiter. It was a welcome diversion and a beautiful still life—red, purple, and bronze lettuces; tiny shrimp; and large pearls of caviar.

With some prompting—from my mother, of course—Richard Quinn took his turn at the how-I'm-connected-to-this-party game. "Like Lyle said, we met in college." And that was that. He speared a shrimp and chewed it.

"Way back in college!" My mother was on automatic make-nice, overcompensating for the engineer's boring monologue, Sybil Zacharias's hostility, and her own daughter's lack of social graces.

And the truth is, her sledgehammer hostessing worked. Richard Quinn begrudged us a few more syllables. "Partners afterward, too, for a while. I was his producer."

"My goodness! Here I've been going on, thinking that Lyle produced *Ace of Hearts*," the former teacher said. "I'm so sorry! What's your name again?"

Quinn shook his head. "Split before he wrote *Ace*. Went back to acting for a while."

He was stingy with words, reluctantly and minimally answering, never truly conversing. And thus ended my shortest and most feeble infatuation since third grade. If there's one thing no woman needs, it's another silent male from whom to beg and wheedle the daily minimum syllable requirement.

"He travels fastest who travels alone," Sybil said. "The Zacharias credo."

I tried to figure out what that meant, or, more precisely, what Sybil meant.

"I did a show with you, you know," Shepard McCoy told Quinn. "*Movie of the Week*. Something about a haunting. Science, faith, that sort of thing. My first doctor role." He smiled, enjoying memories of himself, having forgotten his point and the need to connect his anecdote with the man toward whom he'd directed it.

"Do you remember that show?" I asked Richard Quinn.

He shook his head. He was not a dinner party sort of man. Had he come for Tiffany's sake? He certainly didn't seem to be having a good time. "Don't act anymore," he said after too long a pause.

"What is it you do nowadays, then?" I asked. Free of being even potentially smitten, I now could be socially correct with him.

"This and that." He seemed to consider whether to continue, then decided to do so. "Opening a restaurant."

"With Lyle as silent partner," Sybil said. She had not

been part of this stilted conversation, but that didn't appear to matter to her.

Quinn shook his head. "Changed his mind. Selling off assets, not buying them."

"That's just a pose, that middle-aged hippie blather." Nonetheless, Sybil looked momentarily sober.

"I remember when Lyle really was a hippie," my mother said. "I remember the beads and the fringes and the beard."

"Still has the beard!" the lighting technician said with an air of revelation. "So there."

His wife put her hand to her mouth and laughed silently, secretly, like Madame Butterfly.

Shepard leaned forward and squinted at Quinn. "It wasn't a TV movie. It was when you played that mass murderer on *Second Generation*—the one who terrorized me."

Quinn shook his head. "Never been on Lyle's show. Out of touch with him—"

"Out of touch! How prissy and euphemistic," Sybil said. "Don't be so damned *civilized*! You two didn't speak to each—"

Quinn turned up the volume of his voice and let it roll right over her. "—until he married Tiff."

This time my mother's interest wasn't forced at all. "Your daughter, correct?"

"Step," Quinn said. "Married Tiff's mother." Yet another shrug. "She died." The shoulder went up one more time.

"How touching! You raised that lovely girl, then introduced her to your dear old friend!" Priscilla, the sweet old spinster schoolmarm, head spinning with untested romantic delusions, was nearly giddy with delight. "How *perfect*!"

Sybil snorted and called the waiter over for yet another refill. Somebody had to flag her, take away her car keys.

Quinn shook his head. "Nothing to do with it."

"Then it was *destiny*. And it obviously had a happy ending," Priscilla chortled. "Just *look* at those lovebirds." She smiled innocently at Sybil, whose skin mottled in little patchy blushes. "It thrills me to see that Lyle found happiness at last," Priscilla cooed.

Revenge for Sybil's attempts to muddy the image of her

great triumph and former student, Lyle. "I've never *seen* a happier couple," she added, in case the salt hadn't yet rubbed into Sybil's jugular.

The salads were removed, and by some silent consensus, it was decided that it was time for mid-course milling. People stood to talk to diners at other tables or to make use of the facilities upstairs or down the hall. Our table's population declined by half. Shepard, the lighting director's wife, and Priscilla left in succession, and I wondered if there were a social amenity that I, too, should be attending to.

However, as I stood up, Lyle and Tiffany headed my way.

They'd been making rounds from table to table, she looking bored and gorgeous, and he shaking hands and exchanging jokes and pleasantries with each guest. I watched as one by one faces brightened at his approach. The old attention thing again. He bent close to hear what an elderly relative said, looked concerned at another's remarks, laughed along with a third.

When it was our time to greet Lyle, I stood, as did my mother, and before I knew it, I was enthusiastically wishing him happy birthday and saying what a great party this was, and almost believing myself.

"Be honest," he said with a smile. "You're bored silly, but you're a great soul and you're enduring it and helping me have the time of my life. Getting old isn't bad with friends to share the—"

Tiffany did not successfully stifle her noisy yawn.

"Sorry, darling," Lyle said. "I tend to get carried away. Now, if you'll excuse us, Mandy, we want to check how things are coming along in the kitchen. Tiff's a perfectionist." Tiffany impassively watched her husband through a fringe of lashes. She did not seem amused or charmed or feel the need to pretend to be.

After Lyle and Tiffany left, I realized Richard Quinn had at some point drifted to my side. I was mildly flattered. I wasn't interested in him, but that didn't mean I would mind his being interested in me.

Having approached, Quinn stood aimlessly, as if he had

no idea what to do next. Very eighth grade. But I remembered the cure for it. My mother had given me lots of
teen-help books, and all agreed on one universal credo for
success with males. Ask him about himself. "Where are
you opening that restaurant of yours?" I asked.

"On the Delaware."

"Our Delaware? Here in Philadelphia?"

He nodded.

"When?"

"Two weeks. The Scene."

"What scene?"

"That's its name."

"Ever done anything like this before?"

He shook his head.

Oh, Mom, you never said it would be this hard or point-
less. "Tell me *all* about it," I said, bypassing subtlety. And
finally it appeared I had hit oil. Quinn was nearly voluble,
listing problems with building codes, liquor licensing, his
former backer, and the decision to add on an expensive second floor for private parties.

"Private parties?" The God of Proms had brought this
man to me. "How large a private party?"

My voice must have been too urgent, because he looked
startled and needed to think a bit. "Three hundred," he finally said. "Why?"

I waxed eloquent on behalf of my seniors. He seemed intensely interested in me all of a sudden. We made a date to
inspect it for the following day. I was elated. The evening
of my party-martyrdom had justified itself. For the first
time in all history, or at least in mine, virtue would indeed
be rewarded.

Meanwhile, the party tides once again shifted and guests
and waiters filtered back into the room.

A quarter of an hour or so later, once everyone was involved with buttery-soft beef in a dark sauce, tiny crisped
potatoes, and deep-fried baby artichokes, Lyle stood and
tapped his spoon on the side of his water glass. The string
quartet that had been discreetly entertaining us grew silent.

"I don't want to interrupt your meal," he said. "Please,

continue." And people did, so that Lyle spoke against a background of dancing knives and forks. "I want to thank you for being part of this celebration. I don't think you can know what this means to me. In fact, I'm positive that at least a few of you don't know *why* this means something to me and I'll bet you were surprised by my invitation." The line was greeted by scattered dry laughs.

He cleared his throat and continued, looking down at a small stack of three-by-five cards. "Life, I have found, is not one smooth line. There are bumps. But this is a time to declare that once and for all, our differences and difficulties and misunderstandings and partings of the way are part of our histories and nothing more. I've been joined with each of you at certain significant junctures, and you are all part of the mosaic of my life. At a certain age—and certainly fifty is that age—it seems important to relegate collisions and scrapes to history."

I found the beef better than the talk, and much less schmaltzy. My attention wandered around the room. Sybil stared at her ex through slitted eyes, much more engrossed by him than I was.

Priscilla Lemoyes's hands were pressed together at the base of her neck, reverently. He did better with senior citizens than wives. Hattie also beamed and nodded, but Tiffany looked exactly like my students at a stupefying assembly. She examined her manicured nails, one by one, over and over.

"I have been blessed with more than my share of life's gifts," Lyle was saying when I tuned in again, "so there was nothing material I wanted for my birthday. Besides, as I approached the half-century mark, I saw how *cluttered* my life had become. And how I had become too busy to enjoy it. Most of you"—he paused for a moment—"know I'm about to make serious changes"—another breath—"to take time to smell the roses and grow them, too, and to be with my lovely wife."

His not lovely ex-wife snorted and glared. The current missus was too engrossed in her nail polish to react.

Lyle paused for several rapid breaths. He was much

more nervous than I would have anticipated. I was afraid he would hyperventilate by the time he finished his talk. "And my son and friends," he added. "Time with them, too." It sounded embarrassingly like an afterthought. He looked flustered. Perhaps he was flubbing his talk.

"Before I take the next step, I wanted to see you—my life, to look around a room and see the faces that are the landmarks of my adventure through this—through this—" Again he looked nonplussed. Maybe he couldn't read his three-by-five card prompts. "Like this building—almost where I grew up—like all of you—like . . . excuse me," he said. "Overexcited. Can't catch my breath. Must be why they call us old wheezers."

"Geezers," his son corrected him without a smile.

"A few faces couldn't be here because of . . ." Another pause as he breathed, rather raggedly, I thought. "Others . . . no longer among . . . us." His inappropriate stops and starts made his delivery choppy and his meaning difficult to apprehend. I reminded myself that he was accustomed to being behind the scenes, not onstage. He had the right to be edgy.

"For all—of—you here, thanks for—this—that—moment I—wanted." The rhythm was ever more erratic, punctuated by gasps, and he was skipping words. The hairs on the back of my neck prickled. This couldn't be an attack of stage fright. "It," Lyle said, "—the—greatest . . ."

There had been a gradual cessation of background noise. No more clicking knives and forks. People glanced anxiously at one another, checking whether their alarm was shared. When Lyle actually made it to the end of his talk, there was a spontaneous standing ovation, half praise, half relief.

Lyle pulled a handkerchief out of his pocket and put it to his eyes, then wiped at beads of sweat on his forehead and temples. Then he clutched his handkerchief and bent forward.

"Lyle?" Hattie asked.

"Legs," he said. "Cramps. Bad. I . . . oh, boy. Old—all—

at—once!" He rolled his eyes skyward. "Give me a break!"

Feeble laughter greeted his attempt at lightness. The collective mood roller-coasted, dipping into apprehension, murmuring questions like background music, then audibly relaxing when Lyle made light of his discomfort. It was nothing, then. We were still at a party. Life was normal and fun. And then Lyle winced and buckled forward and the anxiety level skyrocketed.

Lyle waved his hand, pushing away his physical problems, but he was bent way over, as if his cramping legs wouldn't hold him. He put his hands to his throat, his face contorted with fear.

"Lyle! What is it?" Hattie cried.

His breathing had become so raspy I could hear it plainly at my table as it jaggedly pumped. "Throat," he said. "Burns—hurts—"

"Is there a doctor in the house?" somebody called.

Shepard McCoy stood up.

"Oh, for God's sake!" Sybil screamed. "You're an *actor*, you fool!"

But no one else had stood. No piece of Lyle Zacharias's life mosaic had gone to medical school.

"A heart attack?" my mother asked.

"I've never heard of one like this," the former schoolteacher murmured.

"Some horrible infection?" I asked. We were still paralyzed by etiquette. Dear Abby, is it proper to suggest that the host is desperately ill if he says he's not and you might spoil his party?

"Baby, what is it?" Hattie shrieked. "Where does it hurt?" Baby was still gasping and the tears in his eyes seemed from pain.

I stood up and began wedging myself between seats, en route to the door, which seemed very far away. I angled myself to watch what was happening while I maneuvered. "Excuse me," I said many times to guests who were too engrossed in the ongoing disaster to respond.

Tiffany stood by Lyle in red-spangled ineffectiveness, her hands half raised in the I-give-up position.

The room buzzed with nervous collective wing-fluttering as we absorbed the idea that the completely unexpected and potentially disastrous had indeed happened.

"Dizzy." Lyle canvassed the room the way a drowning man might look for the disappearing horizon. I could not believe that the self-confident man who'd stood up a few minutes back had so thoroughly and swiftly become this disoriented, terrified creature. He even looked different—bloated and sallow.

"Who—"

I stopped where I was. His breathing was loud and rough, like sticks over heavy metal grating. He was disintegrating in front of us as if he'd been seized by something alien and inhuman. Now, in addition to the breathing, the pallor, the bloat, the buckling legs, and disorientation, his eyes had lost their moorings.

"*No!*" Hattie screamed.

He lurched forward. I made my way toward the dining room door, past the lace-clothed side table where the dark and white chocolate dream of a birthday cake waited.

"Who—" whooshed out of Lyle, "—*kill* me?"

Hattie screamed. The room buzzed with the single word as question and exclamation. "Kill. Kill! *Kill?*"

Wheezing like a fireplace bellows, Lyle forced more words out. "Who . . . poison me?"

I ran like hell for the phone.

Six

"POISONED?" TIFFANY SCREAMED AT THE TOP OF HER LUNGS. Her words reached all the way down the hall to where I stood at the small front desk. "What are you saying?" she howled. "*I* ate the same food!"

I dialed 911. "A man's been poisoned. I think." It was embarrassing making an emergency call with caveats and small print. *Perhaps* there'd been a poisoning—no guarantees. But there was definitely a sick person and, strengthening my case, fifty other people who had eaten the same food. If, of course, the food was at fault.

Nine-one-one didn't remark on my quibbling. Instead, they said to stay calm, that help would be there any minute.

I tried to follow their advice and remain collected, although I was having trouble remembering how, particularly given the commotion in the dining room.

The scene was out of Breughel by way of *Vanity Fair*. Lyle Zacharias, breathing with obvious difficulty, braced himself on the long table that held his ornate birthday cake. Smartly attired party guests wavered between blasé seen-it-all sophistication and a visible desire to stampede. The repeated motif—whispered, shouted, questioned, in deep basso tones and cultivated soprano—was the word *poison* echoing like the dull pulse of mass hysteria.

People futilely sought comfort and reassurance from one

61

another. "Is sweat on my forehead?" a man demanded of his dinner companion. "Wasn't Lyle sweating?" "But what about *me*?" his tablemate answered. "I feel sick."

And so did lots of others. People complained of dizziness, or weakness, or trembling—including me. I hoped I was suffering a simple old-fashioned anxiety attack.

En route to my mother, I passed Hattie Zacharias, who looked almost as ill as her nephew did. Her wrinkled skin was even looser, as if it were falling off. She mouthed the word *poison*, although no more than a hiss of air emerged. She repeated the motion, as if practicing it, working to get it right. It was even more frightening that way, like a silent scream.

Poison. It finally, thoroughly, hit me, and as dreadful as I felt for Lyle Zacharias, I felt even worse for me.

Fear buckled my knees, and then, of course, I worried that this sudden muscle weakness was an early symptom. Had Lyle's legs weakened or simply cramped?

My core temperature dropped. I was freezing. Had Lyle been cold? No—he'd been sweating. Good, good. But I felt light-headed, too. Was that the same as Lyle's dizziness?

While these idiotic brain waves skittled about, Lyle let go of the table and made a staggering lurch in the direction of the doorway. However, he didn't even make it past the cake before he stumbled and again grabbed the table.

People moved between us, so I couldn't see clearly, but it was obvious from the sounds and the sudden general recoil that the man was now violently ill. I remembered his lurched attempt to escape, and realized that despite the desperation of his situation, he'd been trying to exit and avoid social embarrassment. There was a psychology paper in this for somebody: "Terminal Prioritizing: Death or a Major Social Gaffe?"

The people around him backed off some more, so that I could see Lyle pitch forward into his birthday cake, crumpling the lace tablecloth and pulling it down as he and the dessert both fell. The white and dark chocolate cake landed on his upturned face, putting him in jeopardy of layer cake asphyxiation, assuming nothing worse destroyed him first.

My mother rushed forward, which shouldn't have surprised me. She was carrying first aid—a dampened napkin—and before anyone else had gone beyond milling and agonizing, she had cleaned Lyle's face. Under the icing and chocolate crumbs, Lyle was unconscious.

We watched, fifty ticking time bombs. Make that forty-nine, I thought. If Lyle was right, one of us was a poisoner.

A woman in platinum Jean Harlow hair and gold lamé bent over Lyle and began CPR.

I wanted Mackenzie. Unnatural causes was his turf, not mine, and this seemed a case right up his expertise. Probably.

Probably would have to suffice. I wanted, needed, to hear his voice. I went back to the hall phone. Please, I asked the detective gods, just this once, let him be where I need him to be.

Just this once, he was. I began my 911 riff. "Thought you're spendin' the evenin' with your mother," he said.

"I was, I am—she's here. My father—never mind. Mackenzie, I think it's murder. It's so fast and ugly, with these weird symptoms. And other people are complaining now, too."

"He's dead?"

"Nearly. Well, truthfully, I don't know. Does he have to die? Do you come out for attempted murder?"

"Could it be food poisonin'?" I envisioned him watching the dark rain pound headquarters' windows, finding even his utilitarian and bleak surroundings homey compared to a trek to Queen Village.

A man in tails rushed by, clutching his stomach. I had walked into Poe's "Masque of the Red Death." "I've never heard of any food acting this quickly and violently, have you?" I answered. "Besides, if you wait until we find out what's caused this, all the evidence will be gone. They'll wash up and tidy and destroy every trace."

He considered this, or something. "Okay," he said glumly, "somebody'll be there soon. An' Mandy? Y'all got to get your stomachs pumped."

Stomachs seemed such nicely complete items. I couldn't

imagine how they would pump one. I thought of gas sta-
tions and wells and tried to apply their mechanics to my
anatomy and decided to take a pass. "We can't leave the
scene of the crime," I said, rather desperately.

"Don' know there was a crahm!" He was getting emotional—either annoyed with or concerned for me. His
southern roots curled around every syllable, squeezing out
its hard edges, making it barely recognizable. Blurtalk.
"Don' wan' y'urt." I had to mentally race beside his sentences, clipping them into words. He didn't want me hurt.
Either this was for real or it was not, but he couldn't afford
to gamble.

"Yes. Sure. Okay," I said.

"Listen up—I'll find a bus—no, vans. Send you to different hospitals. An officer for each one. But good Lord,
it's gonna be a bitch. The President's in town, know that?
Fund-raiser, and every extra man's on that duty." His sighs
had become epic in scale. "When the patrolman shows up,
have him call me here. I'll explain."

Gallant, yes, but I'd have preferred his personally rushing to my aid. "Maybe it wasn't a poisoning," I said.
"Maybe this is a little . . . extreme."

"You sure enough of that to risk fifty people?"

His round. Back to the dining room as the bearer of rotten news, just in case the night wasn't already sufficiently
traumatic. The entryway was blocked by the chef, still in
her apron and bandanna. She stood, one hand half over her
eyes, as if she didn't want to watch but couldn't resist, and
the other pointing at her guest of honor, sprawled on the
floor while the woman in gold lamé administered CPR.

She screamed, a thin, piercing wail, almost unearthly and
definitely frightening, the sound a machine might make
when important wires snapped.

"Lizzie," I said softly, lightly touching her shoulder. It
was difficult speaking without much of a waver in my
voice. "Please calm down. Help is on the way."

Apparently, she didn't hear me, but then it was hard to
hear one low voice in the bedlam. Only Sybil and her son
Reed remained quiet, an island of immobile silence in the

din. Hattie, bending over her prostrate nephew, shouted his name over and over, sounding as if each repetition ripped something vital out of her. Tiffany stood, mouth agape, said the same name, but angrily, pathetically, anxiously, questioningly—like an actress trying out her lines. Priscilla Lemoyes sobbed loudly. The young couple from our table clutched each other, asking, constantly, whether they were all right. People cried, offered theories: he'd had a heart attack, a seizure, heat exhaustion—despite the temperature. Anything, as long as it wasn't contagious. And running through the babble and cries like a corrosive acid-drenched wire ran Janine's whine, raised now by several decibel levels. "My tongue's numb," she yowled. "I'm achy all over. I don't feel right!"

"You never feel right!" her husband, right behind her, answered, too loudly. "Shut up for once!"

People stepped away from them. We'd reached the point of every victim for himself.

"My legs tingle!" Janine wailed.

"Who *cares*?" her husband shouted. "Look around— nobody else is carrying on this way! Nobody else is sick."

"Lyle is *dying*!"

"And you're making things worse—as usual!"

With a dramatic intake of air, Janine swallowed her screech.

I wondered if I could be held for murder if I told everyone except Janine about the promised emergency treatment. But this was a night for virtue. "Everybody!" I said as loudly as I could. "Listen!" Eventually they calmed enough for me to shout out my message. "Help's on the way! Vans are coming to take us to the hospital. Police escorts. We'll all be fine."

The push toward the exit slowed to an irritated shuffle. I thought some semblance of calm had been restored, but Lizzie once more erupted, this time in words. Three words, to be exact. "I saw him! I saw him! I saw him!"

"Please," I began, but how could she be calm? There was a good possibility that one—I hoped only one—of her dinner guests had been poisoned. This was not cause for serenity.

"I saw him!" she sobbed. "I saw him!"

"We all did," I said softly.

A woman in purple pushed at me. "I'm not waiting for some bureaucratic underling to send help!" she shouted. "I'm out of here!"

"Why? Where would you go? The paramedics and police are on their way, and they can get you to help faster than you can get there alone. Besides"—I hoped Lizzie was listening, too—"food poisoning isn't this fast or acute. What happened to Lyle probably has nothing to do with the food here, if you ask me."

"Nobody asked you!" the angry woman said.

My mother charged forward to avenge her daughter's verbal attacker. "Just because Lyle _thought_ it was poison doesn't make it so," she said reasonably.

"If you leave and nobody else does," I added, "then the police will assume you were the poisoner."

"Me?" the would-be escapee screamed. "_Me?_ I'm his hair stylist, for God's sake!"

I momentarily wondered why a bald man's hair stylist was on his fifty-most-wanted list, but there were bigger issues to consider first.

"What about botulism?" Shepard McCoy's voice was low, TV doc wise and serene. He was used to make-believe medical emergencies, and didn't know real trouble when he was in the middle of it.

"Botulism's from canned food," a woman in hand-painted silk said. "I thought this place said it used all fresh produce. They said that in _print!_"

What was her point? That we'd file a postmortem class action suit against the restaurant for false advertising?

"Botulism symptoms don't start for hours," Reed Zacharias said. Before anyone could challenge him, he shrugged a pudgy shoulder. "I like biology. Microbiology especially. And I know a lot about toxins."

He waited, as if for a challenge, but I for one make it a

point never to cross surly adolescents who specialize in toxins.

"It's caused by a spore," he continued. "Symptoms are
different. Affects your vision. You get paralyzed."

"I don't think that whatever made him that sick was in
his food," I said. "At least not in whatever we all ate." Because, as I didn't say, as they should have been able to figure out themselves, if the culprit was the food we all had
eaten, we should all be cramping and getting sore throats
and dizziness even as I spoke. We should all, frankly, be
dying at the same tempo as Lyle appeared to be.

Nobody else seemed to want to debate the logic of the
situation or to await the police. Instead, they milled toward
the door, maneuvering around and sometimes over Lyle's
appendages. The platinum blonde continued to pump at his
chest. "I'm not waiting around to find out whether I'm poisoned," a burly young man with acne scars and a ponytail
told me. "I'll get myself to the hospital." He turned to the
crowd around him. "Where is it? I'm from New York."

"*I saw him!*" Lizzie again, still stuck on her three-word
groove. Something dreadful was happening to her—a seizure, a breakdown—and she needed attention, but so did
everyone else, so I hoped her particular ailment, which
didn't seem deadly, would keep.

"Let me by!" the ponytail demanded. I did, and I moved
Lizzie aside as well.

However, the burly man didn't make it through the doorway because we had a sudden influx of personnel. Lizzie's
father materialized, pulling his daughter close to him. "I
saw him!" she cried out. "I saw him!" she sobbed.

He made soothing noises and patted her back. "Oh,
Lizzikins," he said softly. "Hush, now."

A fireman raced through the hall and into the dining
room and almost instantaneously replaced the blonde as the
CPR giver. At the same time, two policemen, Tweedle-dee
and Tweedle-dum, draped in identical plastic rain ponchos,
entered, asking questions: "Who made the call? What's this
about? What's going on here? Nobody leave."

Once again, I explained, pointing at Lyle, waving at the

group in the dining room. "And vans are supposed to arrive to take us to the hospital. Hospitals. Need our stomachs pumped," I said.

"What the devil is—I never heard of such a thing. The scene of the crime should never be disturb—"

"There may not have been a crime." I felt odd, parroting Mackenzie. "But there could be other . . . victims."

I was backed up by a vigorous, adamant chorus.

"Regulations say—"

I told them to call headquarters and ask for Mackenzie. One did. The other stood beside me in the doorway.

"Lyle!" Hattie screamed. "Get up! Stand up!"

"This would never have happened if I'd been in the country," Roy Beecher said.

"Excuse me?" I hate it when instead of dealing with the present crisis, people assign blame or adopt responsibility. And what was he saying—that Lizzie had screwed up? No wonder she had problems.

"I need a cigarette," he said in lieu of an explanation.

I shook my head. "Don't smoke."

"Neither did I. Stopped three weeks ago, but this, now . . ." I could see the tremble in his hand as he released Lizzie. And then, abruptly, he pushed his way out of the building.

"Hey!" the policeman said, but with too little enthusiasm. It was still a wet cold mess out there and he didn't seem eager to rush out into it. And in reality, it didn't matter. Roy Beecher had, if I recalled, been resting somewhere all evening, recovering from jet lag, and hadn't had the possibly poisonous meal.

And then, having been radioed the go-ahead by the police, the paramedics raced in, pushing a gurney loaded with tubes and pumps. "Lyle!" Hattie screamed yet again. "Get up!"

But it was the fireman who stood, looking grim. The paramedics didn't seem discouraged. They inserted a curved tube into Lyle's throat and connected it to an air bag and then, in what seemed mere seconds after their arrival, they wheeled Lyle away, the air bag breathing for him.

"Is he alive?" somebody asked.

Only silence answered.

"Dead, I think," someone else whispered.

"Dead," in a flat, horrified echo.

"Dead?"

"Dead!"

The word detonated from every pocket of the room. It was whispered, screamed, silently mouthed, and uttered with solemn finality. Hattie cried inconsolably. The platinum blonde patted her on the shoulder. Tiffany stood well apart from where Lyle had fallen, one hand to her mouth, her brow wrinkled, as if she were trying to figure out what was going on, or, uncharitable as I knew the thought to be, as if she were wondering how she was supposed to feel about it. Next to her stood Shepard McCoy, one hand on her shoulder, patting it sympathetically.

Janine screamed that she couldn't stand this, she wasn't strong enough. She was not about to be outdone in the misery department, not even when the competitor was a clear winner by virtue of being near death.

Priscilla wiped at tears with an embroidered handkerchief. Her other hand held the lace at her throat in an unconscious and horrifying mirroring of Lyle's choking motions. Sybil clutched Reed, who stared impassively at the afterimage of his fallen father.

Richard Quinn, the taciturn former villain, looked green. For a second I thought he, too, was about to be ill, but it seemed more a case of witnessing a nonsimulated dying than of poisoning.

"Okay, they're here," one of the policemen said. "Count yourself out, twelve to a van."

"I never heard of such a thing in my life," the other policeman said. "They could all be suspects!"

"Five—six—seven—"

"Let me get my suitcase." Shepard McCoy went to the stairs.

"No you don't. Nobody goes upstairs without an escort. Nobody goes anywhere but onto the van. Nobody takes anything but himself. Coats if one of us accompanies you to get it. No pocketbooks, either." This was greeted by considerable grumbling, but he ignored it. "Pockets empty, too, please. You'll get it all back. Don't worry."

"What are you looking for?" my mother asked with innocent sincerity.

The policemen glared at her, disapproval of the question pulling their mouths down. They glanced at each other, then both adopted a cryptic, know-it-all expression.

"Haven't got a clue," somebody muttered accurately behind me.

"Officer on the bus will get your IDs," the older one continued. "Take your statements, bring you back afterward. You got it?"

"I haf naiver!" Anna Pacocci, the Golden-Throated Czech, raised her head high. "Naiver in my life treated like *criminal!*"

"Twelve!" And out she went.

"Okay, you." He pointed at me. "You begin the second group. "One—" My mother was ushered upstairs by a constable who said she could retrieve both of our coats. No point in being saved from poisoning only to succumb to pneumonia, my mother had gently suggested. I wondered whether Mackenzie would eventually arrive in the flesh. If so, it would be unhappy flesh, because if this turned out to be the scene of a crime, it was a very messy one indeed. We'd moved and fingered and pushed and rearranged what evidence there might be. In fact, we well may have made it impossible to ever decide whether there had been a crime committed tonight.

I wondered if, given the situation, he could simply say, "What the hell? What's the use?" Or was he obliged, no matter how ridiculous or futile the task, to search the house, the people, their suitcases and pocketbooks? And if so, what then? Could they test every single leftover slice of beef Bernaise? What if the poison had been in a crab puff, already ingested? Or a glass of wine or vodka, long since downed, the glass probably washed and dried?

I couldn't imagine how anyone could have targeted Lyle in the first place. Perhaps there were partners in crime—a poisoner and a waiter, who placed a specially designated plate in front of the guest of honor. Otherwise, what? The hors d'oeuvres had been picked at random from trays. None of this made sense.

"Five—six." The officer counted slowly. I was halfway out the door when I heard yet another fracas. This time, although Lizzie wasn't making the noise, she seemed to have prompted it.

Hattie was the screamer now. *"You!"* she wailed at the chef. "It's your fault! It's *you*! You!"

"Seven-eight, move right on, please." The officer was obviously used to hysterics.

"I didn't do it!" Lizzie shouted the words with urgency.

This wasn't fair. Nobody had any proof that Lizzie's food was to blame. "It isn't her fault!" I called out as the officer put his hand on my shoulder and moved me forward. But no one seemed to hear me.

Even outside, through the rain pounding on the awning above my head, I could hear the old woman's screams. "You! Your fault!" echoed into the night.

It was a relief to get onto the van and let somebody else tell me what to do, at least for a little while.

Seven

"GOOD GRIEF!" THE VOICE CAME FROM THE SEAT BEHIND me. "I always heard Philadelphia was dull, but do they really consider getting one's stomach pumped something to do?"

I remembered him. He was pale, with haughty, aristocratic features, and he was dressed in tails and accompanied by an anorexic woman; a dancer, someone—probably my mother—had told me.

"You shouldn't make jokes," she said. "I'm sick. I feel like I'm dying. They'd better hurry."

"How could you be poisoned?" the man asked. "You don't eat enough for it to work. It would certainly not be my method of choice with you."

She inhaled noisily, then cried, words coming out every two or three sobs. "I—can't—breathe!"

"Then good for you for nonetheless managing to." He was not going to get the chivalry award tonight.

"I knew I shouldn't accept that invitation." A thin woman across the aisle raked her spiked hair with crimson talons as she spoke to her stern-looking companion. "I knew it. Didn't I say so?"

The stern woman nodded her head. Her hair was gray and cut to a half-inch length. She wore heavy silver earrings that clicked when she expressed agreement.

"I've done business with the man," talons said. "And I have nothing against him, but to travel ninety miles in the rain for *this*."

"Helen," the gray-haired woman said, "Helen, he's—"

"Besides," Helen with the talons continued, "we all knew the show was getting the axe, so it's not like we were going to keep on having a relationship or anything, so why drag myself—"

"Helen, really. What's done is done."

"You yourself said that the cancellation was why we were invited. Soften us up, make us reconsider. Save his face with that retirement business. Didn't you say so yourself?"

"Canceled?" Sybil Zacharias called out. "*Second Generation* is going to be canceled?" She was ahead of me, next to her son, who didn't move his head or his shoulders, but sat perfectly rigid.

"Ratings stink," talons said.

"Really, Helen." Her friend's voice sounded like it came from between clenched teeth. "The man is—the ratings don't matter anymore."

"Canceled," Sybil said in a hard whisper.

The elegant man behind me yawned loudly. He obviously wasn't concerned with Lyle's ratings. "If they would only have told me I was going to spend some of the night vomiting," he said, "I would have dressed for the occasion."

"Don't even *say* that word," his skinny seatmate begged.

A police officer who had already written down about half of our names and addresses methodically continued his rounds. He didn't look any happier than the rest of us, although he, at least, wasn't overdressed.

"Don't you want some kind of statement or something?" I recognized the voice as Janine's. I hadn't realized she was on my bus.

"Can't take them when you're all together like this," the policeman said. "Later."

We were the HUP delegation, being trucked to the Hospital of the University of Pennsylvania. Other segments of the possibly afflicted had been taken to Hahnemann, Jefferson, Pennsylvania Hospital, and Temple. It was lucky that Philadelphia was so liberally blessed with medical facilities. Or was it suspicious?

My mother sat next to me, in the window seat, her hands folded on her lap and her bottom lip gripped by her upper teeth, the sure sign that Bea was brooding. As children, Beth and I used to scurry for cover as soon as we saw the old lip-in-the-teeth, although luckily, Bea could only brood for brief periods of time. I checked my watch. Six minutes since we had boarded. Not many more to go.

Then I looked at my watch again and did a mild double take. Only seventy-five minutes—one and one-quarter hour—had passed since we entered the dining room for Lyle Zacharias's gala birthday dinner. It felt more like epochs, great historical subdivisions, but it was not yet nine-thirty.

With nothing to do but sit and ride, the emotional overload of the evening finally had a chance at me, and I felt overwhelmed with exhaustion and sorrow.

"Good thing Lyle was watching his weight," my mother murmured, breaking her brood.

Nothing like your mother saying something completely insane to snap a mood around. I swiveled and stared at her to see if she was serious. She was. "Call me crazy," I said, "but in all honesty, the last thing I'd want to do right before my death is diet."

"No, I mean if he hadn't been, I'd be worried that one of my tarts did him in. Given that they weren't refrigerated."

"Trust me. It wouldn't have done him in, even then." A love affair can become toxic that fast, but not tart topping.

"Except . . ." my mother said.

I waited.

"When I excused myself to go to the powder room—remember?"

I half nodded because I only half remembered.

"I checked them again. Because it was hot in that kitchen and—"

"Yes, Mother, I know. But they were fine, and anyway, nobody ate them, so forget about it."

"I would. Except for the two I took out of the tin. Only half of one was on the plate," she said. "So somebody . . . you don't think the heat in the kitchen could have—"

"Of course not!" All the same, I was glad she'd been whispering, and I lowered my voice, too. "Mom, whipped cream—as spoiled as it can possibly get—can make somebody sick, but not the way Lyle was."

She blinked, fighting back tears. "Are you positive?"

I nodded.

"Did you see, Reed?" Sybil said from across the aisle. I tensed, afraid she was talking about my mother and me. "Did you catch her impersonation of grief? She never could act. Little starlet tramp. And Shepard as the good old family friend. Now *there's* a good actor, given how he felt about Lyle, *and* Tiffany—I'd expect him to be dancing with joy!"

"Mom, please. You're practically shouting," Reed said with the classic agony of a teenager. "Why do you always say things like that, anyway?"

I was on his side. His mother was loud and drunk and extremely indiscreet.

"I'm *whispering*, Reed. You're so *sensitive*! Besides, am I wrong? Is a single thing I said wrong?"

"All I can say," a male voice proclaimed from the back of the bus. "All I can say is that only a fool lets his enemies get that close to him. Only a fool, or a man who doesn't want to be any older than fifty, ever."

"Hear, hear," the man behind me muttered.

"I'm hungry," his companion said.

"You won't be for long," the man said darkly.

"Why are we moving so *slowly*?" Janine's whine again. Luckily, her complaint, whatever it was this time, was drowned out by the sirens of two patrol cars bracketing us.

I finally had an authentic escort for the evening.

The bus riders lapsed into heavy silence. We were like convicts being taken to the chain gang: sullen, grumpy, and lost in individual fears and self-pity. No one had any spare compassion or concern, and no one even mentioned Lyle Zacharias again. At a time when he should have been the center of events, he had become only a footnote.

THE WOMAN SITTING AT THE EMERGENCY ADMITTING DESK WAS engrossed in a crossword puzzle. She glanced up, then squinted warily as we trooped in, spangled, beaded, high-heeled, and tuxedoed. She bent her head from side to side and applied X-ray vision to our intact forms, searching for the maimed one.

"What is this? Some kind of treasure hunt?" she finally demanded.

"It's a *poisoning!*" Janine shrieked. "A *mass* murder! I feel it creeping through my veins!"

"All of you? Poisoned?"

Janine, clutching her midriff, nodded vigorously. I shook my head and shrugged. I appreciated Mackenzie's caution and protectiveness, but the only signals my body was sending out were hungry S.O.S.'s. I was positive I hadn't had any of whatever had felled Lyle, and I was not at all convinced that his collapse was necessarily the result of murder.

My mother wrinkled her brow. "We *think* that *maybe* somebody else was definitely poisoned."

"Come again?" The name on the admissions woman's plastic tag had less than the standard basic allotment of vowels. African, perhaps. "Ma'am" seemed easiest.

"We were at a party, ma'am," I said.

"Didn't think you were digging ditches in those duds."

You would think he had troubles enough of his own, but a man waiting for treatment, a bloody rag pressed to his head, guffawed at our fashion blunder. We were incorrectly dressed for the occasion.

"Now Ralphie," the woman said to him, "don't you always be making fun of people."

I wondered how often a person had to stagger in here

to become a known quantity and a regular. Ralphie's face had zipperlike scars on the forehead and chin, not to mention whatever he was covering with the rag. I suspected that Ralphie had a revolving charge account with the E.R.

"And a man collapsed—got really sick—"

"*Died!*" the skinny ballerina said.

"When he collapsed," I continued, "he said he'd been poisoned, and we were all eating the same food, so the police thought we should be checked out."

She rolled her eyes ceilingward until they were nearly gone into some recess behind her brows. Then she counted us and opened a file drawer and counted again until she had a satisfactory number of forms.

"Okay," she said. "Everybody take one and fill it out."

"Fill it out?" Janine screamed. "We could *die* while we fill it out."

"And please have your insurance information ready when it's your turn," the woman said.

We all, pretty much in unison, did a double take. If there was one person among us who had really tucked his Blue Cross card into his cummerbund, I thought we'd make the *Guinness Book of Records*.

While Janine continued to whine, the emergency doors flew open and two attendants wheeling an elderly woman on a gurney raced by and through a second set of swinging doors.

"Wait a minute!" Janine said. "We were here first! You aren't making *her* wait!"

"Uh-huh," the admissions woman said. "Yo, Ralphie, you can go in now," she told the man with the rag on his head. "An' don't you bleed on my floor again!"

He grinned and went through the swinging doors.

"My good woman," the elegant man in tails said. "Is it at all possible to speed this process along?"

"Not really," she said.

A pale and bulky man who looked like a refrigerator with red hair was steered in by a small lump of a woman who spoke around him, in the general direction of the desk. "He's hurt. He was with the guys, and you know how they fight when they have a little too much to drink, and—"

The red-haired man tilted forward and smashed down onto his face.

"That's what I mean," his little pilot said calmly.

The woman behind the desk buzzed someone.

The elegant man in tails turned to our group. "Now we all know that old joke. First prize: a week in Philadelphia. Second prize: two weeks in Philadelphia. Third prize: three weeks. But I ask you, what precisely did *we* win? The booby prize?"

His cadaverous companion still sniffled about her impending end.

The film student/critter consultant also looked concerned. "I'm getting vibes from my babies. They need me. I have to get back to Connecticut," she said.

"Babies?" The man in tails pronounced the word as if it were foul. "How many do you have?"

"Dozens!" the young woman said, perking up. She was definitely the happiest person in the emergency room. "Not *people* babies," she chortled. "*Critters.*"

"Is that like varmints?" the receptionist asked.

"Nonhuman companions. That's what the language Nazis call them these days." The sophisticate in the tuxedo raised an eyebrow.

The girl in black blinked and wrinkled her forehead. "Critters," she said in a small puzzled voice. "Doggies and kitties. I have this gift."

I didn't want to hear what the man in tails would make of her telepathic talents. Luckily, Sybil Zacaharias once again erupted and averted doggy-shrink redux.

"This whole business is completely and utterly ridiculous!" she said, quite loudly. "Disgusting, too. I'll bet Lyle did this out of pure spite. Poisoned his own damn self and set it up to look like it was one of us. It would be just like him, especially now that I know he was losing his job." She chuckled, a bit madly. "That's what those stupid, saccharine invitations should have said: *It's my party and I'll die if I want to*."

Her son looked at her as if she were a mutant life-form. "Get it?" she asked.

"No offense," my mother said, "but that's a bit . . . hard-hearted, don't you think?"

I was still plodding through the form when a young Asian woman in a white jacket came out holding a clipboard. "I'm Dr. Lee," she said. "And you are the . . . poisoned?" She looked at us, one by one. "What is it you've taken?"

We shrugged.

"Why do you think you were poisoned?"

"Because a man at the party we were at said he was."

"Said?"

"Then he died. Or something. He certainly got sick."

"And we ate the same food."

The emergency room doctor, or resident, took off her glasses and rubbed her eyes, probably wishing for a nice, comprehensible knife fight or heart attack. "What, please, are your symptoms?" she eventually asked.

Janine cut to the chase and begged for a stomach pump while the dancer and a grumbly male voice overlapped one another with dire signs and my mother dithered, saying she actually felt fine, and Sybil Zacharias said the words *patently ridiculous* at least twice.

The doctor put up a hand. "One at a time!" She pointed at me. "What are your symptoms?"

I shook my head. "I don't have any."

She scowled. Then she asked each of us in turn the same question. Aside from boredom, hunger, and being pissed off, the worst we came up with was shortness of breath, dizziness, and nausea.

"Those could all be symptoms of anxiety, which is understandable if a man has collapsed near you." Her voice was flat and precise and not particularly enamored of us. "I want you all to take seats."

Janine—theoretically close to death by now—elbowed
her way to the chair nearest the swinging doors. "And
then?" she asked.

"And then you will sit on those seats. *If* you develop
any symptoms whatsoever, we'll try to help you. But in
the absence of any knowledge of what was ingested—if
anything, by anyone—and with no symptoms, no distress, I
cannot authorize gastric lavage, which is an invasive proce-
dure."

"I demand my rights!" Janine was back on her feet. "I
pay taxes! We should have gone to a different hospital. This
place has no respect!" Her husband seemed to be shrinking
inside his ill-fitting suit. I kept imagining a male and innocuous version of the Wicked Witch of the West puddling
down into nothingness. Since his outburst back in the dining room, he'd contented himself with no more than baleful
glances.

"It is not your civil right to have a tube put down your
esophagus," the doctor said.

"But the police sent us here to—"

"If the policeman who sent you here has a medical degree, then have him join this hospital's staff and I will
definitely defer to him," she snapped.

Poor Mackenzie. He'd meant well.

Janine continued to sputter. I wondered what rule of nature had decreed that there had to be an obligatory jerk in
any random assemblage of people. I further wondered if
Janine was aware that that was her function.

"You want an uncomfortable, gratuitous tube down your
throat?" the doctor asked imperiously. "You want to have
water pumped through you and out so that your stomach
contents land in a bucket over and over again until the water runs clear? Do you know how you'll feel afterward, let
alone during?"

"I know how I feel right now," the man in tails said. "I
feel excellent! I feel marvelous! I can walk, I can breathe—
Lord, Lord, a miracle!"

"Sit down." The doctor's emotionless voice now seemed
writ in capitals. "Furthermore, just so you'll understand: if

the poison—if indeed there was ever a poison—is a corrosive, then lavage is contraindicated and potentially dangerous because the tube could perforate your tissues."

Sybil looked horrified and even more outraged than she'd been.

"Tell me, precisely, the dead—the ill man's symptoms," the doctor said.

In a depressed voice with no affect, Terry Wiley listed Lyle's symptoms with the professional precision of a high school science teacher. "Leg cramps—possible muscle spasms, sore throat, shortness of breath . . ." And on, including the rapid onset of both Lyle's symptoms and collapse.

The doctor nodded.

"Food poisoning?" the dancer said in a squeaky, terrified voice.

"I can't stop thinking," my mother said. "What if my—"

"Shh!"

"But maybe the doctor would know if it's possible for whipped cream to—"

"They'll need to run tests," the doctor said. "This man's symptoms sound extreme. A purgative of some sort, perhaps. But if it's food poisoning, and you've been eating the same foods, then by now somebody else should show real symptoms. That is generally how we recognize food poisoning, by the numbers of people getting ill."

"But I have symptoms!" Janine insisted, immediately huffing and gagging, although for the last few minutes she'd been asymptomatic—too preoccupied with her right to be purged to have time to be ill.

"Otherwise, it could be something he ate earlier in the day, something nobody else had. Or it could be a stroke, or a heart attack, or a convulsion of some sort. There is no point second-guessing."

"But!" Janine half rose.

"Sit down and wait!" The doctor turned on her rubber heels and went inside.

We didn't all always stay seated, but we did wait. No matter how desperate you may ever be for something to do on a Sunday night in Philadelphia—don't consider your neighborhood emergency room an option. At one point a brunette in hard labor was wheelchaired by. Her medical crisis, if not the woman herself, was at least cheery. But with that, the evening peaked. Three minutes later, a new entry was rushed in—something gory surrounded by police.

"Gunshot," the admissions woman said. "Crack, I bet. Crack or booze." But the next entry in the night's sweepstakes was neither. Two men braced a third, who slumped between them, an apple-sized lump on his head. "We were playing Nintendo," was all they said by way of explanation.

A woman limped in, one arm dangling and a massive shiner puffing and discoloring half her face. "Fell down the stairs," her male companion declared like a challenge. Eau de drunk filled the air.

And so it went. There may be a million stories in the city, but the ones that wind up in the emergency room are depressingly similar.

The elegant man in tails stood and bowed to the admissions clerk. "One hell of a party," he said. "Hate to tear myself away, but hey, I appear to be not dead, and if I'm alive and intact, this is the last place I want to be. Are we dismissed? Discharged? Do we have to fill out some more forms to get out of here? We're in a hurry to return to our wild whirlwind evening, you see. Our bus and further questioning awaits."

She looked at the rest of us. She buzzed the doctor behind the swinging doors on an intercom. It appeared that none of our hosts this interminable night was eager to stay with us for long. We were out of there.

"Do you think they'll let us finish our meals now?" asked the man in tails who'd made all the anti-Philadelphia remarks.

Janine bonked him on the head, hitting him—accidentally, I assumed—with a clunky bracelet cuff, a formidable business that looked made of chain mail and that behaved like a small saw. The poor man had to stay behind to be sewn up, and, perhaps, call his lawyer.

One should never antagonize a whiny woman who has been thwarted in her quest for a stomach pump.

Eight

EVEN FROM INSIDE THE VAN, SEVERAL THINGS WERE OBVIOUS as soon as we pulled up to The Boarding House. Our cool welcome at the hospital had not been unique. All the other vans had also been turned back with their revelers' stomachs unpumped. Second, since we were all still alive, albeit grumpy and hungry, it seemed probable that none of us had been poisoned. Third, our places in the bed and breakfast had been usurped by the city's finest, which meant that the party was emphatically over, and only the bureaucracy lingered on. And finally, since the process outside and inside seemed to indicate that an investigation was under way, it appeared Lyle Zacharias had not miraculously recovered.

The bedraggled guests avoided the rain by huddling in the vans until it was time to open umbrellas and dash out and under The Boarding House's bright green awning and identify themselves to the police waiting there.

Locking the hotel door a little late, I thought. They might as well let us in now. We'd done all possible damage earlier, long before they'd arrived. All we could do now was drip on whatever evidence we hadn't already obliterated. But the police nonetheless kept party guests outside the crime scene, and dutifully requested vital statistics, individual accounts of Lyle's collapse, and whatever other gossip people felt compelled to share. Only after the drilling

was payment given—their own searched purses and suitcases, as well as permission to leave the premises.

The out-of-towners who'd been booked into The Boarding House looked especially distraught. Wet, dripping, and
now homeless. This was not going to help our city's tour-
ism business.

I looked out the rain-smeared window of the bus, watching a woman's gown hem wick up an entire puddle.

I waited while guests moved out from under the green
awning like long-legged turtles under the domes of their
umbrellas. Finally it was time for my mother and me. We
raced to the awning and our policemen and recited our
names, addresses, and visions of the night's events.

I heard my mother convey an amazing body of irrelevant
details, such as each guest's marital status and the geo-
graphic locations of their grown children.

"Yes, ma'am," her policeman kept saying to her, long
after I was finished. "Thank you, but I think we have everything we need. Now this address here, that's Boca
Raton, right?"

"That means mouse mouth," she said. "Boca Raton."

The policeman's expression was untranslatable.

"In *Spanish* it means mouse mouth," she said.

"Yes'm. Florida, isn't it? I was wondering if you had a
local address as well, that's all."

She wrote Beth's phone and street numbers on the form.

"Please don't leave town without notifying us," the policeman said by way of farewell.

"Why?"

He played deaf and ignored her. I pulled at my mother's
arm like a two-year-old. She moved a few steps, then
stopped and asked again. "Why? Why can't I leave town
without telling the police?"

"It's routine," I said. "Don't you watch cop movies?"

"They didn't say anything like that to you!"

"He meant it for both of us."

She clenched her hands. "It's something about me."

"You're being silly, Mom. Paranoid." The rain pounded
on the green canvas above us. "Let me take you home."

But as we walked by the front door, I heard suspiciously Southern vowels and my pace slowed. Mackenzie himself was on the scene. Seeing him would be the one good thing about tonight, but I wasn't sure I wanted him to meet Bea of Mouse Mouth or vice versa.

"I demand to know what that policeman was insinuating," my mother said. "I'm from Florida, yes, but I'm a citizen, too! I—" She stopped herself short because Richard Quinn had completed his taciturn tête-à-tête with the police and had noticed us.

"So," he said to me, "are we—this Lyle business makes it . . . but—you know, tomorrow?"

"What about it?"

"The restaurant."

Slowly, the brain gears and levers cranked up. The prom site. "I think so," I said.

I could almost feel the strain as my mother tried to translate our klutzy syntax. Was this good or bad for her daughter? Was this, in fact, anything at all?

"I'll be around," Quinn said. "They told me not to leave town."

"Ah!" my mother said. "You, too!"

Quinn smiled somewhat uneasily. He rubbed his chin, as if checking his shave. "Six okay?" he asked.

I nodded.

"See you then." And he loped off.

My mother smiled with delighted miscomprehension. A man, a time, a meeting—it must mean a date. The distress of being a possible murder suspect evaporated in the balmy warmth of the idea of my having an assignation with Richard Quinn—or, frankly, anyone. "Nice young man," she murmured after he had blended into the rain.

I looked at her sharply. I don't mean to be an ageist, but although fifty was a splendid age, it was not one generally equated with youth. And who had any idea of whether he was nice or not? Did my mother automatically equate *nice* with *available*?

"And obviously interested in you," she added.

"He's opening a restaurant. On the water, with a big room to rent for parties upstairs."

"How *lovely*," she said. "Much more stable than acting, too."

"This is not what you think. This is about business."

My mother waved away my words. "Age becomes irrelevant once you're a grown-up," she said. "Don't you agree?"

What was this *grown-up* business? A euphemistic reminder that I was getting *old*? My thirty-first birthday was imminent, true, but surely that was not *old*. Or grown-up. Grown-ups do not obsess about the meaning of every little phrase their mothers utter. "You know the expression *too stupid to come in out of the rain*?" I asked her. "Let's go home."

"Perhaps we should use the powder room before we set out," she said in true motherly fashion.

"Perhaps not. It's a crime scene, Mom. That's why they're interviewing everybody outside. I don't think we can just bop in and ask to use the facilities."

Talk about ambivalence. I really wanted to hear Mackenzie's bayou-dusted sentences, but considering my mother's misguided ecstasy when Richard Quinn mentioned seeing me again, what excessive, mortifying behavior would greet a man who had demonstrated actual interest in me for nearly a year? As bad as this evening had already been, it was possible for it to skid even further downhill. "We'll stop for coffee somewhere else, okay?" I said. "Somewhere clean and crime-free and with a bathroom."

She agreed and we both poked our umbrellas out in front of us and opened them. I'd manipulated her out of the danger zone.

But as observed by a famous philosopher—one of the Beatles, I believe—life is what happens while you're making other plans. I was so busy congratulating myself, I barely heard him say, "That you? You're okay, then?"

My mother heard, however. "Me?" she said. "Oh, God, is that a policeman? Is he talking to me? He isn't wearing a uniform, but he's *in* there, so—"

I could no longer pretend not to hear. I turned and faced him. "Hi, there," I said. "I'm fine. We all are, it seems."

My mother applied her elbow to my rib cage. I felt it all the way through the down. "Oh, right," I said. "This is my mother, Bea Pepper, and this is, ah . . . Detective Mackenzie."

"Pleasure to meet you, ma'am," he said. "Sorry it has to be under these circumstances. My job's not too . . . sociable, unfortunately." Light blue eyes fixed on her, he continued with more of the same, his voice soft and soothing as a summer night.

My mother apparently found looking at Mackenzie as pleasing an experience as I did. Her face softened into bedazzled appreciation.

Having conquered her, Mackenzie switched personas. The once and future cop was back. That balanced out the long lean frame and abundant charm. "By the way," he said, "was Roy Beecher on your van? The man who owns this place?"

I shook my head. "Why?"

"He's missin'. Last seen, took off for cigarettes. Never came back."

I remembered the leave-taking, but I was surprised that he hadn't returned. He'd been so protective of his daughter. Besides, permanently disappearing in pursuit of cigarettes was a husband's ploy, not a father's.

"Daughter's in a bad way."

Physically, Lizzie gave an impression of so much life and vitality—scrubbed fair skin and red curls popping out of the bandanna head cover—except, it appeared, she wasn't fully inhabiting herself at all. "She seems really fragile."

Mackenzie belatedly noticed the rain and chill air. "Whyn't you come in?" he asked. "Dry off. Warm up. Besides, you're good with kids. Maybe she'd talk to you more easily than to us. Can't make any sense of her."

We entered a building where somebody had just died, where even now sobbing could be heard, but my mother, ordinarily a sensitive woman, suddenly lit up and beamed.

"You're *Chuck!*" she said with delight. "Chuck Mackenzie. I didn't realize!" She cooed, she simpered. "I'm thrilled to finally meet you! Mandy has told me so much about you."

Behind her back I shook my head. I hadn't. Not even that his name wasn't Chuck. It's difficult knowing a man for nearly a year and not yet knowing his given name. It's impossible to explain to my mother, so I had one day declared him Chuck. I thought he'd be so offended, he'd break down and confess the real name, but he only laughed. The no-name business has become a joke between us—but I knew it wouldn't amuse Mom.

"An' Mandy's told me lots about you, too." The faux Chuck maneuvered her into The Boarding House living room. "An' I sure hope we can clean up this ugly business fast so"—I couldn't believe it; he was using TV cop dialogue on her—"we can spend time together under less taxin' circumstances real soon." His accent was being troweled on so that his words were thick liquid honey.

"Oh, my." My mother had been lobotomized. "Please—your work is so important, you must get back to it!"

Mackenzie made a good show of reluctance about the prospect of leaving her.

"So Roy Beecher didn't put himself on any of the vans, then?" he said to me. "Didn't think so. Accordin' to his girl, he didn't eat dinner, anyway. Too jet-lagged."

"Is that Lizzie I hear?" I asked.

Mackenzie nodded. "Actin' real odd. Not hysterical, really, but distant, disoriented."

"In shock, perhaps?" my mother said.

Mackenzie shrugged and nodded at the same time, wordlessly conveying agreement and confusion at the degree of shock, perhaps.

I remembered Lizzie's peculiar reaction to seeing Lyle sprawled on the dining room floor. And then there'd been the odd scene in the kitchen before dinner, when she seemed to slip out of gear. "Does she have a history of epilepsy?" I asked. "I once had a student whose attacks were like a needle getting stuck on a record. Maybe Lizzie—"

"That sweet child." My mother stood up. "What a dreadful thing to happen. Her reputation and her career at stake—this certainly isn't going to help anything. Let me see if I can be of any use."

"Mom, listen, you aren't supposed to—" But Mackenzie nodded at her.

"Maybe she'll tell you her doctor's name," he said, "or tell us if there's some medical condition. She gets crazy when we suggest takin' her to the hospital. Won't leave until she finds her father." My mother left the room, her cheeks flushed with purpose.

"What's going on?" We both said it the second she was gone.

I deferred. "I can't get a straight story," he said. "Maybe fifty straight stories, but who am I to—"

"How come you let everybody leave? The police didn't ask all that many questions. Wouldn't you want to know where—what—whatever it is that you always want to know?"

Mackenzie ran his fingers through his salt and pepper hair. It's a good thing it's curly and rearranges itself or he'd look like a spiked rock star at the end of the day. "We have their names," he said. "We have their accounts of what they saw and heard. But even though I'd like it to be like an English country house mystery, too, with all fifty of us sittin' around comparin' accounts, don' see how we can. Fifty witnesses . . ." He shook his head. "Fifty witnesses, when I don' even know what they witnessed, what to ask about, whether there even *was* a crime, or whether whatever somebody tells me is a lie and a cover-up. I'll tell you, if I were goin' to murder someone, I'd do it just this way. It's a mess. An' even if we knew what to ask more'n we did, we don' have the manpower to do it. The President's in town."

"Right. Fund-raiser."

"So we have fifty people we don' know what to ask, an' a missin' man, a kid on some weird trip, and an old lady—"

"Oh, Lord—Aunt Hattie? She was hysterical when we left. Screaming at Lizzie, blaming her for Lyle's death. I know she's distraught, Lyle was her very life, but all the same . . ."

"Under sedation now," Mackenzie said. "Couldn't get a worthwhile syllable out of her while she was awake. Had to take her to the hospital. I hope she's strong enough to pull out of it." His sigh was enormous. "So you tell me, Mandy. What happened? What'd you see?"

I tried to remember everything potentially relevant, although everything I said had already been told to the patrolman outside, and nothing I said was what we needed to know. All I'd seen were the aftereffects.

"Should have been the best night of his life," Mackenzie said. "Instead, it was his last."

"Those aren't necessarily contradictory ideas, you know."

"You mean Housman's poem?"

"And people complain about cultural illiteracy. Can you imagine?" "To an Athlete Dying Young" was a favorite of my students. The issue it raised—whether it was better to die at the moment of triumph or to trudge on through a life where "glory does not stay"—intrigued adolescents, who love the idea of going out in a melodramatic blaze, and never intend to age, anyway. But postadolescent, graying Mackenzie still remembered it well enough to paraphrase:

> "Now he will not swell the rout
> Of lads that wore their honors out."

Although he was a cum laude graduate of Rice University and some pretty effective schools before that, I always pictured him memorizing poems from a chalk slate in a one-room shack down in the bayous of Louisiana, and the image, false as it is, touches my heart. Nonetheless, this particular poem was inappropriate. "Lyle was hardly a lad, Mackenzie. Nobody calls a man of fifty a lad." Why did I have to keep reminding people that fifty was a considerably grown age?

"Did anybody leave at any point?" Mackenzie asked.

"What? When? Leave where?"

He looked disappointed. It was a breeze for him to leap

from Housman to homicide, and he expected me to follow without a stumble.

I felt insulted, but I plodded on. "Leave what?" I asked. "The living room? The dining room? The building?"

"All of the above."

"I do wish somebody had told me there was going to be a murder. I would have paid more attention to what was going on around me and less to how much I didn't want to be there in the first place." I recited what I did remember, although I didn't know if what I said was in any way relevant.

"Very helpful," he said when I was finished. "Let's see if I got it." He tried to imitate my mid-Atlantic accent. He sounded like a Southerner with a sinus condition, and I would have laughed had I been in a more humorous mood. "Just about everybody got up and milled around between courses—and maybe also left the room. And"—he pushed hard on the final *d*, talking Yankee—"an*d* everybody was in and out before dinner, too. That it?"

"I told you. I didn't know to be on red alert."

His expression made it clear that he'd have noticed and remembered each detail no matter how tedious the evening.

"These questions," I said, "and the fact that nobody except Lyle was affected—it was deliberate, then, wasn't it? He was poisoned."

He shrugged. "Tha's the assumption. We'll know soon enough. Took samples of everythin' edible, even candy and gum in people's bags. If it was poisonin', we have a head start, which is unusual. Don't customarily know what people ate, or else we can't get actual samples."

"I can't imagine you'll find anything in that food—or why didn't anybody else get sick?" We walked toward the back of the building. "How do you justify having these men here—especially with the President in town—investigating what might not be a murder in the first place?"

"I'll find some way, but the real justification"—he made that word gorgeous and somehow sexy—"was I was worried about you." He looked at me so directly, it felt like an embrace. I was glad my mom wasn't in the room. His genuine concern had the same effect on my central nervous system as his southern elision had on my mother. The same effect his southern elision had on me, now that I think about it.

"Real worried," he said. "But maybe I overreacted."

"The emergency room people were not amused."

"Pity. You'd think they could use a laugh, an' there is definitely somethin' comic in a passel of people dressed to the nines charging the stomach pumps—or am I warped?"

"Not warped, but a little overprotective, perhaps."

"Protective," he grumbled. "Not excessively so. Besides, when a guy says he's poisoned, then crumples up and dies, there's enough presumption of a crime for me." He looked relieved, as if he'd just this second finally found a solid rationale for his actions.

The dining room had yellow crime-scene tape across its entry. I wondered what anybody expected to find or prove at this point. A few steps ahead, on the other side, the kitchen was similarly proscribed. We went into a small bedroom behind it, once probably meant for the kitchen maid, now seemingly Lizzie's.

She sat on an old-fashioned and unpretentious white chenille bedspread. My mother sat beside her, offering an ignored glass of water, and a blue-uniformed officer across the room leaned on a chest of drawers. I had the feeling nobody had moved in a long while.

"I want my father," Lizzie whispered as we approached. Her normally fair skin looked spectral, as if the blood had been drained off, with freckled punctuation marks in high relief. Her hands were folded on her lap, on the white apron she still wore.

"I'm sure he'll turn up in a moment," my mother said, continuing to hold out the glass of water, as if it were a cure-all.

I stayed at the doorway. Lizzie looked as young and vulnerable as the kids I teach. Only four or five years out of high school, she looked defeated as well. "Is there anything I can do for you?" I asked softly.

She turned her head in my direction although her eyes seemed unfocused.

I went closer to the bed and took her hand in both of mine, unsure of what to say.

"Did you see?" she whispered. "All down there on the floor, on my floor, at my feet, all . . ." She shook her head and bit at her upper lip. "I can't breathe, I . . ." She pulled her hand out of mine and put it to her temple. "Head hurts, and my stomach . . ." She whimpered, hands still to her head. "All down there on the floor. Like that."

Mackenzie looked at me, raising his eyebrows, his chin pushed forward. I read the expression easily. This is how she's been, he was signaling. What do we make of it?

I truly didn't know. I wondered if Lizzie had always, or at least of late, been unbalanced, although I doubted that her father would have left the hotel in her control while he flew off had she always behaved this bizarrely. Tonight had pushed her off the edge. Maybe she needed to be taken somewhere for psychiatric help. "What happened is terrible," I told her, "but nobody blames you." Except Aunt Hattie, I silently added.

Lizzie's sob was heartbreakingly thorough.

"What's the name of your family physician again?" I asked, taking unfair advantage of her misery.

"Dr. Burlinghouse?" she asked. "What about him?"

Mackenzie looked as if I'd found the cure for the common cold. I stored that look away for future use.

Thank heavens Lizzie's doctor had an unusual name. Now if only he was in town and not on vacation, and willing to accept middle-of-the-night phone calls. I looked up. My mother had disappeared, and I knew she'd gone in search of a telephone book.

"Miss, um, Chapman," Mackenzie said, "we'd be glad to take you to the doctor, and I'm sure Miss Peppah here would go along and—"

"No!" The wail was stretched tight with impending hysteria. "Don't make me leave! Don't take me away! Please!"

I looked at Mackenzie, wondering if he found her responses as peculiar and inappropriate as I did. My first-hand crime-scene experience was distinctly limited. Perhaps people often became semicoherent and regressed to near-infantile speech and behavior.

"Don't be afraid," Mackenzie said to her.

"I didn't do it!"

"Do what?"

A worried line appeared between her golden-red eyebrows. "My father knows I didn't."

"What?" Mackenzie asked again.

"What?" Her eyes were wide and fearful now.

"Didn't what?" he said. "What didn't you do?" They sounded like a bad Abbott and Costello routine, and we were getting nowhere.

"I didn't . . . I don't know." She slumped and became almost slack-mouthed, as if her brief burst of confused energy had drained her. Shaking her head, the confusion line between her eyebrows etched even more deeply, she retreated into a remote semistupor.

My mother returned with the Yellow Pages. But she returned by a side door.

"Mom?" I said. "Where were you?"

"The phone book was in the kitchen. There's a door that leads directly in here."

"Did you notice that yellow police tape on the kitchen doorway?" I asked.

She looked insulted. "Of course. I didn't disturb it. I crawled underneath, very carefully. Anyway, I have Dr. Burlinghouse's number." She handed the information to Mackenzie, who looked about to say something, but apparently decided against it. He went into the hall instead.

My mother jerked her head, signaling me to come close, which I did, afraid of what she'd say out loud otherwise.

"The tarts are gone," she whispered.

"You told me before."

"Not just the ones on the plate, although even that plate's gone. But the tin, too. The entire tin. They suspect me."

"Mom, they took everything. Just to be sure. Relax." If I wasn't careful, there'd soon be two women keening on the bedspread.

I heard dialing at the nearby front desk, and then Mackenzie's soft voice. "Have him call soon as possible," he said. Burlinghouse was elsewhere.

"I never *meant* to," Lizzie said. "I never *meant* to!"

"Of course you didn't," my mother said, as if this were the most normal of conversations. "And in fact, you didn't mean to and you didn't. Do it, I mean."

"Didn't I?" Lizzie asked as Mackenzie reentered. "So what? My head hurts. I'm so mixed up."

Me, too.

I tried for a reality check. I was of no use here; Dr. Burlinghouse would be found without me and would provide pharmacologic relief; Mackenzie would continue to be otherwise engaged; I had to teach at dawn, and my mother and I were behaving like obnoxious guests, overstaying our welcome.

Which I said, more or less, trying for a little levity.

I wrapped my down coat around me, poised my umbrella at the ready and made my exit, my mother trailing one step behind. Mackenzie, our allotted portion of the city's finest, escorted us. Then he detained me for a second. I thought he was going to compliment me on extracting the doctor's name. I thought he might say how happy he was that I had not been poisoned. I hoped he might say that he'd be over later, waiting for me after I dropped my mother off.

But what he said was, "Listen. Thanks for the help."

"Is there a *but* waiting in the wings?" Of course there was, but I wanted to give him a chance to retract it.

He didn't. "But—no offense, all right? I need to make sure that this is the end of it for you. No Nancy Drewing. No Jessica Fletchering. You have this tendency—"

"Thanks for the warning, officer, but I don't have anything to do with this, and I don't want to."

"Good," he said. "Keep that in mind. No Miss Marpling, either."

And that was all he had to tell me.

I didn't want to think of what the city's worst might be if this was what it considered its finest.

Nine

NEXT MORNING I FELT HEADACHY AND QUEASY, WHICH SEEMED distinctly unfair and definitely unearned. There had been no overindulgence whatsoever. I had post-traumatic shock disguised as a hangover.

Entering the school office was not much of an upper at the best of times. I emptied my mailbox of assorted inane messages and flipped through them. Next to me, Harvey Porter, a part-timer teaching psych while he finished his Ph.D. dissertation, did the same, histrionically. Harvey works a twenty-six-hour day and radiates pure irritable tension for at least twenty of them. Our low-quality mail wasn't helping his mood.

Junk today, yesterday, almost always. Nagging reminders and make-work from the principal, or his handmaiden, Helga the office witch. But it was bad form to dump it into the wastebasket before pretending to look it over, so I glanced through.

A notice on Day-Glo orange paper was headed IMPORTANT!!! It seemed staff was to be ever-alert and prevent false alarms. I had no idea how we were to do this, since the gongs inevitably were set off while class was in session. In fact, emptying classrooms was their entire point.

Another wasted piece of paper reminded us that seniors in danger of failing were to be notified by mid-April, and in writing. Pro forma. Nobody whose tuition was paid in full failed to graduate.

A slick brochure described an exciting, sure-to-entice grammar text, but alas, even if the hype were true, we had no budget for new texts this year.

My professional journal had arrived, bulging with breakthroughs in the teaching of our native tongue. As usual, I felt an idiotic, unjustified flare of hope that this issue, at long last, would contain the magic secret that actually worked.

"At least there aren't any bills," Harvey said as he rather violently tossed the entire contents of his mail slot into the trash can. And, swinging a hand-knit scarf over his shoulder—teenage girls love his affectations—he left.

No bills, but other irritants: a note from a student—never was a note left with good news in it—asking for an extension for her paper, no reason or excuse offered; a pink telephone message slip requesting a parent-teacher conference; another note on three-ring paper that said, *Miss Pepper! The Cavanaugh burned down last night!!! What will we do?????* At least on this issue I had an ace up my sleeve via Richard Quinn.

I opened a sealed envelope with a great deal of curiosity. My mailbox generally contains reminders and brochures, not envelopes of any sort—and this one was unlabeled. I pulled out a piece of heavy bond and several newspaper clippings. The white paper had a drawing of a tombstone with an apple sitting on top of it. *R.I.P. Teach* was written on the stone. *Makes you wonder who's next, doesn't it?* was printed on the bottom of the page.

I looked up, looked around, to see if the practical joker was watching. But everyone else in the office was intent on his or her own mail and looming day. I had an immediate, unpleasant conviction that this was not intended as a joke.

No signature. The clippings all concerned violence to teachers. A college student who'd killed his professor because he didn't get a fellowship. A high school teacher held hostage. A junior high coach stabbed. Etcetera.

"Helga," I asked, "did you notice who left messages in my mailbox?" I knew it was a stupid question as it left my mouth, perhaps before.

The school secretary looked at me as if I were vermin. "She thinks I have time to monitor every to and fro to the mailboxes!" she told an invisible friend—the only sort of friend who'd have her.

I tossed everything but the manila envelope and its contents and went to my first period class, my false hangover now doubled in intensity and my legs slightly unsure of where they were landing with each step, as if I'd suffered a mild stroke.

R.I.P. Teach. Who on earth had sent that to me? I thought of my teacherly sins—disciplinary actions, bad grades, harsh words, boring lessons—but I couldn't think of anything I'd done, or anything a student had done, that warranted such an extreme reaction.

I didn't know what to do about the packet. I didn't know the point of telling anyone else at school yet. Anybody I'd show it to would only repeat my unanswerable questions, add to my fear. I told myself that I was overreacting, that the afterimage of Lyle Zacharias's death was still blinding me, making me see menace everywhere, including a note that surely had some rational, nonthreatening explanation.

It was nearly impossible to believe what I told myself.

I had to squelch the urge to enter the classroom as a person with problems, rather than as a teacher. I wanted to say that a man had died in front of me last night, and that now someone was threatening my life. But that wasn't my role—or my students'. Luckily, I had a low-energy morning ahead. Two sections were having exams—could that be what had ticked somebody off?—and the ninth graders were spending the week rehearsing their adaptation of Oscar Wilde's *The Picture of Dorian Gray.* I had lots of passive time ahead in which to speculate and tremble.

The eleventh graders moaned through yet another S.A.T.

Prep drill, this time on analogies. This is to this as that is to what? Tests are to hell like school is to . . .

R.I.P. Teach. Why? Who? How?

I was mixing up the letter writer and Lyle Zacharias's killer, making their dark thoughts and impulses one and the same. I tried to shake the ensuing confusion out of my head.

Makes you wonder who's next, doesn't it? I felt nauseated as I corrected the analogies next period while my tenth graders wrote what they insisted on calling an *S.A. exam* about *Lord of the Flies*. I had tried to disabuse them of their error, explaining the meaning of the word *essay*: to try, or a trial, its roots in Latin and Old French.

S.A. they insisted.

I asked what on earth they thought the initials could stand for. Stupid Ass seemed their hands-down favorite, although there were riper suggestions as well.

The ninth graders were behaving with atypical seriousness about their *Dorian Gray* playlet.

"The things one feels absolutely certain about are never true," a character told Dorian.

I listened. I tried to apply the Gospel according to Wilde to my own situation, to wring some reassurance from it. The problem was, I didn't feel absolutely certain about anything this morning, including the meaning or message in the epigram.

End of easy morning.

En route to the teachers' lounge for a cramped and spartan lunch, I composed a mental to-do list. I had the S.A./essays to mark, two more sections to teach, and a free period which was anything but since I was the faculty advisor for the school paper, which met in my room, under my supervision, every Monday.

Faculty was required to have outside interests: hobbies, sports, or nonacademic pursuits that so enchanted us we needed to share our passion with a herd of adolescents. If you didn't happen to have a congenial interest that minors could share, you were assigned one. I had been offered either girls' basketball or the school paper, and as the latter sounded less noisy, sweaty, and desperate, I picked it.

Today, I knew, the work of the paper would be put on hold while the seniors discussed the really big news, the catastrophe at the Cavanaugh. We might as well make the hunt for a new prom site the big story in the next edition. I was already hopelessly involved, anyway, as I was not only the newspaper advisor, but this senior class's prom advisor as well. Being so selected by the students is said to be an honor, but only by those who were not so honored and who therefore get to stay home and enjoy themselves on prom night.

I was absorbed by my agenda and by paranoid fears that I'd encounter the note-writing teacher terminator as I made my way down the wide marble staircase to the first floor.

Somebody called my name. My unvarnished name, sans the usual *Miss* or *Ms.* that students add, even here, in these informal halls. I had a rush of panic, but the woman waving at me would never be coy or oblique about her threats. "Sybil," I said with real shock. "Mrs. Zacharias." I remembered that she wanted Reed to come to Philly Prep—had wanted me to pull strings if possible—but *today*?

"I'm early," she said as she approached. "My appointment isn't until one. Reed's coming separately. His cab hasn't arrived yet."

Had she forgotten that her husband—ex or not—had died the night before? The father of the boy who would soon taxi in? I would have assumed that the business of life, including private school applications, would take a rest stop, in memoriam. A moment of silence. Twenty-four hours of not pursuing temporal goals? Time for a thought or two about the transience of life?

"Surprised to see me, aren't you? Want me to be a hypocrite, but if I skipped this appointment, it would have been for appearance's sake alone. Am I supposed to act like I'm stricken with grief?"

I couldn't think of a response that would be both honest and polite, so I said nothing. She seemed cold to the core, capable of operating on a purely intellectual, pragmatic, and self-serving plane.

Students swirled around us en route to the lunchroom or the great and freshly scrubbed outdoors. A few nodded in my direction or called greetings. Most completely ignored the two of us. Sybil returned the lack of concern and seemed neither to hear nor notice them. "You're reading Wilde," she said, with a half nod to the book I was carrying. "I didn't realize people still did."

"My students—" I began.

"My mother named me for a character in *The Picture of Dorian Gray.* Sybil Vane. She said it was because Sybil was so pure, so beautiful, so perfect." Sybil Zacharias laughed impurely, unbeautifully, imperfectly.

"But she was all those things," I said.

"So what? She was also *dead. Ruined* by Dorian. Destroyed by the man she loved. She *murdered* herself because of his corruption and vanity and stupidity. The name was like a curse on my head, a prediction."

"I'm sure your mother meant well." She had reduced me to inanities. How did I know what her mother intended? Maybe her mother was stupid, or illiterate—or truly malevolent. In any case, Dorian's first victim was a peculiar inspiration for a name.

"Destroyed," Sybil repeated. "But this Sybil refuses to be. No matter what he does. And I won't let Reed be destroyed by him, either. The truth is, I can't afford—figuratively or literally—to wait. I have to protect my son."

"I'm sorry, I don't follow." We stood outside the opaque glass doors of the office, away from human traffic. My stomach walls rubbed together, found nothing, and growled a protest, but Sybil probably couldn't hear it above the student racket. She probably wouldn't have cared if she had heard.

"Her." Sybil made the word sound like something foul she'd been forced to swallow. "The Merry Widow herself. The luckiest bimbo on earth. God *knows* she wanted to get rid of him and keep the money."

"I really don't understand," I murmured, very intrigued.

"She hates Reed. She's always been jealous of him, of every second his own father spent with him, and there weren't that many seconds, believe me. And of every cent Lyle spent on him, as if he took each penny out of her pocket. And Lyle was so afraid of his baby wife's tantrums that he was pushing Reed right out of his life."

Had Sybil decided that her son would be better off with a dead father and an inheritance rather than a living, weak father and a stepmother who was chipping away at fatherly support? Or had, perhaps, the microbiology-loving Reed himself felt that way? Maybe they were a team, in collusion. I took a step backward.

"And all the while," Sybil said, "she was only using him."

"Him? Who? I'm afraid I don't understand."

Sybil eyed me as if I embodied human ignorance. "Tiffany was using Lyle, of course. Everybody knew." She spoke half as quickly as she normally did. I was, after all, a slow learner. "It isn't like they even tried that hard to hide it."

I shook my head. "Tiffany and Lyle? Hide what?"

"I mean Reed, poor dear, his voice is still high. Hasn't changed yet. Once, he picked up the phone and said hello and was mistaken for Tiffany herself. Reed was flabbergasted. The man on the other line went on and on about being all alone an entire night with her—with *you*, he kept saying, of course. He talked about where to meet and what to wear—and not wear, like undergarments."

"I take it the man on the phone was not Tiffany's husband, Reed's father."

Sybil sneered. "You take it right. Lyle might—in fact has—shocked his boy by being inappropriately romantic in front of him. But no, it wasn't his father on the telephone. Not at all. It was Shepard he heard."

My mouth opened, ready to ask if she meant the *McCoy* Shepard, but what other one could she mean? It was hard to find the ones who guard sheep here in Philadelphia. I readjusted my lips.

She shook her head with irritation. "Wasn't it *obvious*?

Good Lord, it's been going on for nearly a year. No surprise, really. Almost no secret. That's how she is about men. That's how she got my—got Lyle. That's how she'll get whoever's next."

I am always amazed at how long the fury of betrayal burns. I could still feel the heat of Sybil's rage.

"Even last night!" Rusty blotches stained her cheeks. "Like a dog in heat. Did you see when she left the room between courses and he trotted right after her? I couldn't believe my eyes for the blatancy of it! At her husband's birthday party! If Lyle wasn't such a blind, egotistical, self-centered fool, he'd have noticed. Everybody else did."

Except me. I'm embarrassed to admit it, but the news depressed me for many wrong reasons. Not only because Lyle Zacharias had been another fool of a middle-aged man, in deep trouble even before he died. Not only because his young wife was unfaithful or because I was suffering metaphysical angst for the meaninglessness of contemporary marriage vows.

No, I felt a stab of grief for having thought that Shepard McCoy had been coming on to me last night and that I had skillfully kept him at bay. In retrospect, with this new information, it was obvious that I had been sitting on a direct eyebeam line with the voluptuous Tiffany, and that by nuzzling my shoulder, leaning over me, pointing his face in my direction, Shepard could view his beloved clearly. The moony eyes had been aimed past, not at, me. How humiliating to resent attentions that weren't for me in the first place.

"I warned Lyle, tried to wake him up," she said in a low voice. "He told me I was a dried up, bitter old . . ." She looked away. "But that's beside the point now." Her voice became brisk again and back to business. "Now the problem is what Tiffany will do with the money. Lyle agreed that Reed would be happier in a smaller academic environment where the special needs and individuality of each child is respected." She had memorized our brochure. "Honestly," she said. "I'm telling the truth."

Is it possible to believe anybody who says that?

Sybil's face was like the satellite weather map on TV. Strange clouds suddenly shadowed what had seemed an impervious terrain. Unstable conditions.

"Yo, Miss Pepper!" Raffi Trulock is the star basketball player in our school. His real name is Gavin, but his neck is long and his legs begin at his Adam's apple and continue for about a week. He had been compared to a giraffe for so long that a diminutive form of the word became his name.

It gives me a crick to look up at him, but once I do, his goofy smile and stalky clumsiness are oddly and instantly endearing. "What's up?" I asked.

"Did you hear the Cavanaugh burned?" He looked from Sybil to me. "Didn't mean to interrupt, though," he added with a forward dip of his neck.

"I have a lead on a possible new place," I said. "We'll talk later today."

"*Great!* I knew you'd do it. You're the—that's *great!*" And with a duck of the head, towering over the classmate who'd been waiting for him, he bade farewell. His buddy gave him an elbow to his side. I watched a mock scuffle, then both boys looked back at me before truly departing for lunch. For a flicker, less than a second, I wondered if they could be the note-writers. They seemed so intent on me. But then I discarded that theory as ludicrous.

"That's why I have to get Reed placed *immediately*," Sybil said. "Like, um, as of last week. At least then my lawyer can make a case for keeping the status quo. It isn't fair to take things away from an orphaned boy, is it? But if I wait, that bitch will refuse to pay for it, won't admit that this is what her husband wanted for his son. She wants every penny. She probably *did* it."

"You mean because of . . . Shepard?" Good thing Sybil worked with plants, not people. A begonia can handle angry incoherency a lot better than most folk.

"Because of Lyle's life-change," she said. "You know—the *simple* life he talked about last night, just before . . . *Retiring.* Quitting his job, selling his house—everything. Of course, now I know his show was being canceled. He was saving face. Or maybe he was really burned out, or going crazy. He told me he was through with all the leeches—meaning me, of course, and his own flesh and blood, his son."

"He said that? He called Reed a leech?"

"First he called Richard the leech. After Richard's partner had a heart attack and dropped out, he came to Lyle for a loan."

A little slowly, I targeted her *Richard* as Richard Quinn.

"Lyle said that was the final straw. That everybody wanted something from him. Everybody was a leech. Guess who else he meant. But of course the simple life business was an excuse to screw me and his son. He was going to deliberately make himself poor—at least as far as the courts could see. Can't get blood out of a stone. A farm in the unfashionable country. Vegetables. You think his bimbo wanted that? Lyle without bucks? Without parties?"

And what about you? I wondered. What good timing, what good luck, what a coincidence that Lyle died before he could hide his assets. "Good luck to you and to Reed," I said briskly. "My lunch hour is about to end and—"

"Do you think this principal of yours, Haverwhatsis—"

"Meyer. Havermeyer."

"Whatever. Is he—how much of a stickler for . . ." She straightened her shoulders and became almost belligerent, as if she were preempting predictable objections. "I mean," she said emphatically, "what *difference* would it be to anybody except poor Reed if he had been officially enrolled here say, two weeks ago? It's not as if it's any crime I can think of. He's quite bright. He'll be an asset to the school."

I didn't know which way to bobble my head to show that I couldn't see how it would matter, either.

"Then do you think he—Mr. Haverstein, will—"

"Meyer. Havermeyer. Doctor."

"—object? I mean I did *call* several weeks ago. I *might* have come sooner. It wasn't *my* fault that he didn't have an appointment open until today. At least not one that fit my schedule. It's no more than a technicality. If he's a rational man, this Mister—Dr. Haverman, he'll have to agree."

I didn't correct her this time. I wasn't her tutor. And I didn't tell her that Dr. Maurice Havermeyer was willing to bend any rule, particularly if the weight used to bend said rule was a heavy check. My principal's principles were simple and focused: goodness was money. Goodness incarnate was a person who brought money to his school. He wanted good people's children around him, and the rules—especially picayune ones like the date on the acceptance—be damned.

Sybil looked at her watch. "I've been standing here talking and I'm nearly late now!" She looked at me accusingly. "The *last* thing I want is to make a bad impression!" We reversed places. I moved away from the office door and she entered it without a fare-thee-well.

I wondered if she had ever been gentle, or subtle, or likable. Did a man's defection warp a woman's personality or simply heighten what was already there? In any case, I was glad to contemplate lunch and gladder still to see the last of Sybil.

I wanted to be rid of the Zachariases. The living Z's were exceedingly unpleasant, and if Sybil was to be believed, the deceased had trundled around on two feets' worth of clay. If I didn't want to think ill of the dead, I'd better stop thinking about him at all. I had promised to take my mother to visit Lyle's aunt Hattie in the hospital, but after that I would be finished with that family except for Reed. But I'd cross that Zacharias when I found him in my roll book.

The afternoon passed almost gracefully. The newspaper meeting was actually fun, as the reporters behaved like Clark Kent hot for the Cavanaugh Hotel fire scoop. I told them about The Scene and also was coerced into finding out whether, by chance, the Bellevue had an available night—a cancellation, perhaps. They, in turn, listed a dozen other possibilities—improbabilities, in truth, but places they'd investigate.

I walked out of school into the dazzle of poststorm purity. If it had not been for the definite damper of having a faceless kid's threats feel like a chronic ache, I would have been tempted to do a soft shoe down the school staircase. It was that kind of afternoon.

But then I saw Mackenzie unfold himself from a park bench across the street. I don't mean to imply that the sight of him is anything but pleasurable, but he looked so deliberately casual about this unscheduled visit that it was obvious something significant had happened. And Mackenzie's variety of significant news is always, inevitably, bad. The intimation of doom that began last night and bloomed poisonously at the mailbox this A.M. grew so thick and tight, I felt as if I might suffocate.

"This has to do with the note, doesn't it?" I asked as we walked toward Broad Street.

"Don' know what you're talkin' about."

"There was a creepy anonymous note in my mailbox this morning. And clippings."

"Kids you teach have the worst sense of humor," he murmured, obviously thinking about something else. My Mackenzie—the noncop part I irrationally filter out and think of as the *real* man—was missing in action.

"Then what brings you here, officer? I know I'm irresistible, but during business hours?" Was anybody still home in there?

There was. "That you are, lady," he said. "And only irresistibility could have made me willingly sit there an' be giggled over and unsubtly examined and discussed by three dozen teeny boppers. Felt like eighth grade schoolyard all over again. So what the hell—might as well be crazy and bold." And he took my hand, even though teenage mutant spies could be lurking anywhere.

"So this is a social visit." Relief is one of my favorite feelings. "A beautiful day for a stroll."

"Not exactly," he said softly. He could walk and produce anxiety at the same time. "Wanted to tell you in person. Because of the irresistibility."

And immediately I wanted to be very resistible for at least a few trauma-free hours. What I didn't want was whatever news Mackenzie had chosen to deliver in person. I took a deep breath.

"It appears," he said slowly, his deceptively soft voice like background music, "that your friend Lyle Zacharias spoke the truth, much to all of our distress. Didn' die of indigestion or stroke or heart attack. Something, somebody, somehow, poisoned him."

I was surprised and flattered that he'd come all this way to tell me that in person.

"And there's somethin' else."

Now I got it. "Don't worry. I was annoyed the way you said it last night, but in truth, I agree. I have no interest. I don't like what little I know about those people, and I have no ties with them, so there's no problem. I'm not involved and I'm not in any danger. Except, maybe, from the crazy kid who left me that note."

"The somethin' else is kind of major," he went on, as if my words had been no more than dust motes. "It appears that Lyle Zacharias left the dinin' room during dinner and did some serious nibblin'. Guess you reach a certain age, nobody warns you about ruinin' your appetite." He sighed again, such an enormous intake and exhale of air, I was almost ready to administer CPR—but I wasn't sure whether he'd need it or I would.

"He ate some tarts," Mackenzie said. "That's the only food we know he and nobody else ate. An' then he died."

I disengaged my hand from his. "That's absolutely ridiculous and you know it."

"Maybe."

"My *mother*! In all the world, of all its people, my mother is the *last* person who would deliberately hurt anybody!" A plump woman in a cherry-red coat clutched her Wanamaker shopping bag and edged away from me. I knew I was not completely in control, but so be it. "My mother is not a murderer!"

Mackenzie looked sad.

"Are you *crazy*?" I screamed.

The woman in the cherry coat's eyes showed white all around. She backed into the recessed entryway of a store, my words bouncing and echoing off the brickwork around the window.

Crazy—crazy—crazy.

Mackenzie continued to look sad.

Ten

MY MOTHER THE SUSPECT. MY MOTHER THE POISONER! IT WAS too ridiculous to give a moment's thought. It made me furious, in fact, that Mackenzie had even let the idea slip into his brain, the words through his lips.

My mother! All her life her single crime had been overconcern. A sort of obsessive nurturing that tilted dangerously toward meddling—but only because she was convinced that she could make things better for people.

"Do you realize," I demanded, "that my mother devotes every single Wednesday to trying to save the Florida manatee from speedboat propellers? Does that sound like the kind of woman who would *murder* someone?"

He looked befuddled, like my students working on their analogies. Bea Pepper is to manatees as a murderer is to . . .

"Why would she?" I asked while he slowly pondered. "What on earth would be her motive?" I upped my walking pace, implying, I hoped, that his outlandish suggestion hadn't given me even momentary pause.

"Did I say I *believed* it? I don' get it, that's all."

"Then I'll help. *If* the tarts had anything to do with Lyle's death, then somebody else tampered with them. Get it now?"

"When would that have happened?" he asked in an infuriatingly mild voice.

"You figure that part out."

"Hey, Mandy," he said, "don't kill the messenger, okay?"

I didn't kill him, but I didn't have much to say to him, either. We meandered down Pine Street in silence, stopping now and then to admire an antique store's display, although I couldn't really focus on anything except this ridiculous suspicion. Debris—mostly early leaves from distant trees—had accumulated against the buildings in last night's storm. I kicked at a soggy piece of newspaper, reluctant even to speculate, for fear it would be incriminating—erroneously incriminating, of course, but not worth the risk all the same.

For example, my parents' dispute yesterday afternoon, which I had forgotten until this minute. It replayed in my head like a poorly received radio station, full of static and omissions. I should have listened more carefully because all that was coming through was my father's continued anger and grief over his foster sister's death. But that was so long ago, surely he wouldn't have . . . and use my mother as knowing or unknowing accomplice? I shook my head.

"What?" Mackenzie said.

"Nothing." I couldn't believe I was even hazarding these thoughts, but I was definitely not about to share them. I had never suspected how nightmarishly easy it was to plant a seed of doubt and have it flourish in even the least hospitable ground. "What kind of poison?" A ludicrous question because the answer would mean nothing to me. All I knew about poisons was that in mysteries the victim smelled of bitter almonds, a variety I certainly never heard of. Were they anything like smoked? Dry-roasted? Why were they bitter? Were they the almond-reject crop? And how did everyone who found a corpse acquire such familiarity with the aroma of those bitter nuts to recognize it, never confusing it with bitter peanuts or pecans?

"Dunno yet. Takes time. But it doesn't look like the standard ones."

"No smell of bitter almonds, I take it."

Mackenzie smiled. "An' no little bottle with a skull and

crossbones clutched in his death grip, either. What's a detective to do?"

"That about covers what I know about poisons," I said. "Except for household cleaning agents, but surely Lyle didn't unwittingly drink ammonia or gnaw on room freshener."

"Ah, well, there are a couple more common things, but so far, no trace of barbiturates, opiates, arsenic, or cocaine."

I had forgotten those, although imagining my mother trying to score some coke in order to kill Lyle Zacharias made me giggle.

"Wish your mother hadn't put all those warnin's that only Lyle should touch the tarts. Like a great big finger pointing in her direction, don't you think? That is, if the tarts turn out to be the problem, an' the lab sure thinks they might."

"She meant it as a joke," I said. "Years ago, he'd told her he hated sharing her baking. Maybe her sense of humor isn't the best, but that's not a criminal offense."

We walked a half block farther while Mackenzie looked as if he were searching for words. Finally he found them. "Now I'm the only one's made the connection so far, an' I haven't said a word. But when somebody does think of your mother, what'll I do? Say she can't be the perp because her daughter's my . . ."

His . . . ? If I'd been a bunny or a puppy, my ears would have pointed sideways, toward him. Eleven months past our first meeting, we were underdefined, so even though our relationship was not the relevant issue at the moment, all the same—I was his what?

". . . you know," he said.

His you-know. "Boy, do you have a way with words, you old flatterer, you."

You are my you-know, my only you-know. How could two stupid words be so depressing? If our real subject, my mother as killer, weren't too serious for diversions, I would have declared time out for semantic analysis and emotional pulse-taking. But Mom as murderer had priority.

"I'm not goin' out of my way to point out who the tart-baker is," he said. "but I can't stop it once somebody else does. It'd look like a cover-up. In fact, it'd *be* a cover-up."

We'd define our relationship after my mother was cleared, which shouldn't be too far in the future. Maybe by then I'd know what I wanted the definition to be. We turned left on Broad onto Philly's answer to Hollywood, our own Walk of Fame. Ours honors the city's musicians and music makers, of which there has been a staggering abundance.

"You're not takin' this too seriously," Mackenzie said.

"Because, of course, my mother didn't do it." I stepped over André Watts's bronze plaque. "She couldn't and she wouldn't. She came up a day early to bake for him. She was so proud of her present. She arrived carrying the ingredients, in case Philadelphia didn't have exactly the right fruit." I realized that what I'd just said could also be used against her. "Ah . . . she worried about the whipped cream. Was afraid it would turn and make him sick," I said. "Does that sound like a poisoner?"

We trod over Todd Rundgren and Teddy Pendergrass and were almost on top of Harold Melvin and the Blue Notes before Mackenzie said, "The issue is, who killed Lyle Zacharias?"

"Why are you so hung up on the tarts?"

"Didn't we already do this?" He sounded weary. "First, it's the only food that Lyle ate and nobody else did."

"Which doesn't make it poisoned. Also, that isn't necessarily true. Maybe it's the only food you know about that he ate that way. He might have eaten something at home, or something he brought with him—a candy bar, a flask of bourbon, who knows?"

"And second, the old woman started screaming about them, probably after you left—"

"Aunt Hattie." I shook my head in annoyance.

He glanced at me with a mild frown. "Pulled at her hair and screamed that Lyle ate the tarts, and then she fainted. Which helped point in their direction."

We passed Samuel Barber, Stanley Clark, and Al Martino before I had a suggestion. "Maybe Hattie did it herself and she's trying to point the blame elsewhere." I knew I was grabbing at a pathetically weak straw, but I kept clutching. "Last night, she accused Lizzie. Said it was all *her* fault, not my mother's. And now this. It doesn't make sense."

"You think Harriet Zacharias killed her boy Lyle? Harriet, who nearly died of the shock of it? For whom— according to a source none other than Amanda Pepper— Lyle was her life? Tell me—why would she? Give me one reason and I'll think about it. But meanwhile, third is that once the lab was directed to the tarts, particularly the remnants of one on a plate in the kitchen, there indeed seemed to be somethin' unusual—haven't said what yet—inside them. Fourth thing: it does appear, from preliminary tests, that Lyle Zacharias died of a poison. A purgative, they think."

"But even so, *if* it was the tarts, it's only those two, which were out of the tin—"

"Lab hasn't had time to go through the entire contents of the tin yet. Don' make assumptions."

"Well, however many, like I said, anybody could have put something into them." When I stopped walking, I realized I was on Ed McMahon's plaque. I have never understood what he's doing on a musical Walk of Fame, unless I've missed the part of his biography when he played something besides second banana. "The tin of tarts was out on that counter for hours," I said, continuing the dreary discussion. "She sent them by messenger in the afternoon. Anybody could have put something in them."

His sigh was a huff of exasperation. I didn't respond while we crossed narrow Bach Place. At Pearl Bailey's plaque, Mackenzie finally looked my way. "You're sayin' Lucretia Borgia was on the guest list, and she gets there, dressed to kill, literally, includin' a phial of poison—just in case some other partygoer happens to bring Lyle a gift of food into which she can then dump her potion? That what you're sayin'?"

It didn't seem quite as probable when spelled out that way, but I couldn't go down without a fight. My mother was at stake, after all. "Maybe Ms. Borgia thought she'd put it in his dinner, and then she suddenly saw this better, easier opportunity. Why not?"

This time he kept his reply and his thoughts private and simply shook his head back and forth, slowly.

We moved toward the Bellevue, past stars highlighting the city's gifts to rock 'n' roll. Bill Haley. Chubby Checker. Bobby Rydell. "You saw how she was last night when we came back from the hospital," I said. "All she was worried about was everybody else—Lizzie and Hattie. Remember? And later, all the way to Beth's, she tried to figure out how she could help, what she should do. That isn't how a murderer behaves."

She'd been so agitated, so empathetic, that I'd agreed to chauffeur her to the hospital tonight. "Good God," I said out loud. "She's planning to bake cookies for Aunt Hattie."

"Maybe not the best idea. Harriet Zacharias seems a little nervous about Mom's cookin'. Isn't goin' to help her heart."

The musicians' names grew more august and serious, befitting their position in front of the venerable Academy of Music. Bessie Smith, John Coltrane, Dizzy Gillespie, Mario Lanza, Eugene Ormandy, Marian Anderson, Anna Moffo, and Leopold Stokowski. How had I grown up so untalented and unmusical in this city? It was almost unpatriotic. And then we were past the wide steps to the Academy, and the classical imperative no longer held. Plaques for Dick Clark and Frankie Avalon provided a finale to the parade of stars.

"Why do you think Ed McMahon has a plaque?" I asked.

"What?"

"Ed McMahon. Everybody else was a musician. They make sense. Eddie Fisher, Jeanette MacDonald, Ethel Waters—all the rest—but why Ed McMahon? He sat on Johnny Carson's right and laughed and did commercials. Why him? I mean, if Ed McMahon has a plaque, where is the justice? Where is the *sense*?"

Mackenzie stared at me.

"I am attempting to make civilized conversation," I said. "I think we've exhausted the other ridiculous subject."

I continued toward the Bellevue feeling a sudden flulike malaise, a sort of foretaste, or fore-flu, of impending, inevitable grief.

We reached the impressive gray hotel, the heroine of buildings. At her debut she was the most opulent in the country, and even after the flush of youth, she led a dignified existence as "the grande dame of Broad Street." And then Legionnaire's Disease coursed through her air-conditioned arteries and left a raddled hag, ugly, devalued, and shunned.

But now, a decade and a half later, she was back with her face lifted, body resectioned into shops, offices, a health club, a garage, and a smaller hotel. My hat's off to any dame who holds her ground. It gives me heart.

We walked into the little courtyard and entered the elevator for the fourth floor ballroom. There was no way, barring another attack of Legionnaire's Disease, that the hotel was going to have an open date for a prom. I knew this was a futile investigation, so of course I became really irritable when Mackenzie suggested the same.

"Why are you doin' this?" he asked.

"The kids thought the hotel would take me more seriously. It wasn't out of my way. I don't want them to have the first homeless prom in America."

"It's their responsibility." He was not excited at the prospect of co-chaperoning, and he made it known in a variety of situations and ways. "Shouldn' coddle them," he grumbled. "You're not their mother, you know." He paused and looked at me, one eyebrow raised. "An' you're not *your* mother, either—are you?"

"You can portray my mother as either a coddler or as a murderer, but not both," I snapped. "And you can remember that being an adult entails certain responsibilities concerning children's welfare."

"My, oh my," he murmured. "Feed 'em, clothe 'em, and find 'em prom sites?"

"Help them when you can. This is an extenuating circumstance." He, whose overprotective needs had involved the Philadelphia police force, several vans, and dangling stomach pumps, did not get it. "You want the prom canceled so that you won't have to sit through it," I said.

He laughed. "Curses. Found out again."

Upstairs, outside the ballroom, a petite woman introduced herself as Penny and explained with hyperactive enthusiasm that she was filling in for the regular special events coordinator who had chicken pox of all things and, gee, but she was sorry for any inconvenience this might mean.

"I'm interested in reserving the ballroom in late May, early June," I said. Penny beamed so widely, her smile threatened to completely encircle her head and split it in two.

"Congratulations to both of you!" She leaned close. "I just *love* working with people who are so *visibly* in love."

I looked around. Mackenzie was checking the exits. Penny needed to have her vision and sincerity retooled.

"Of course," she continued, "June is a busy, busy month, booked well in advance, a year ahead lots of times, but let's see if we can't find . . . as long as you're flexible . . . there are options like a weeknight reception. It's quite chic, you know. How large a guest list do you anticipate?"

"This is not about us," I told Penny. "Not a wedding."

Her eyes grew squinty and suspicious. "Engagement?" she asked with dwindling enthusiasm.

I shook my head.

"Then what?" Her voice was now small and nervous.

I did not want to tell her. Proms were hotel nightmares. Who wanted adolescent revelers? Kids getting sick in the stairwells. Kids wallowing in high puberty hormones. Kids renting hotel suites for extra-prom partying. Non-kids complaining and never returning to the hotel. "Never mind," I said.

And then my you-know charged to the rescue. "A *ball*," Mackenzie said.

Penny stood on tiptoe, the better to understand the man. "A what?"

"Y'know, like we always have down home? Maybe you call it a cotillion up here? Lotta folks dancin', fancy dress . . ." He looked misty-eyed and wistful for the old family plantation. If only he'd had one.

"Like *Gone With the Wind*?" Penny whispered.

"Precisely!" How did he manage to get so many syllables into the word? How much magnolia scent and Spanish moss? "We plan to have us a few hundred guests," he added. "That is, if you can find a slot for us in this magnificent hotel."

She twinkled and glittered and beamed up at him. A ball. Scarlett O'Hara lived, even though Mackenzie's accent was born of the wrong state and certainly the wrong era and social class. Didn't matter. He murmured on. My own genuine Bubba-you-know, and irresistible. I could feel my own self twinkling at him.

"I *know* we'll work something out," Penny said as Mackenzie gathered up brochures and price lists from her. "I'm just sure of it!"

"Bless you," I said when we were back on the street. "That was truly altruistic, inspired, and saintly. Not to mention funny as hell."

"Yankee women would probably be much happier if the South had won the war and ever'body talked the right way." And then he added, as if it had some logical connection, "But y'know, I've been thinkin'. There's a whole other way of goin' at this."

"Another way of finding a prom site? Or do you mean another way of getting Yankee men to talk the way you do?"

"We've been lookin' at opportunity here, and method—maybe—but we haven't been lookin' at motive."

Good-bye, Rhett Butler. Luckily, I didn't have to answer him, because it wasn't a question. If I had been specifically asked to consider motives, I'd have felt even worse about not mentioning that the first Mrs. Lyle Zacharias had been my father's foster sister. I knew that was irrelevant to Lyle's unfortunate death, but would Mackenzie?

"So the question is: who'd want to have killed him?" he asked. "Who had a good motive?"

The flinty eyes of Sybil Zacharias flashed like a blinking danger signal, although I still thought she'd have wanted him alive at least one more day, until after she enrolled her son in private school without needing to fudge about the date. But maybe the opportunity had popped up with his party—a chance to be in the same room with him, and she took it. I kept her filed as a possibility and then looked at the objects of her bad-mouthing. "According to his ex-wife, his current wife has been having an affair with a soap opera actor, Shepard McCoy," I said.

"I'm not sure ex-wives are overly reliable on the subject of current wives," Mackenzie said. "Although that is interestin'."

"And Lyle was going to quit his job and live the simple life. Shuck his possessions, go native, which his current wife would not like at all."

"A few decades late for that sort of thing, isn't it?" Mackenzie said.

"And there's maybe somebody else, a whiny woman named Janine who was pretty obvious about not liking Lyle."

"Not likin's not the same as killin'. Lots of people I don't like." He raised his right shoulder in a quiet statement of dismissal.

Whining, obsessively self-pitying Janine was certainly a more likely killer than my poor old mother, and I said so. "And what if there really was something seriously wrong between them? A long-standing feud. Just because she was obnoxious doesn't mean she was wrong."

He walked a few steps. "What I don' get is that it was his birthday. His best friends, right? Why would any of them do him harm?"

I tried to explain the odd invitations and Lyle's desire to "see his life" whole before his eyes, to heal old wounds, forget old grievances. It had obviously been a desire best squelched. It was possible that Lyle Zacharias had no authentic, tried and true friends, but what a way for him to find it out.

"Tell you what," Mackenzie said. "Let's get our priorities straight. Why don't we go find two brimful plates of pasta, and while we're ingestin' them, you tell me everything you recall from last night. We can thrash out the goodies, the maybes, the baddies. Know it's early, but I'm starvin'. Haven't had time for anything since six A.M."

"Damn," I said. "I can't."

"The invitation holds even if you can't remember a single one of them. I wasn't serious about that sorting out."

"I mean I can't have dinner." I double-checked my watch and it confirmed what I'd said. "I promised my mother I'd take her to visit Hattie."

"Can't Beth?"

"The two kids' schedules make it complicated."

"A cab, then?"

"My mother would consider that a serious breach of faith on my part. Besides, if it was Hattie screeching about the tarts, then maybe I should be there to . . ."

"Protect your mother?" he asked softly.

I nodded. "She wouldn't dream she's in danger. She might say or do . . . I don't even know what I'm talking about." Because, of course, last night she *had* dreamed she was in danger. She'd said, at least once, that she was a suspect. But she hadn't *meant* it or believed it, I was sure. "Anyway, I have an appointment after that, too. Another prospective prom site. My last—I promise."

"You need my good ol' boy routine for that one, too?"

"I think a mid-Atlantic twang will work this time." We hugged, exchanged kisses—no students about—and I turned toward the parking lot where I keep my car.

"By the way," Mackenzie said. "Just why were your folks invited to that party? And what does it have to do with the way you call Harriet Zacharias 'Aunt Hattie'?"

I brushed away his annoyingly logical questions. "Some other time, okay? I'm late already."

When I glanced back, he was staring intently after me. So now I knew how to rivet the attention of my you-know.

All it took was having him believe that there was a murderer amongst my relatives.

Would even my mother approve of this method of snagging a man?

Eleven

THE KILLER GRANNY WOULD NOT BE TALKED OUT OF VISITING her accuser. I didn't see the point of notifying her of the cloud of suspicion over her head, so my excuses were fairly lame, and definitely not persuasive.

"But she's out of the hospital. She's okay," I said. Hattie Zacharias had suffered grief and agitation, not a heart attack.

"Mandy! The woman lost her son. It's nothing more than *decent* to offer condolences."

I was being petty and selfish because Hattie lived in Society Hill, which was all the way on the waterfront. I couldn't shuttle my mother there and back to the Main Line then retrace my tracks and arrive at Richard Quinn's waterfront restaurant in time.

"Poor old woman," my mother shouted. We were in the family room, where my father sat, almost regally, with the encased foot on a low stool and an afghan over his lap. My niece, Karen, was the floor show, dancing to recorded ditties in a convulsive but enthusiastic style. The background music was the same squeaky white-bread version of rapped Mother Goose that had caused my father's precipitous slide across the living room twenty-four hours earlier, but he did not appear to make the connection and/or care, proof of how heavily he was sedated.

"It's the least I can do," my mother bellowed, trying to be heard above the din.

". . . *went to the cupboard to get her poor dog a bone . . .*"

It was the worst excuse for music I'd ever heard, and I wondered how the woman who'd cut the record had fallen to the nadir of show-biz.

Still, as sorry as I felt for what had become of her, I felt even worse about what was happening to my auditory nerves. I put my hands to my ears and charaded aural agony, and way, way after she should have, my bright niece caught on and lowered the volume microscopically.

"Poor Hattie never had anything, anybody in the whole world except Lyle," my mother said. "Now, what does she have at all?"

"The Queen of Hearts she made some tarts . . ."

Even at a slightly lowered decibel level, the voice was grating. Besides, I didn't want to hear about any tarts, even the Queen's, at the moment. My father didn't wince or flinch. He grinned beatifically. The drugs he was taking were obviously the secret hope for peace on earth. Unfortunately, he wasn't sharing them. "Karen!" I shouted. *"Please!"*

She looked shocked and examined me with a face that clearly was redefining me as seriously old and out of it. Nonetheless, she lowered the volume to an acceptable level. She was going to be an interesting challenge as a teenager.

"Okay, Mom," I conceded. "We'll go. But we have to leave now, and I might have to send you back in a cab, because before I knew about . . . this, I made a . . ."

My mother's eyes widened, her mouth opened slightly. I could imagine her expression on someone lost in the wilderness who finally spots a sign of life. "Yes?" she asked softly, hopefully.

"A . . ." I gagged over the word, but my mother looked so expectant, so *innocent*, that I tried to give her this. "You know, a—a—"

"A *date*!" she said. "Of course! I nearly forgot in the confusion—that nice, um . . ."

"Actually, it's more an appointment."

She beamed. "Richard Quinn. I remember. He said he'd see you at six." She looked at her watch with a troubled expression.

I couldn't believe how much attention she paid to the trivia of my life—the social part of it, anyway. We had to deal with this, but right now we were in too much of a hurry. "It's not a *date* date." Why did I have to explain that to my mother? Why did it matter so much to her? "He's buying into a new restaurant the kids at school might be able to rent for their . . ."

She wasn't interested in small print, but she was willing to hustle out and get me to the appointment/date on time.

"Mom," I said while en route, "you're so *eager* for me to get married—"

"Yes, dear." Her voice was pleasant and untroubled, and she sat with her hands folded comfortably on a red and white tin of homemade cookies. "I'm your *mother*. That's what parents are for. To take care of their children. I want you to be *safe*. Protected."

Amazement kept me silent. Protected? Safe? I mean if men are the protection, what on earth are they protecting us against?

My mother observed the passing city through her window and continued. "Nothing unusual about that. But I know that sometimes it can become a problem."

"Yes," I said quickly. "I'm glad you realize that. I wanted to talk about—"

"Like Hattie," my mother said. "That was too much. She was an overprotective mother."

I could not envision what that word meant to my mother, short of a lioness, teeth bared. Hattie roaring.

"She didn't approve of Cindy, of course."

"Why not?"

"Well, Hattie had plans for Lyle. She was even picky about his friends, and then Cindy came along, one of those

who had definitely made love not war, complete with her
. . . love child."

Isn't that a cute expression? And what's its opposite for
children born within the institution? Habit child? Contrac-
tual obligation child?

"Hattie thought Lyle could do better than a hippie with
a baby, and Lord knew who its father was, and she made
her objections *very* clear. Of course, once Lyle married
Cindy, Hattie accepted the situation, but she was like that
about everything and everybody that had to do with Lyle.
Planning, arranging for what was best for her boy. Sometimes, like with Cindy, it was too much. It was . . . meddling. Interfering."

"Ah," I said. "Yes. I understand meddling. In fact—"

"Still and all, she only wanted the best for him, like any
mother. And she was his mother, even if she didn't give
birth to him. He was the absolute center of her life. Everything, everything revolved around him and what was best
for him. And now . . ." She sighed and shook her head.

Hattie lived down by the Delaware River in Society
Hill's only high rise, which loomed over the two- and
three-story brick colonial buildings and disrupted the illusion of standstill time in Olde Philadelphia.

"We're back where we were last night, aren't we?" my
mother asked. "Except I don't remember such a tall building. My mind's going." She chuckled, but she sounded a
little nervous, too.

I explained that the already arrived denizens of Society
Hill would probably not like being confused with the still
upwardly mobile of Queen Village, where we'd been the
night before, a few blocks to the south. The mistake, however, was understandable. It's hard to tell one gentrified
brick row house from another.

It wasn't until I had finally located the parking entrance,
and we had ridden the elevator talking about neighborhoods
and apartments versus houses, that I realized I hadn't made
a dent in my mother's implacable campaign to meddle until
she married me off.

* * *

HATTIE SAT WITH HER LEGS UP ON A CREAM-COLORED SOFA, covered by a throw that looked spun of softness itself— cashmere, I guessed. Twenty-four hours of bereavement had accelerated the aging process. She was ancient and translucent with pain.

Even so, she looked out of her withered face with sharp eagle eyes that sized up the soft doviness of my mother. Easy prey.

"I baked cookies for you," my mother said. I cringed, waiting for a horrible showdown and accusations, a replay of what Mackenzie had told me, but Hattie seemed too stunned or grief-stricken to connect yesterday's baked goods with today's. At least not openly. Yesterday, she had bragged to me about her ability to remember everything. Apparently, there had been some major changes overnight.

Hattie smiled, rather weakly, and when my mother opened the tin and offered the contents to her, she delicately extracted one, a swirl of chocolate and vanilla strips whose kin had brightened many of the lunch boxes of my childhood.

"Very pretty, Bea." Hattie kept the cookie in her hand the entire time we were there. It never visited the neighborhood of her mouth. Maybe her memory wasn't shot, after all.

A flabby woman with thin pinkish hair introduced herself. "I'm Alice," she said with a peculiar animation that was first cousin to hysteria. "A neighbor *and* dear friend. Helping out in this time of grief, so let me make you comfortable." She proceeded to bustle around making intrusive efforts at hospitality, offering us our cookies and repeatedly urging the housekeeper, Maria, who looked offended by her directives, to bring us coffee or tea, no matter that we both declined the offer.

"The most perfect boy who ever lived," Hattie said. We seemed to have arrived in the middle of a discussion. "I cannot believe he's gone."

"Always was an angel," Alice said. "And now he's one for real."

"Kind to everyone," Hattie said. "Generous to a fault."

Perhaps we hadn't interrupted anything except a never-ending Lylesong in two-part harmony.

"A saint," Alice said.

"Sometimes he was too good. People took advantage," Hattie said. "Expected too much, too often."

The leeches? I wondered. Alice tsked and shook her head. Maria the housekeeper sulked. I checked my watch.

"Bright as can be from day one," Hattie said.

"And quite the athlete, too," Alice added.

"And of course, so talented in his writing," my mother said.

I couldn't endure the round-robin, which felt programmed and potentially interminable. I stood up and walked to the large picture window.

"The shame was, *Ace of Hearts* made him famous, and he got so involved in producing, he never really wrote again," Hattie said from behind me.

"Well, this way he was more of a Renaissance man," my exceptionally gracious mother said. I wished Mackenzie were here—I wished the entire force were here to observe her and dispel any lingering questions about her innocence.

While the three women began a new cycle of competitive praise, I looked out over the river. Although the city of Camden on the other side is not often listed as a scenic wonder, it does have a skyline, and the Delaware flowed in front of it, reflecting its night lights. It wasn't half bad. The most perfect boy who ever lived had done well by his auntie.

"He was the best. The best," Hattie repeated. Her criteria were simple. If something involved Lyle, it was the best. Period. "I would have done anything for him, so how can I still be alive while he's—he's—"

My mother made comforting noises and Alice uttered grating homilies about the good dying young, and I felt useless and awkward and tried to concentrate on the wall that adjoined the picture window, a montage shrine to the late Lyle Zacharias.

My mother had a similar wall in Boca Raton, and I had spotted the beginnings of one at Beth's house. Apparently, the real umbilical cord is strung between the delivery and dark rooms.

There were Kodak moments of Lyle on a bear rug and on a pony, dressed for baseball, tennis, swimming, and high school graduation; with a toothy prom date in taffeta, with a grin a mile wide under the marquee of the theatre that had premiered *Ace of Hearts*. There was a snap of a blurred trio of happy faces in matching jackets—Wiley-Riley and Lyle—and there was a picture of boyish Richard Quinn and Lyle grinning nervously from behind matching wooden desks. There were travel snaps: Lyle and Hattie in the surf, on a mountain with a small Asian guide, on board a raft in a dark jungly setting, at a Thanksgiving gathering.

There was a remarkable absence of females, except, of course, for Hattie. I searched for someone who might be my father's foster sister, but couldn't find a likely subject. Couldn't find Sybil, either. Couldn't find Tiffany.

It was Lyle she cared about and for. Period. Even Reed was barely present, and always a sidekick, never the real subject of the photo.

The housekeeper, urged on by Alice, offered me a cup of coffee for the third time in perhaps seven minutes. She looked desperate to end this impasse, so I accepted the flower-sprigged, nearly transparent cup. I grappled with its too-small handle, and as this seemed a particularly inappropriate time to destroy anything else Hattie cherished, I looked for a place to put it down.

I was standing next to a table with a display-case top. Not a suitable coffee-cup rest, but intriguing in its contents' brilliant colors and convoluted shapes. I had expected to see bibelots, man-made treasures. Instead, the glass covered a purple butterfly, an orange and black shedded snakeskin, a fern frond, two small pressed flowers, a red-armored beetle, a large gray-green pod, a thickly veined leaf, a bird's wing that varied from scarlet to buttercup to azure, a chambered nautilus shell. I leaned close and read a tiny brass plaque: TREASURES COLLECTED BY HARRIET ZACHARIAS.

I turned and was surprised to find Hattie watching me appraisingly. "Wonderful," I murmured.

She nodded agreement. "When I was a girl, I dreamed of two things. First, I wanted to be a naturalist, but of course, girls didn't get to do such things in my day. The closest I came was working at the Academy of Natural Sciences from the time I received my Secretarial Certificate until . . ." She paused and bit at her lips. "After *Ace of Hearts*, I was able to retire." She sighed and pressed a handkerchief to her mouth.

So she had saved the little orphaned nephew, and then he had saved her.

"What was the second thing, Hattie?" Alice asked, much too brightly, as if she were the host of an afternoon talk show. "You said you'd always wanted two things," she prompted.

"To travel." Hattie answered so softly I had trouble hearing her. "But of course, once I had a little boy to raise, I couldn't. When Lyle was five, he said, 'Aunt Hattie, when I grow up, I'm going to send you all over the world. Every place you ever wanted to go.' And he did. Even back then, when Lyle said he was going to do something, he really meant it. I've never doubted his word once."

She suddenly sobbed, then wiped at her eyes while Alice annoyingly repeated, "There, there, mustn't get riled." Alice had a lot of undeserved self-confidence and was never at a loss for words, although the words she found were clichéd, meaningless, and irritating.

My mother made sympathetic clucks and held Hattie's free hand. The housekeeper stood in the doorway to the kitchen, studying us impassively.

Hattie resumed her one song. "Such a good boy and such a good man," she said.

"Lyle was too good to live, is what I say," Alice added, just in case Hattie wasn't feeling bad enough already.

Hattie sobbed into her handkerchief.

"Wasn't Mr. Lyle just the kindest man who ever lived, Maria?" Alice persisted.

"Yesss," Maria said sibilantly, her face sullen.

"Sound a little more like you mean it!" Alice laughed,

then turned to us and rolled her eyes. "The man was a prince!"

"Mr. Lyle he was a prince," Maria said with no conviction. Her expression remained as impassive as it had been since we entered.

"How could this have happened?" Hattie sobbed.

I awaited the next blow, Hattie's theory of how, indeed, it had happened. But instead of pointing at my mother and yelling *"J'accuse,"* Hattie looked toward the ceiling. "It's that girl!" Her voice cracked with emotion. "It's all her fault!"

"What girl?" Alice asked.

Hattie waved her away. "You weren't even there last night." And then I knew which girl Hattie meant, and I wondered why she was again fixated on poor Lizzie.

And then I wondered why the police weren't.

And then I was ashamed of myself all over again. The young chef was as ludicrous a killer as my mother was. The Boarding House was her business. She'd been flushed with creating a successful party and with what it could mean for her future.

Of course she had behaved bizarrely ...

But again I argued myself down. Something might be neurologically or emotionally wrong, but that wasn't the same as having either a motive or the temperament to murder and self-destruct.

Alice looked mortified, either about being excluded last night or about Hattie's reminder of the same just now.

Facing me across the room, a crimson and gold mask, vaguely Indonesian, contorted in confusion and pain. It seemed to capture, in one ambiguous expression, the sadness, unfairness, and waste of Lyle Zacharias's death.

Hattie saw me studying it. "We bought that in Bali. The artist called her the Queen of Hearts. Not like in our playing cards, but like in love and heartache." She sighed, heavily.

"Take some comfort," my mother said sympathetically, "that at the end he was surrounded by his friends, the people closest to him on earth."

Alice snorted. "With friends like that, who needs ene- mies?" Her face flushed with excitement, as if she'd in- vented the expression that very moment. "I've known that boy from the time he was a toddler, and the one thing wrong with him was that he was too trusting. Thought ev- erybody meant him well. It was his fatal flaw, I'd say. Right up to that last day."

"Alice," Hattie said. "Please."

"Well, it's no more than the truth, and I for one am *sorry* he was so eager to see them all again. Let sleeping dogs lie, I say."

Was Alice truly Hattie's friend, or merely a grief vulture who fed on misery? Maybe Hattie, ill with mourning, lacked the energy to throw her out of the apartment.

"Couldn't pick friends, couldn't pick wives," Alice said. "Starting with that little hippie girl—"

I saw my mother's spine straighten. So, apparently, did Hattie.

"Alice!" she said sharply. "Bea was related to Cynthia. Cynthia was a very nice girl. And pretty. Reminded me of Maureen O'Hara."

"Did I even hint that she wasn't nice or pretty?" Alice asked with a fake smile. "She was an *angel.* But surely you'll agree that Lyle was unlucky to have his child—"

"That was not Lyle's child." Hattie turned to my mother, who had been watching the two women as if they were a sporting event. "I wonder what became of that girl," she said. "A bad seed, if you ask me."

"No, just a baby," my mother murmured. "The accident must be a terrible burden to bear. I hope she turned out all right."

"So you haven't stayed in touch, then?" Hattie asked.

My mother shook her head. "I'm ashamed to say we wouldn't know Betsy if we bumped into her on the street."

Hattie raised her eyebrows and looked as if she had more to say, but Alice pushed back into the conversation. "All I mean is that Lyle's own flesh and blood is a different breed of cat. Reed is certainly not the kind to pick up a pistol and—"

"Alice!" This time Hattie's voice was nearly a growl.

"I didn't mean—" Alice looked upset for a moment, but she had a quick recovery time. "Then how about his *other* wives? You'd agree that they were not lucky choices, wouldn't you?"

Hattie glared wordlessly.

"All right! Not another word," Alice said. "My lips are sealed." And she made a motion—I could have predicted it—of zipping her mouth shut. Only the zipper broke immediately. "Wasn't that coffee delicious?" she chirped. "Maria is the best coffee person in the city!"

Maria glowered. I couldn't remember what I'd done with my cup.

"Mrs. Pepper and her daughter are ready for refills," Alice said. "Do you think that might be possible, Maria?"

What I thought might be possible was hurling Alice out the window if all the rest of us cooperated in the effort. If we got our angle and swing right, she might even sail all the way into the river. Become part of the view. "None for me," I said.

"Oh, my! The time," my mother exclaimed.

"You can't leave yet!" Hattie looked alarmed and somewhat put out.

Accusation time at last. I tried to avert it, tried to hurry my mother by talking right over her voice, offering my sympathy again and asking for my coat.

"Please, don't," Hattie said, teary-eyed. I thought her misery must at least partially be fear of being alone with Alice.

"I promised Mandy, you see," my mother said.

Maybe this sort of thing went on all the time. Maybe my social life was always the mainstay of her conversation. But she was usually a thousand miles south of Philadelphia, so at least I normally couldn't hear it.

"She has a . . . a prior *commitment*, you understand," my mother insisted on saying as I scrambled into my coat.

Given their emotional states, I don't know how my mother expected them to react to her coy euphemism, but

I knew how I had, and, feeling like a great oafish toddler, I tugged at her sleeve.

Hattie stood up, the cashmere throw falling around her feet as she lurched forward and clutched my mother's coat, and the slightly dazed, mostly benign expression she'd worn hardened so that her wrinkled old face was more crazed and crackled than ever. "You're not really leaving, though, are you?" she asked.

"Well, as I explained, Mandy—"

"I mean back to Florida." The hand clutching my mother's coat had long nails painted an incongruous scarlet. It reminded me of a tropical bird's foot.

I couldn't decide if she was hostile, or angry, or if her cracked vocal cords were in need of oiling. But there was a note of urgency that seemed misplaced.

"You mean right away?" my mother spluttered. "We meant to, well, the tickets were for . . . but you know, Gilbert had a little accident, his foot, and we can't. . . ." Her words accelerated, one falling on top of the other. She was afraid she wasn't being kind enough, sensitive enough. "Besides, I wouldn't leave now, not until after the . . . I'll be here. I'll come visit you again, too, if you like."

She wasn't paying proper attention to that hard-coal stare of Hattie's. She thought Hattie was asking for company, and instead Hattie preparing a trap, a subtle snare. The *j'accuse* was just around the corner, I was positive. I only wished I could see through her game plan.

"If there's anything I can do," my mother said, "bring you, take care of, drive you . . ."

I particularly liked that last offer, as she hadn't a car, only a chauffeuring daughter.

"Please," my mother continued. "Don't hesitate to . . ."

Stop, I wanted to shout. Run back home. Did Florida have extradition?

"Let me help you, Hattie, however I can," my mother babbled on. "We go way back, after all, there's no denying . . ."

No, no! Remember Hattie? The overprotective? She thinks you killed the light of her life!

"If there's an errand I can run, something I could cook—"

"No." Hattie was loud and final, all tension abruptly gone. "Nothing. But it's good to know you'll be around." Her hooded eyes fixed on my mother with a predator's grip. My breath caught as she nodded, satisfied that the quarry was near at hand and all hers.

Twelve

My dear mother. I saw it again, that dreadful optimistic innocence lighting her face. And all would be well, all would be well, some tiny spirit sang inside her.

She was not only capable of walking into the lion's den, but of petting the lion while he devoured her.

While she devoured her.

I drove away from the apartment building, unable to shake the image of Hattie Zacharias X-raying my mother. I couldn't imagine why she was playing cat and mouse instead of acknowledging her suspicions, but whatever her reason, her actions made me queasy.

My mother broke off her humming. "Drop me off anywhere," she said. "I'll hail a cab."

"Of course not!" Where were her brains? What had happened to her self-preservation instincts, all the warnings and precautions she directed my way?

"You can't be late for your—"

"It's not a—" I couldn't bear to hear the word, to realize once again that this sweet woman was stuck in a Judy Garland movie time warp. "I'll drive you to the Sheraton," I snapped, rather more harshly than intended. I smoothed my voice, tried to keep the frustration out of it. "It's close, on Dock Street. Right here in Society Hill. There'll be a cab outside, or we'll have them call you one and you can wait in their lobby."

I was late for my appointment with Richard Quinn, but all the same, I waited outside, needing to be certain my charge didn't wander out into danger. I had to control the urge to remind the cabbie to drive safely.

I was becoming just like the woman.

CONSCIOUSLY OR NOT, RICHARD QUINN HAD MATCHED THE walls of The Scene to his eyes. It was a good choice. They—the eyes and the walls—were a silver-blue counterpoint to the dark night river and sky outside the oversized windows. The focal point here, as in Hattie's nearby apartment, was a head-on view of Camden with a bonus peek at the lights of the Ben Franklin Bridge.

"Sorry I'm late," I said. "I hope nothing's ruined." Nothing like arriving out of breath, flustered, and mildly sweaty from anxiety, but, I reminded myself, this was not a date. Not the way my mother meant. I was here to check out the room and the food. "I was paying a condolence call on Hattie Zacharias. Got delayed," I offered as excuse for my tardiness.

He tilted his head. "You know her?"

"My mother does. Did. I chauffeured."

"Bad, huh?" He helped me off with my coat.

"Why's that?" Your mission, I told myself, is to wrestle nouns and verbs and even more than one sentence at a time out of him.

Quinn shrugged. "The way she was about Lyle."

"So you knew her, too?" I examined the restaurant-to-be. It was washed in marine colors, from the silvery walls to the aquamarine upholstered chairs to the deep-sea, blue-green carpeting.

"She checked me out."

I waited.

He gave up and released an entire set of sentences. Victory for my side. "Checked everybody near Lyle out. Had to approve. Lyle didn't mind." He shrugged, then put my coat in an empty cubicle lined with bright blue pegs and lifted off a numbered tag hanging from it.

"I don't think I need the check," I said.

He put it back. No smile. No sense of the ridiculous. Boring. "Didn't mean to go on that way," he said.

"When?" He needed remedial going-on-that-way help.

"Like it?" Quinn opened his arms to embrace the room at large.

I stated my approval at length—more length than I honestly meant to provide, much more length than he'd ever manage, certainly. But each time I paused, thinking I'd concluded, Quinn raised his eyebrows and looked as though he hoped for more. He was stingy with his words, a glutton for mine. If it had been money instead of language flowing between us, I'd be the U.S. deficit and he'd be Midas.

It wasn't that easy finding subjects to praise. After all, the main item to appreciate in a restaurant is the food, which was conspicuously absent. I trusted that Quinn had it squirreled away somewhere, as a treat after the compliments, and at least as a sampler of what the place would offer, and so I went on about how much I liked the color scheme, the way the tables weren't overly close to one another, and the quality of the linen and china samples Quinn showed me. Growing desperate, I even said how much I liked what wasn't there, such as fishermen's nets and fake sea gulls and the hard surfaces that make too many restaurants uncomfortably loud. He handed me a menu, and I complimented the prospective variety of entrées and even the teal-blue leather folder that held the list of offerings.

And then I hit the compliment wall. "Must be scary to start a new venture," I said, in search of a new conversational tack.

"Shows, huh?" He rolled his head back and pushed at his neck in a classic, but probably futile, attempt to ease the tension. "I'm pretty rattled."

"Well, even if you weren't just about to start something new, last night would leave you jangled." I chitted, he chatted. Whenever I think longingly of marrying, it is primarily to avoid this tiptoed tour of forced cheer. But then I look at old marrieds' silent meals in restaurants and I stay happily single. We made our way to the glassy end of the room, where all three walls were windowpanes and water lapped at the sides of the pier. "I mean, losing a friend— and losing him that way . . ." I pulled my attention away from the view of glamorous Camden and looked up at Quinn, who stared out over the water, his face as unrattled as a face can be.

I wondered where everybody else was. Shouldn't people be rehearsing? Stocking the pantries and the bar? Setting the tables?

"Want a drink?" Quinn asked. "Not everything's here yet, but—"

"Mineral water, please." No alcohol on a stomach that felt cavernously empty. I checked the room again for signs of dinner, even sniffed for aromas, and felt a little like my cat when there's no food in sight and he's anxiously convinced there never will be again. I wondered what Quinn would do if I rubbed against his leg and mewed.

I was so absorbed in visual foraging that I nearly missed a murmur about Lyle and long ago and their partnership, although it was followed by a silence needing to be filled.

"Too bad you split up before *Ace of Hearts*," I said, hoping I was responding properly.

Hitherto, I hadn't known a face could change dramatically without visibly moving a muscle. It was as if each of his cells contracted and grew hard and his river-water eyes sparked like flint.

"Wouldn't have, if I'd known. But we'd agreed we weren't going anywhere. No ideas, no projects, no money. He said he was quitting the biz, too. Then four months after we split, *Ace of Hearts* was ready to roll." His voice was icier than the Delaware River running outside. He handed me a Perrier, clutched his glass of bourbon and water, and seemed to stare into his past.

That had been a veritable oration for Quinn, startling for its verbosity and passion, relatively speaking. I looked at him. His anger wasn't visible; he'd been an actor, after all. But it was definitely there, boiling the pale marine world he'd created. How angry Richard Quinn still was, decades after he'd made his badly-timed exit.

Except, I remembered with a hot shock to the system, there was a new anger, new fuel for the fire. Sybil Zacharias had told me that Richard Quinn's first restaurant partner had become sick and had backed out. Then he'd wanted Lyle to help with this place—recompense for past injustices?—and had been turned down. Lyle had called him a leech.

I wondered whether his obsession about the disparate fates of the Quinn and Zacharias halves of the former partnership was enough to lead to a twenty-year, time-delayed poisoning, particularly after further insults and injuries had been inflicted. And if you needed more capital for your restaurant and were refused, what happened? How much trouble was Quinn in?

And how much trouble had I put myself in?

The damned place was empty, and what was I doing here? I felt stupid and nervous. Could I blame this on my mother? Why wasn't anybody else here? Surely, a restaurant's opening needed the same sort of ensemble effort as a Broadway play.

"Water under the bridge." Quinn didn't sound overjoyed about that, either. "No point looking back. Come see my room."

I pulled back, clutching my Perrier as a potential weapon until I realized he meant the room where the burned-out prom might be held. This was a business-as-usual night. I had nothing to fear from Quinn, except, it appeared, hunger.

We returned to the entrance and I followed him up a flight of stairs.

He'd been a failed producer and a minor, not overly successful actor, and I didn't know what else. Now he was trying to become a restaurateur and already hitting bad luck in the effort. This could well be his last real chance, and he had every reason to be nervous. I wondered why Lyle had decided against investing. I wondered what the scene between them had been like. I stayed close to the exit from then on, never letting Quinn block my path toward the door. Just in case.

Upstairs was a perfectly wonderful potential prom site. The view was even better—as long as Camden continued to be considered a view. The space seemed right. I could see it bright with summer formals and tuxedos, the corners junked up with Senior Prom decor.

"We have small tables and lots of chairs. As many as they want," Quinn said.

And in one corner, amongst the balloons and streamers, Mackenzie and I would be drinking the legal punch, knowing that the students had managed, no matter our vigilance, to spike theirs. "No alcohol, you know," I told Quinn.

"No problem."

"And the food?" The more nervous or anxious I get, the more hungry I also get. I hoped mention of sustenance would prompt him to offer me something. My stomach echoed the hope—audibly.

"The best. Good prices, too," he said. No samples.

We would have to make sure that the restaurant was actually opening on time and that it would still be open in June, given Quinn's financial problems and lack of personal charm as a restaurateur. Never had the school newspaper been presented with such an interesting investigative challenge.

It was very quiet. We had run out of conversation.

I told him that I was personally sold on the space, told him the prom date, asked him to hold it for twenty-four hours, and reassured him that lots of people would want to hold their significant parties upstairs at The Scene and that his future seemed assured. Then I headed back to the stairs. I had two goals: to go home and to eat, in either order.

"Lyle's aunt," Quinn said from behind me. "Is she okay?"

It was the first time he'd asked about somebody else, extended himself. "Understandably grief-stricken," I answered.

"She say what killed him?" We were back in the entry-way of the restaurant, next to the coat-check cubby.

As what she'd said pointed toward my mother's head, I decided it was privileged information. "Nope," I said, practicing taciturnity.

Richard Quinn gave me my coat. I had half expected him to charge me for its storage. I put it on, hoping it would muffle my stomach's growls. I considered Quinn's chronology with Lyle. "Did you know Lyle's first wife, too?" I was eager for information about my mysterious semi-relative.

"Uh-huh."

Did he think that answer sufficed? "What was she like?"

He rolled an imaginary toothpick around in his mouth. "She's dead. Don't like to speak ill."

Of course, by saying that, he already had, only indirectly. "Please. I'd really like to know."

He seemed on the verge of asking me why, and then seemed to stop caring. "Very Sixties. Peace and love, but intense about it. Holier than thou."

"Interesting," I said. "What do you mean?"

He shrugged. It was a tic with him, a substitute for emotion. "Wanted people to be perfect. *Other* people. Fought with Lyle all the time." He shook his head, perhaps believing that I could see what was going on inside his skull. "Last dinner together . . ." More head shaking. "Like *Who's Afraid of Virginia Woolf?*"

"Why?" I cued him once again. "About what?"

He—surprise—shrugged. "Don't know. Called each other names, like *idealistic idiot*. That would be for her. And she called him a *pig*. Back and forth."

So much for my father's sweetness-and-light vision of Cindy.

So much, too, for Quinn's interest in the subject.

"Take my card," he said. "And extras, to pass around. So I'll hear from you tomorrow?"

Accepting a small pile of cards seemed easier than protesting. But I couldn't resist one last question. "Why did you go to Lyle's party?" I asked softly, one hand already on the front doorknob. "Was it for Tiffany's sake?"

"No. Tiff didn't want to go, either."

"Then why?"

"To see."

"See what?" We sounded like one of my niece's stupid riddles.

"Who else he needed to let bygones be bygones with. How many."

"But surely not everybody there—"

"Can't say. Not the young ones, the new ones. But people who go back a while." Quinn leaned against the front of the coat-check cubby. "Like Sybil said, Lyle doesn't have old friends. Once you get to know him . . ."

"For example? Anybody specifically at last night's party?"

He nodded. "Terry Wiley, for one. He's no friend anymore. Lyle ripped *Ace of Hearts* off him."

"No," I said. "If that were true, he would have gone to court, would have—"

"Did. Poor slob lost. No proof. Who keeps carbons from high school?"

"Maybe the claim was fake. Wiley's a science teacher, not a writer."

"Meet his wife? Ruined him. He gave up trying."

I could believe that.

"Lyle *sounds* good. Pure salesman, pure talk, but no ideas and no talent. Knockoffs. *Oklahoma!* on the moon, or Double O Seven with Siamese twin agents. Junk. His whole career: a show, TV series, revival, and spinoff—all from that one idea. Terry Wiley's idea. Terry Wiley's old script, too." Quinn's dislike of speaking ill of the dead—in fact of speaking at all—did not extend to the newly dead Lyle. I wondered when I was going to hear someone besides Hattie and her sidekick Alice speak well of him.

I considered Terry Wiley as the possible murderer, but was stymied by his wife's insistence on having her stomach pumped. Possibly the ties that bind have an escape clause when one of the partners is about to commit murder. Maybe Terry simply didn't tell Janine what he was up to. Or maybe Janine's performance was only that, designed to deflect suspicion.

And perhaps Quinn's sudden willingness to talk about Wiley was also a way of keeping attention elsewhere and off himself. Quinn had been robbed, too, or thought he'd been. If Lyle was going to steal a show, a hit, then the least he could have done was share the spoils with his partner.

Quinn. Wiley. Sybil. Tiffany. Shepard. Even Reed. Good grief!

How could anyone suspect my motiveless mother when there was a covey of potential villains at hand?

And what the devil was I doing with one of them? In an eyeblink and one taciturn farewell, I was out of there.

Thirteen

MACAVITY WAS PLAYING FELINE FAMINE, EYEING ME BALE-
fully and yowling pitifully, although his starvation act was
a hard sell, given both the size of his belly and the brim-
ming container of dry food on the floor.

"I'm hungry, too," I muttered. I nonetheless opened a
can of his beloved glop before I dared to take off my coat.

I wondered if I should talk to my brother-in-law about
my parents' potential legal problems. Sam specialized in
corporate law, but surely he'd have a better idea than I of
what to do in case of impending criminal disaster.

Perhaps my parents should flee back to Florida. Maybe
even a quick trip across the water to the Bahamas. Didn't
all manner of shady characters gamble and gambol there
with no danger to their persons? Could a nice but wrongly
accused couple from Florida join them?

Meanwhile, I studied my refrigerator, which featured the
rank remains of what had once been broccoli, a plastic-
wrapped wing that worried me because I couldn't remember having broiled chicken since mid-January, an extremely
hard circle that had once been a cold cut slice, and cheese
that had mutated into a St. Patrick's Day ornament.

I jealously eyed Macavity's full dish. Where was the eq-
uity in our relationship? I always thought about his welfare.

It was high time he thought about mine. He needed sensitivity training.

"Cat," I said, "I'm going to tell you a true story. A *parable*." I didn't wait for permission, or even for Macavity's attention. "In the time of King Richard the Third," I said, "there lived a nobleman named Sir Henry Wyat. Sir Henry was accused of political crimes and sent to the Tower of London, condemned to die of starvation."

Macavity snarfed his food without glancing my way, but I persisted. "Sir Henry would definitely have starved, except that his brave and true cat crept down the chimney every single day for months, each time bringing him a freshly killed pigeon.

"The King heard about it, thought it a miracle, and released Wyat. Now what do you think of that heroic, clever cat?"

Macavity eyed me with a baleful yellow glance. If he'd known how to snicker or say *sucker*, he would have. "Thanks a lot," I told him. "You were supposed to become inspired."

I therefore faced another cereal night without so much as a raw pigeon to liven things up. Damn Richard Quinn. Damn me, for assuming my restaurant appointment might include food.

I dialed Mackenzie and spoke with his answering machine. "I'm home," I said, "and in case you haven't yet polished off that pasta, I'm interested." I wasn't counting on it, though. He's a detective, after all. If he wanted to find pasta, he would have, hours ago.

Macavity sauntered off to the living room to digest his repast. He was, I had to acknowledge, neither heroic nor particularly handsome. His fur is an odd gray-brown that looks like the contents of a vacuum cleaner bag. His feet are enormous. But all the same, he was mine.

I filled my bowl with Cheerios, poured in the half inch of milk remaining in the carton and vowed to start keeping shopping lists, to become my own wife. I make that vow at least once a week.

The mail was the bleak, generic stuff of life: bills and

discount coupons for services I never requested. No one had dialed my number all day. I took my potage into the living room, my feet dragging like a drab character in a Russian short story. A Chekhovian clerk with an answering machine.

"C'mere, cat," I cajoled, but Macavity is proof of my mother's old warning: give a guy what he wants, and then he won't want you. Once fed, Macavity was less committed to our relationship, and he stayed in the middle of the floor and groomed himself.

The Long Night's Journey into Self-Pity had begun. No mail, no calls, no food, no cat, and a mother who's a murder suspect. Woe was me.

The Russians were better at bleakness. I was boring even myself.

Besides, maybe Mom wasn't a suspect anymore, or at least not the only one. Hattie had blamed my mother yesterday and Lizzie this afternoon.

I looked longingly at the phone. It wasn't his pasta that made me yearn for Mackenzie. Among other parts, I craved his brain, needed to talk with him about all this. Where was he?

On the other hand, if he returned this minute and picked up the phone, what was I going to do? Point a finger at innocent Lizzie? Her chubby and somehow pitiful face hovered like an ungrinning Cheshire Cat in front of me. Not a killer's face. I would swear to it.

But perhaps she was a witness. Had the police been able to get her calmed down enough to question her?

I tried to think, although it was difficult being thoroughly logical on a bowl of Cheerios. But whenever I decided not to bother, I saw a vision of my mother peering out from between bars.

So, then. If somebody had doctored the tarts—and if I refused to consider that the doctor had been one of my parents—then who could it have been? I started at the beginning with the messenger service, but that was so far-fetched, so completely reliant on coincidence, that I put it at the bottom of my list.

More logically, the tampering took place at The Boarding House, most likely in the kitchen, and if not at Lizzie's hands, then probably under her nose.

Perhaps she'd seen something out of the ordinary, even if she didn't recognize it as such at the time. Perhaps I'd recognize it.

Information gave me the number of The Boarding House, and I dialed. "I was wondering how you're doing," I said. "Last night I didn't really have a chance to—"

"Last night. Oh, sure. I remember you!" She sounded as if I were the Mounties come to save the girl and the day. "*Thank* you for calling me. I feel like I'm—I feel like—he isn't *back*, and I'm going crazy and there aren't any guests today but I don't know whether—I mean if I leave and they find him—"

I had to say her name three times, increasing volume and force with each repetition, before she seemed to hear, and even then it took her a while to decelerate and catch her breath.

"Are you all alone?" I asked, softly.

I heard a sniffled intake of breath, a stifled sob of agreement. Poor child, I thought, although she wasn't a child. But she was nonetheless needy. "Tell you what." Mackenzie had not answered my phone message, the cat was having a postprandial nap, and breakfast cereal did not a dinner make. "If you feel in the mood for company, and if you won't take it as an insult to your excellent cooking, how about I pick up hoagies and soda and bring them to your place?"

You might have thought I had offered to bring over the Holy Grail.

I felt gratified, but if asked, I couldn't have said whether my motive was a desire to provide comfort and companionship, to drill her silly about what she might have observed in her kitchen, to more carefully aim the beam of suspicion onto her bright red hair, or to simply have a strong reason to go out and snag a hoagie.

"Wait." She sounded mournful again. "My diet! I can't eat that kind of stuff."

Anyone who remembers a diet does not qualify as distraught in my book. I no longer quibbled about my mixed motives.

LIZZIE APPEARED TO HAVE DISCOVERED THE FIRST HONEST Overnight Weight Loss Method. Although she was still roly-poly, she looked dramatically diminished, as if the past day had devoured her.

I handed over one of the Styrofoam boxed salads and a small container of oil-free dressing, miffed that her food virtue had made me too guilt-ridden to buy myself the much-desired hoagie. This is a female form of macho— who can desire less food, be less hungry?—but this time it was no game for Lizzie. Only for me.

"Oh, miss!" She was reverting to her Dickensian meekness.

"Mandy. Please." I followed her into the kitchen, which seemed her spot, whether or not she was working, and pulled a high stool up to the center butcher-block table. The room around us was clean and smooth-surfaced, and not half as alive as last night, when the counters and ovens had been filled with lovely edibles.

Lizzie and I opened our salad containers and wielded plastic forks above unthrilling leafy greens. "I don't think you should be here all alone," I said. "I thought—last night, didn't you say you were going to see somebody today? A doctor?"

"I did. He prescribed pills to calm me and made me see another doctor, too. A psychiatrist. He said I had suffered a traumatic shock. I'm supposed to go back tomorrow, but I don't know. Bad enough I left today—but what if he came back while I was gone?"

"Your father? If you were gone, he'd come in or wait, Lizzie." There was a final bit of solidity and adult logic missing from the girl, keeping her a child.

Her deep brown eyes widened. "I can't leave again. How would he find me? And what's happened to him? He never disappears like this! I don't know what to do about anything. We've had two cancellations today, even though it wasn't my fault—you know it wasn't my fault, don't you?"

I decided that I did know that. It wasn't my mother or father's fault, and it wasn't Lizzie's.

"I'm sure he's sick," she said. "Heart attack or I don't know. Whenever I see him, in my head, sprawled out on the floor like . . . like . . ." She closed her eyes and shook her head and seemed to have trouble inhaling.

Wait. We had switched *him*s in mid-sentence. "Like what?" I whispered, sure she meant Lyle, spread out on the floor, dying.

Her eyes opened wide and she looked at me as if I might have the answer. "I get so scared if I let myself see it. I know something horrible, horrible has happened—and I know it has, it did, but I don't mean that. Something *else* horrible, do you understand? Do you think I'm crazy?"

I sidestepped both questions and speared a curly-edged lettuce leaf. "Is this the same feeling you had yesterday? Here, in the kitchen before the party. Remember? You became frightened and felt ill and you didn't know why."

She looked puzzled. "I can't remember. Only something like not being here for a while."

"Then where were you?" I was nearly whispering.

"Somewhere scary." I could barely hear her. "What's happening to me? What's going on?" Her voice regained some strength. "And what's happened to my father?"

"You're very close, aren't you?"

She shrugged. "We're all we have. He'd just never scare me by staying away on purpose. He knew I was nervous—he was nervous, too. That's why he went for cigarettes. He was trying not to smoke, but he was too shaky after . . . after . . ." Her voice rose into the dangerously thin air of hysteria again.

"I'm sure the police will find him."

She shook her head. "He's not a suspect and they're real busy—"

"Is the President still in town?"

"They told me that lots of men walk away from their

families that way. But he wouldn't. He was just so nervous after Mr. Zacharias fell down."

She had odd and childish ways of describing events. *Fell down* did not seem the appropriate way to describe a dying man.

"I called all the hospitals and asked for him, but he isn't registered anywhere. All he did was go out for cigarettes. I'm sure he's been mugged or even—" She couldn't say the word.

"Don't assume the worst," I said. "Hang in there." The words sounded hollow and futile. The girl had problems. Her father was missing, her livelihood was disappearing, and, even before a man had died after eating her food, she'd shown signs of a serious panic attack, cause unknown. I hoped she didn't know that as of this afternoon, Hattie was also blaming Lyle's death on her.

"And that old lady—that old lady *called* me today," she said.

There went that last hope.

"She said she knew that everything was my fault. That I knew it, too. What did she *mean*? She sounded—I feel sorry for her, losing her son and all, but she was cruel. It wasn't my fault. Why didn't anybody else get sick if it was my fault? Why would she be that way?"

"People are not themselves sometimes when they're in a state of grief." I felt like one of those old-fashioned arcade dolls—put a nickel on the lever, push, and I'll hand you back a platitude. I could become a team, along with Hattie's friend Alice. "She's old," I continued. "Needs to blame somebody for this tragedy. Ignore her."

"I told her—I told the police—he ate a tart. He came in after the salad course and said they were irresistible and that he had to break his diet and have one and I shouldn't tell. There was a little plate of them, you know?"

I knew. I remembered my mother pulling out two of her favorites and saying he could nibble away if he liked. I wondered if Lizzie also remembered.

"Nobody else got sick. It has to be that. But they think I could have poisoned it, and I guess I could have." She propped her head on her hand. "Of course I could have." She sighed. "But I didn't. Why would I?"

My cue. "Maybe you could help figure out who else could have tampered with the tarts."

"Here? In my kitchen?" She looked astounded by the concept, and was probably too sweet and polite to say the obvious—that the tarts had arrived poisoned by the hand of Bea Pepper, who had selected out the deadly culprits and presented them to Lyle.

"A tart could be muddled around pretty easily, couldn't it?" I persisted. "Add something, stir the filling, then redecorate the top, sprinkle nuts, squirt whipped cream—"

"I *gave* them the can!"

"Them? The police? What can?"

"It wasn't mine. I don't know where that spray can came from! I saw it in the trash while the guests were eating the beef and I was cleaning up. Everything is fresh here. I would have whipped my own cream, if I'd needed any. I wouldn't use a squirt bottle!"

A can of whipped cream. Good. Didn't it prove the tarts were tampered with after the fact? And surely the can would have a solid fingerprint on the place you push. I could imagine somebody taking advantage of a time when Lizzie's back was turned, but I couldn't imagine them donning gloves for the job.

"Think, Lizzic. Who came into the kitchen after the tarts were delivered? Were you alone much of the time or were there always people coming in and out? I know that when I was in here the first time, so were my mother and Hattie Zacharias and Lyle himself and his current and ex-wives. Did a lot of people come in?"

"What does it matter? Do you think somebody came here carrying poison? To kill Lyle Zacharias?"

"I don't know. The only question I can deal with right now is: who was in the kitchen?"

She shook her head. "I don't know most of the guests' names."

"Think. Describe whoever you remember." I had a small

notebook in my pocketbook, and, feeling vaguely foolish like a sleuth in a B-movie, I pulled it and a pen out.

"You were there. Twice. You came back to see if I was all right." She picked up a carrot slice and nibbled at it with little interest. "And Mrs. Zacharias."

"Which one? The dark-haired one or the blonde?"

"I meant the blond one. She was in a few times. With her husband once or twice, and by herself, and with Doctor—Shepard McCoy. She said she wanted to open a kitchen shop. Wanted to know if I liked copper better than stainless. That kind of thing. But the other one was there, too, not at the same time. Once when you were here, then later, when she wanted to know if I used preservatives, or artificial sweeteners. She told me she was Mrs. Zacharias. 'The *former* Mrs. Zacharias,' she said, so that's how I know who she was. Her son was in with her, and then I think he came back. Wanted to know if I had any cream soda. That was during the cocktail hour. Kid was a pain."

"Anybody else?"

"Well, yes. But I don't know who they were. Some lady who wanted an aspirin and who was allergic to dairy products. You know, Mr. Zacharias had asked everybody to say if they had any food allergies or preferences, and she never said. What was I supposed to do then, with dinner almost on the table and me running all over the place? Luckily, this man came in and told her to stop bothering me. Said it nicely, but she got the message. Boy, was I ever grateful."

Janine. I'd bet on it. I wondered how often Wiley had to put the clamps on her obnoxiousness. "Is that it?"

"To tell the truth, it felt like people never stopped coming in and out. I was surprised, because when we're just serving dinner normally, that doesn't happen. But between the guests asking questions and the waiters in and out and trying to get everything on the table at the right time, I nearly burst into tears twice. Had to leave the room and pull myself together, take deep breaths and count to a hundred."

"Literally? A hundred?"

"Three hundred the other time."

Great. Not only was everybody capable of tampering with the tarts, but there were now obvious gaps when nobody supervised the kitchen.

"Some lady who spilled wine on her dress," Lizzie said. "A green satiny thing. Another lady who wanted the recipe for the crab puffs. I didn't know what to do. Should I give out my recipes? What do you think?"

I thought that anybody could have taken the opportunity to doctor the tart and that we were back to square one, which is to say, nowhere.

Except in the kitchen of The Boarding House, where the telephone abruptly broke the silence. Lizzie rushed to answer it.

"Yes?" she said. Then "Oh!" and "When?" and "How did—" and a "Where?" and a "Now?" and a rushed, intense "Thank you."

"My father!" she said when she hung up. "He's alive. At Jefferson. He got sick on his way to buy cigarettes—really sick. People thought he was a drunk or a junkie and left him alone." She stopped to absorb this for a moment, wrinkling her brow and biting at her bottom lip. "They left him to die," she whispered. "He probably looked awful, but they could have called an ambulance, couldn't they?"

I nodded and sighed.

She brightened a bit. "This morning, a policeman noticed he wasn't a regular street person and realized he was sick, so he had him taken to the hospital. He'd been rolled and had no wallet or ID. Now he's conscious, and he told them who he was and what happened. And they think he's going to be okay!" She pulled a ring of keys off a peg on the wall and looked close to jubilant.

I supposed this was, more or less, a happy ending. Except for the growing suspicion that the timing of Roy's sudden illness was no accident—or rather, part of the same accident that killed Lyle Zacharias. "Does your father have a sweet tooth?" I asked Lizzie.

She smiled, as if this were a part of their affectionate history. "Does he ever! Anything with chocolate, nuts, whipped . . ." She heard herself. "Oh, my," she said.

"That's who ate some of the second tart." She took a deep breath. "There was a tart left on the plate. Mr. Zacharias was very precise about that, eating only one. 'Have to show some self-control,' he said. But then, by the time the police came, there was only part of one left. My father never eats all of anything. Always leaves a portion on the plate. Says it's why he doesn't get fat."

This time it was why he didn't get killed.

Fourteen

MACKENZIE'S CAR WAS PARKED ON THE SIDEWALK IN FRONT OF my house. Bad timing was becoming our trademark.

"Your message said you were home," he murmured by way of greeting.

"I *was* home when I said that." Macavity curled on his lap, purring. Such behavior might not be exceptional for normal cats, but even years after I rescued him from our mean streets, Macavity prefers to show affection subtly. He believes in being nearby, on call, or on anything you're try-ing to read, but otherwise he mostly swats the stuffing out of anything that tries to get closer. However, all bets and truisms are off when my gentleman you-know appears.

"Said you were hungry, too," Mackenzie mumbled.

"I was. I still am." I almost yearned for the withering remnants of the uninspired salads back on the butcher block in Lizzie's kitchen.

"So I brought food over. Ravioli, garlic bread, salad, wine. Thought to impress you."

"Well, hey. You succeeded." My mouth watered in antic-ipation. "I'm impressed as can be. And ravenous, too." I tried to control myself from drooling while I circumspectly looked around, but the edibles were even more discreet than I.

"Well, since you didn't show . . ." He looked sheepish.

157

"I, um, figured you were out eating. There wasn't much of anything here. So, I . . . well . . . I ate . . ." His sigh was final. The topic—and the food—were both history.

Then he brightened. "Your salad's still in a container in the fridge."

I should have known. Lettuce was my karma tonight, but I'd just as soon pass. "I had salad with Lizzie, the cook at The Boarding House. They found her father." I explained all that had happened and presented my summation. "Which makes three things clear," I said. These were not items that made me, daughter of Bea, particularly elated, but they were so obvious, I might as well be the person to say them. "First, it had to be, indeed, a tart that poisoned Lyle, and second, the tart was poisoned on site by the whipped-cream can carrier, and third, Lizzie isn't the poisoner."

C.K. nodded. "Already knew about the tart."

"How?"

"That leftover bit had odd seeds in it. There aren't that many seeds people would put in a sweet tart, and these weren't sesame or poppy or sunflower or pumpkin or anything anyone in the lab had seen, so they went after them. Normally, findin' poison, testin' all the different foods for all the different possibilities, would take ten times as long, but since we were pointed right at the tarts—"

And their baker, too. "By Hattie, right?" I could have told him that Lizzie was now her suspect of choice, but of course I'd just declared Lizzie not guilty, so why bother?

"Pretty much, yes." He nodded and extracted a notepad from his pocket, disturbing Macavity, who jumped off his lap. "You know," Mackenzie said as he brushed off his slacks, "if there's still a market for hair shirts anywhere on earth, you could make a fortune off that cat."

He flipped notebook pages until he found what he was after. "What they think it is," Mackenzie said, "is *jatropha curcas*, or Barbados nut, sometimes called purge nut, for obvious reasons. An unusual poison because it tastes good, which most do not. It wouldn't particularly seem out of place in a gooey, puffy, nutty tart. But enough of it—not too much—three seeds'll do you in—and that leftover bit was loaded with seeds—only had to nibble, and Lyle gobbled—and you're history within the hour. Used as rat poison some places."

"Never heard of it." My scope of information didn't have any particular relevance, but I hoped to subliminally plant the idea that such an exotic, ridiculous poison was completely out of range for any normal, civilized being's knowledge. A normal, civilized being like my mother.

"Why would you? It doesn't grow here, so it's nothing you have to be warned away from in these parts."

"Where would somebody get it, then? How would anybody even know about it?"

"Golly, Mandy." His pale blue eyes opened in fake astonishment. "Just because somethin' doesn't flourish in Philadelphia doesn't mean it's uncommon. Whether or not you're aware of it, there are other places in the world that grow things. Nice warm travel-destination places, in fact, the kind that people, people who were maybe at that party, enjoy. Places like Hawaii and Mexico and Central America and Africa and Asia and South America."

"Great. That eliminates only those people who came straight to the party from Scandinavia or Antarctica. Or people who never get out of Philadelphia. Like me. And Lizzie, most likely."

He shook his head slightly, left to right, then back, as in no, wrong, not so. "Lizzie's father was just over in Vietnam."

"So what? Why would that be of any relevance?"

"Who knows? But who also knows if he was really sick and alone last night, or setting up an alibi instead? I couldn't have done it, officer, because I was a victim, too. Luckily, I ate just enough to keep me alive but away from the cops, on the streets—I say—where nobody could identify me. Wouldn't be the first time people pulled that. I've seen guys shoot themselves, cut themselves up, all to prove they—"

"But he didn't even know about the party. He was away when it was booked. So even if he had access to poisoned

whatsis nuts over there—and even if he had some kind of
grudge against Lyle, which is doubtful because how would
he even know him? They definitely don't move in the same
circles—but even if that were true, are you saying he'd
bring back poison just in case he someday had a chance to
use it? And then someday came the very day he returned
home? Isn't that a bit of a stretch?" And then, having
shown how illogical it was to suspect Beecher, I suddenly
remembered something about him that didn't compute.
"Except," I said, "just before he left the hotel, he said
something to the effect that none of this would have happened if he'd been there when this party was set up."

"Interestin' remark. Ah, but . . ." Every Gallic dollop of
DNA in Mackenzie's Louisiana ancestry is visible in his
shrug, which, with great world-weariness, made it evident
that my thinking was pedestrian and naive. "He said this,
he said that. We'll see."

"Wait a second!" My mother could now be crossed off
the list of suspects because of geographical impossibility,
and I told Mackenzie so. "My parents' travel itineraries are
limited. Destination: here. Boring, yes, but also an alibi!"

Mackenzie repeated the left-right-left head swoop, his
expression compassionate, but all the same, dreadfully, cyn-
ically cop-like.

"Don't be ridiculous!" I insisted. "How could she have
gotten those seeds? Are you going to tell me she made a
buy? Met some guy on a seamy Boca Raton street corner
and bought herself a lid of jatro—whatever? Come on!"

"It happens that it grows in one place in the continental
U.S., too," he said softly. "Only one."

"Not Florida," I whispered. "Please?"

"Southern Florida, to be exact. Used a lot as an orna-
mental plant." He stood up, unstretching his long, lanky
frame, running his fingers through his curly hair. "What
puzzles me is this: why not poison one of the tarts in the
box instead? That way, Lyle'd go home and kill himself
some random day when he hit the target, and the odds
would be way against anybody knowing what or who had

done him in. It's a rare poison, and all the other tarts would be clean. But this way's so obvious. Too obvious."

He turned to face me, something important on his mind, pointing his index finger like a mother about to chastise her child. The gesture annoyed and vaguely frightened me. I could understand the annoyance, but not the fear, which further annoyed me.

"Nothin' unusual, far as anybody can tell so far," Mackenzie went on, "about any of the tarts in the tin. An' since these seeds that seem to be the culprit are pretty easy to spot, unless more than one type of poison was used, it appears that nobody's about to find anything unusual about your mother's tarts. Except for the two she put out on that plate." He let that last sentence ride on the air and fill the room, reverberating with ominous import. "If Zacharias had finished off both of them, we would still be way far deep in the dark."

"Somebody doctored the tarts. It would be witless of my mother to publicly offer up the only tarts she'd poisoned. Are you saying she's not only a murderer but stupid, too?"

"No, of course not, I only—"

"Then case closed. I hate to mention food after so much talk of poison, but would you consider an expedition to the all-night market?" I wanted to dig into something besides chlorophyll. I began a mental shopping list.

But Mackenzie and I were on such different wavelengths, we weren't even playing in the same city. "The thing is," he was saying when I finally tuned back in, "that it *would* make sense if she wanted to humiliate him."

"What *she* are we talking about?" I asked, bristling.

"Correction. Make it a theoretical question. If A hated B so much that she didn't want him to die quietly offstage, but publicly, in front of everybody he held dear—to be humiliated, then die—then if murder ever makes any kind of sense, this design for one would, too."

Theoretical question, my foot. Mackenzie isn't one to wallow in hypothetical constructs for long. I gave him six seconds to cut to the chase.

"So," he drawled after only three seconds, even though

each subsequent word dripped nectar-slow over his tongue, "your mother have any old grudges against Lyle Zacharias?"

I shook my head. She didn't. She was the one who had dragged my father up north to do some active forgiving and forgetting, or at least the forgiving part.

"Your father, maybe, then?"

My heart did a little syncopated movement. He'd read my small print.

"Some long ago feud?" he asked mildly. "Business? Or a woman?"

I overreacted, as I am wont to do when something comes within shouting distance of information I'd rather keep to myself. "Why mention my father?" I glared at Mackenzie and crossed my arms in what I hoped was an assertive no-nonsense stance. "He wasn't even there!"

"True," Mackenzie said. His question still dangled between us.

But when people mention trouble over a woman, they don't mean problems concerning a foster sister. I intended to use that linguistic convention to maximum advantage. "How could my father possibly have a problem over a woman with Lyle Zacharias, who is—who was—ten years younger than my dad, when you realize that my father has been married for thirty-seven years, which would make Lyle thirteen when my father stopped dating. So what are you implying about my father and women?"

Mackenzie shook his head in amazement. "Why're you reacting that way? It was only a question."

"An incredibly stupid question!" I felt a bit smug. I had dithered and carried on and in general detoured around the real issue of whether my father had unresolved differences with Lyle.

As I heated up, Mackenzie reacted by turning down his emotional barometer, entering a kind of walking hibernation, all systems on low, his voice the lowest, slowest, and scariest of all. "It is," he said, "within the scope of human possibility that one spouse might act in the other's behalf. Even you could imagine that with a little effort. Haven't I heard that your parents can be just a little overprotective of their daughters and grandchildren? Why not of each other? Maybe your mother wants to take care of something that's been eatin' away at your father." He paused, and looked at me. "It's even possible that a daughter can be overprotective of her parents." Then he put his hands up in mock self-defense. "Only an idea. A passing idea."

"You don't believe any of this, do you? You don't truly believe that my mother—or father—could be a murderer, do you?"

" 'Course not."

I was surprised at the degree of relief I felt, at how many of my muscles began to unclench, at least until he spoke again.

"But I don't disbelieve it, either. The thing of it is to not have any preconceived notions. If you know what you're lookin' for—or if you *think* you know what you're lookin' for—then sure as not, you miss what's actually there."

"But my *mother*—"

"Look here, Mandy. I don't know your mother. I know you, at least a little, and I'd be real surprised if you killed somebody. But the truth is—without getting all metaphysical or anythin'—we none of us know anybody. You want to be surprised about the human condition? Become a cop." He looked directly at me, his blue eyes and his voice both clear and unsurprised as summer sky. "Have a little faith. The truth will out."

I sighed. "Maybe, then, we should stop theorizing, and wait for hard facts, like *motives*. Everybody seems to have one if you poke around a little, get past that nice facade."

Mackenzie had lost interest again, except in Macavity, who was back again, purring and kneading his paws while the great detective scratched what would be feline armpits, if only cats had arms.

"Yo!" I snapped. "Over here!" He barely glanced my way. "I saw Richard Quinn this afternoon."

Being Mackenzie's you-know obviously doesn't necessitate the giving of attention, let alone actual concern as to why I'd seen Quinn. Mackenzie merely scratched Macavity more slowly and waited for me to complete my thought.

This relationship was never going to make it. I bet he'd demand custody of the cat, and I suspected that Macavity would happily agree.

"He's the one who's opening the restaurant—the place the seniors could use for their prom."

"Told you. In a few weeks those kids are going to be on their own out there. Stop bein' such a mother hen. They should have checked the site, not you."

It was possible that he was right. I was getting increasingly confused about who was supposed to do what for whom, so I changed tacks altogether. "He says that Lyle's big breakthrough, *Ace of Hearts*—from which he's still making money, and which is about to become a second TV series and make skedillions more—was ripped off Terry Wiley, who brought suit, but lost. Didn't have enough proof. And Quinn himself feels robbed in the same deal. This restaurant he's opening is probably his last chance, and Lyle refused to help with it."

"Uh-huh." If Mackenzie emitted any less energy, he'd be reclassified as inorganic material.

"And Lyle's wife, Tiffany—"

"You told me this afternoon. And about the angry old wife, too."

"But those are motives, C.K. Those are real motives."

"Right." He stood up, which always seems a more intricate process for Mackenzie than for other people. He unlocks and stretches one section at a time as though rebuilding himself.

I finally noticed that while Mackenzie's edible offerings were mostly gone, his potables were not. A bottle of Chianti Classico was on the counter next to the sink. "Wine," I said.

"Whine?" He gave the word two and a half syllables. "Me? I do not. You, on the other hand, are showin' a definite tendency toward it lately."

I ignored him. Anyone who puns and insults in the same sentence does not deserve an answer. "Wait. I'd better not get my hopes up. That's probably an empty, resealed bottle." But it wasn't. I poured us both glasses and anticipated settling in for a nonmurderous, amicable evening of being each other's you-knows.

He sipped wine, smiling at his own good choice, and at me.

I smiled back.

"Tell me somethin'," he whispered.

"Whatever you want to know." It's corny and learned by osmosis from bad movies, but verbal foreplay is nonetheless my favorite parlor game.

"How come earlier today you referred to Harriet Zacharias as *Aunt* Hattie? I notice that you've dropped the aunt part, so how come you did that, too?" He smiled again. "Her name to the rest of us is Harriet, y'know."

I drank wine and sighed.

"Whose aunt is she?"

"Lyle's." Macavity wedged himself between us. I made it an easier job by moving farther away from the detective.

"This makes me sad, Mandy. I thought at the very least we were on the same side. That we were—"

"You-knows, right?"

"How's that?"

"Mackenzie, you're forgetting that this isn't some abstract criminal demon we're talking about. It's my *mother*."

He looked taken aback. For a moment I thought he was still puzzling through the you-know business, but then I realized that on some level he really didn't understand what I had said. I was afraid he was going to ask what the woman's having given birth to me had to do with the issue, but he didn't. Still and all, I knew he thought it.

Amazing how ambiguous he could be about affairs of the heart when professionally he was only interested in right and wrong, true and false, crime and punishment. It was probably advantageous to know this about him, although just then I couldn't decide if I was impressed or depressed by the realization.

I looked straight ahead and said nothing.

"Didn' answer, Mandy. How come you called her Aunt Hattie when you were talking about the visit to her?"

I shook my head.

"Because your mother calls her that, right?" He sat back, legs out straight from the sofa, proud as hell of his deductive ability. "Because there's a relationship. What is it?"

"They aren't related." The stepmother of the husband of your foster sister-in-law couldn't be considered a relative. Maybe in the South, where Mackenzie came from, but certainly not in Philadelphia.

"Let me put it this way. Why were your parents invited to that particular party? What was their place in Lyle Zacharias's life or history?" He looked at me, all innocent blue-eyed wonder.

We froze into position, neither saying a word. Anyone passing by and peeking in might have misinterpreted that long impasse. They might have thought we couldn't get enough of the sight of each other, that we liked what we saw, that the exchange had anything whatsoever to do with affection.

Finally, I decided that I might as well come clean. He'd find out later, anyway. I wondered which fate my mother would like less—to be accused of murder or to be responsible for breaking up her spinster daughter's one semireal relationship?

Fifteen

I spent a goodly portion of Tuesday morning in a paranoid funk. Entering school and being in range of the note-
sender gave me the creeps. Even though there was no
follow-up in my mailbox and no further signs of danger,
every motion and sentence by students or faculty seemed
ominous, every one of my fellow human beings potentially
the psychotic who wanted me to become the next news
story about violence against teachers. It made for a twitchy
morning. Luckily, the annual Junior Journalism Conference
occupied the afternoon. I had only a half day's paranoia to
face.

I had meant to talk with Mackenzie about it. I had, if I
recalled properly, even tried to on our afternoon walk. But
both then and last evening, Topic A had been the case
against my mother. Besides, what would Mackenzie have
done but ask me the same questions I kept failing to answer
myself—who? why? what could it mean?

I was eager to get out of the building and the foggy
sense of ill will growing around me. I had trouble concen-
trating on the ninth graders, who really didn't care, as they
were having a high old time with their play. I sat at a desk
at the back of the room and tried to listen, but whenever I
stopped obsessing about getting out of school and away
from the note-writer, I began obsessing about my mother's

167

jeopardy, and when I couldn't handle that one, I switched to Lyle Zacharias, alive and dead, and a mess both ways.

My various preoccupations made me repeatedly zone out and miss the rehearsal. I faced forward and, for the forty-fifth time that period, tried to listen.

My class hadn't been drawn to their adaptation because of Oscar Wilde's witty epigrams or dark morals about beauty and the soul. What they were crazy for was the special effects potential in the novel's grand finale, when Dorian's portrait regained its beauty and Dorian himself was revealed in all his monstrous corruption. Somebody's mother knew somebody's cousin in New York who had access to masks that had been used in a horror movie. This rehearsal and the work that preceded and would follow it were all for the sake of flashing a cinematically hideous face at the audience.

Still, along the way, the adaptors and actors ingested an interesting classic, and I say whatever works, works.

The foppish Lord Henry was played by a spotted and square young man who would have given Oscar Wilde hives. "Why should Basil have been murdered?" Lord Henry wondered with a flounce of his head. He wore his hair long, in great clots held together with gel, so his head-shaking was indeed something to behold. "He was not clever enough to have enemies," Lord Henry concluded.

Well, I decided, I must be clever. I'd garnered enemies. I was, after all, on somebody's academic hit list, even if I wasn't clever enough to figure out who my enemy might be. And Lyle Zacharias had been clever enough for enemies, even if Quinn said he'd been a no-talent fake. Maybe Wilde had stretched too hard for a witticism. Maybe enemies were an equal-opportunity employer.

"The things one feels absolutely certain about are never true," Lord Henry said. The line seemed a message sent directly to me, a warning. What was it I felt absolutely certain about? Why did it sound so familiar?

I was losing it. Of course it was familiar. I'd heard it here, twenty-four hours ago, the last time Lord Henry declaimed, and it meant nothing. Just another clever line.

More to follow. Once again, and rather desperately, I tried to pay attention.

Lord Henry continued:

> "Life is not governed by will or intention. Life is a question of nerves, and fibres, and slowly built-up cells in which thought hides itself and passion has its dreams. You may fancy yourself safe, and think yourself strong. But a chance tone of colour in a room or a morning sky, a particular perfume that you had once loved and that brings subtle memories with it, a line from a forgotten poem that you had come across again—I tell you, Dorian, it is on things like these that our lives depend."

That wasn't pure epigram or fun with words. That meant something, and the something it meant shuddered over me like ghostly fingers on my flesh. I almost saw the cells, each propelled by a passion and puffed with secrets piling up through history, encapsulating the past and finally exploding from the weight of the burden.

As if nothing was ever truly over, only etched on a revolving drum that sooner or later rotated back into the present when those history rich cells must, reflexively, act on what they have known for so long. *You may fancy yourself safe and think yourself strong.*

How foolish of Lyle Zacharias to have summoned his ghosts, all those waiting passions, injuries, and secrets.

That's what comes of not reading and heeding the classics.

But I had, and even so, what was I to make of it?

"There is no evidence against me," Dorian Gray, a.k.a. Jack Clancy, said to himself after Lord Henry left. Jack favored hand flapping for dramatic emphasis. But the production wasn't Broadway bound. It would have an extremely short run at a Philly Prep assembly, and Jack was having a wonderful time, so I let the student director handle the spastic motions and silently apologized to Oscar. He'd understand. He had a great sense of humor. Besides, he'd coped with much more serious issues in his time.

"Except for the picture," Dorian continued with an extravagant wave of both hands. "The *picture*!—my conscience, my enemy. As I killed its painter, so will I kill *it*!—and then at last I will be at *peace*!"

He brandished an imaginary knife at an imaginary portrait and let out a bloodcurdling, agonized scream.

"Jack!" I shouted. "Hey! Keep it down. There's a class in the next room!"

"Carried away. Sorry," he said, then he dropped to the floor, sprawled on his belly, the better to put on his mask when the time came.

The door to our room whipped open. "Everybody okay?" Flora Jones called out. She was followed by a half dozen of her computer students. She gasped and put her hands to her heart as she saw Jack on the floor, then rushed over and dropped to her knees beside him, but by then I was up the aisle and vastly annoyed.

"Come on, get up! You're scaring Miss Jones. Don't worry," I explained. "It's only Dorian Gray, where he stabbed himself."

Flora Jones was a formidable woman, a computer whiz, working part-time at our school while she completed her MBA at Wharton. She was also a marathoner and a former Miss Black Teenage Philadelphia. None of which necessarily made her familiar with Oscar Wilde's work.

"Dorian needs an ambulance," she snapped to one of her students. "Quickly. Do you know CPR?" she asked me.

"No!" I shouted to the retreating student. I prodded Jack with the tip of my shoe, controlling the urge to give him a swift kick. "Jack! Cut this out!"

"Jack?" Flora said.

"Up!" I shouted at the inert body while Flora watched with horror, then growing relief as Jack finally stood up.

"Gotcha, didn't I?" He bowed to the class. "Talk about acting!" He strutted back to his seat.

"It's a play they're rehearsing." I glared at Jack. "Talk about *over*acting. Forgive us."

She exhaled with some deserved exasperation. "I thought something had happened to you," she said.

"Why? Why me?" Asked too intently, my paranoia index setting new highs. What did she know?

"I don't know. Guess you just hear about it so much . . . Plus," she lowered her voice to avoid offending Jack, "the kid's voice is still pretty high. I thought it was a woman's. Yours." Her own voice back to normal, she continued. "Anyway, the scream and the body must have rattled me, else I'm losing my mind. How could I forget Dorian Gray? The guy with the picture that got old instead of him. I've always wanted to find that artist and commission my own portrait. How could I have thought it was your student's name?" Laughing at herself, she left the room.

I laughed, too. And tried to believe that it was Jack's high-pitched voice that had made her think I was in danger, and not any special intuition of impending danger on her part—or intimate knowledge of the note I'd received.

LAST YEAR THE HIGHLIGHT OF THE JUNIOR JOURNALISM CONference had been a strawberry-blond history teacher with dark eyes. Once he opened his mouth, it was obvious there was precious little behind the splendid facade, but he was so aesthetically pleasing, I'd hoped for a second viewing.

However, his school was now represented by a tidy woman in a dress-for-success suit. The businesslike power ensemble had a certain ridiculousness, given the realities of teaching, where success is largely intangible, and certainly nothing that good tailoring can assist. I murmured something about the missing strawberry-blonde.

"You talking about Douglas?" She had a brassy voice that clashed with the suit. "He left teaching. Went to L.A. to *act*, can you believe?" She rolled up her eyes so that I'd get it that there was something fishy about his new profession.

I waited to find out what was on her agenda.

"From what I hear," she continued, as I'd known she would, "he mostly acts sexy. Entertaining dirty old women. One of those male exotic dancers." She pursed her mouth in distaste and waited for me to concur.

"Glory be, *un*dressed for success," I murmured. Before we could debate the hunk's career path, a student tapped my shoulder and whispered that she couldn't find the page makeup room, which problem provided me with an acceptable excuse to move on.

I saw the student safely into a room of earnest seniors arranging and trimming columns, like paper-thin jigsaw puzzles that didn't interlock, and then I stood by the door, deciding what to do. I scanned the workshop list: editorial writing, news coverage, copy editing, photography, sports writing, features, and columns, and then, finally, the faculty advisors' workshop, scheduled for a half hour from now. I had time to search for coffee.

I spotted the machine, and the man currently using it, Terry Wiley. He was bent over, retrieving a cup of what looked to be cream mixed with a little coffee. "Oh!" he gasped upon seeing me. "It's, ah, Pepper, right? Amanda. I had forgotten that you—but of course, you did say . . . well, in the confusion, who could remember anything?" He sounded as if the sight of me had literally taken his breath away. He pulled a stirrer out of a container on the counter and worked on the contents of his cup, treating the mixing of coffee, cream, and sugar as a major project. "Let's see— Philly Prep, I think. What a surprise—a nice surprise to see you again. So soon."

The oddest thing about him was not his spluttering but my absolute conviction that his befuddlement was an act, a lie, that he had known full well I'd be here and yet felt it necessary to deny it. I could not for the life of me figure out why.

"Well," he said. "Well, well. You, ah, busy right now?" I shook my head.

"Then would you," he shrugged with one shoulder, "like to sit down or something? I mean after you get your coffee. I mean I'm assuming you want coffee or you wouldn't be here." He laughed nervously.

I couldn't envision him part of that high school trio Lyle had described, but I knew it was possible. I see unlikely combos like that at school—kids who need sounding boards and audiences so much they confuse them with friendship.

I put change into the machine and received a cup of bitter black brew, and I sat down at a small cafeteria table across from Terry Wiley.

He ran his tongue nervously over his lips and looked around the room as if searching for a topic of conversation.

"It's unusual for the science teacher to be the newspaper advisor," I said, trying to fill the conversational abyss before the man had a heart attack. I felt tired already. I seemed to be on a roll—Inarticulate Men R Us. Quinn last night, Terry Wiley today. Mackenzie had his faults, but at least speech wasn't a controlled substance with him. He talked funny, but he believed in words, thoughts, communication, and I gave him points for that.

"Unusual? Well . . . I guess. But, um . . ."

I peeked at my watch. Twenty-four more minutes of this torpid tête-à-tête. My heart plummeted.

"I was a writer once," he said. "Reporter. *Philadelphia Bulletin.* Remember that? Afternoon paper. Gone now, of course."

I wondered whether his news stories had also emerged in two- and three-word gulps, like stuttered telegrams. Even more than that, I wondered why I made him so nervous.

"Science stories. Health. Inventions. You know." He gulped. "Paper folded. Didn't want to move." Major swallow of air. "Offered job teaching." He looked abashed, then focused on his cream with coffee and drank from it.

"Lucky journalism students you have," I said when it appeared that Wiley had drained his conversational reservoir. "To have an authentic pro as their advisor. The rest of us spout theory, but you know the real world of journalism."

I should have said, "And did you like it, Wiley? Do you miss it? Did you think about your other writing—the one opening on Broadway and making somebody else famous? And did you fester about it after the lawsuit, before the party Sunday night? Would you please confess now and get my mother off the hook?" Instead, I drank more coffee.

"Journalism's risky," Wiley said. "That's what I know.

Bulletin went out of business. Now I'm a teacher. A lot safer."

The sum total of his knowledge of two professions. How depressing, and not much to dig in the flat-surfaced landscape of his world.

How to leap the chasm from that to whatever murderous impulses lurked inside his twitchy exterior? I debated techniques for a moment, then decided to proceed the only way I could—straight on. "There was a teacher of yours at my table last night," I said. "Priscilla somebody. She said something about your having been a playwright." I was proud of getting to the point via an almost truthful route.

"She said I was a playwright?"

I nodded. "She said you wrote something back in high school."

"Lemoyes changed her mind? *Now*?"

I had the horrible realization that Priscilla Lemoyes must have testified on behalf of Lyle. I would have given anything to unsay my words.

"Wrote the senior show in high school," Wiley said. His speech had become less nervous, so much so that it was without affect. It sounded as if he were reciting memorized lines. "Tried to, that is. They only used one skit." He looked bemused. "Can't believe Lemoyes changed her mind, after all. A little late for me, but all the same . . ." He didn't seem angry because of my lie. In fact, he looked relieved. Exonerated, perhaps?

Now that he was relaxed, what could I do but push at him a little more? "Never tempted to go back and tinker?" I asked. "Write another play or fix that one up?"

He shook his head.

I had pushed us back into silence. Terry's eyes repeatedly darted toward the door, as if awaiting the posse who would rescue us. Since we were both headed to the same advisors' meeting, and since I obviously had no other commitments, I didn't know how to gracefully excuse myself. I silently counted off the seconds.

But then, miracle of miracles, just as I reached fifty-nine-one-thousand, Terry spoke spontaneously. "Well!" He sounded breathless again, but pleased at having discovered a new conversational lode. "Awful, wasn't it? Lyle, of course."

"Awful." And did you do it? Why couldn't I think of a single other thing to say about the death of Lyle Zacharias? We stared at each other. "Awful," I said again.

"Scary," he added.

More silence. "Guess we didn't have to go to the hospitals, after all." My voice emerged with an unfamiliar, high-pitched perkiness. "The police are pretty sure it wasn't the food that was poisoned." And then I clamped shut my mouth—a few sentences too late. I couldn't believe I'd blurted out privileged information.

I once dated a headhunter, an executive recruiter who, over dinner, explained his method of getting people to divulge things the law didn't allow him to ask, but that he nonetheless wanted to know. "If you keep quiet," he told me, "there is an almost irresistible impulse to fill the silence, keep the conversation going. People get uneasy and blurt out incredible things, often not in their own best interests."

He then proceeded to use the technique on me, and even forewarned, I became one of his suckers, babbling nonstop while the recruiter grew pensive, or took forever to light and tamp his pipe. By the end of the evening, he knew everything about me and I knew nothing about him, except that I didn't want to see him again. Another Dater's Digest's Condensed Relationship: a first-date/last-date all-in-one sandwich.

And now I'd done it again, repeating what Mackenzie had told me in confidence, what had definitely not been meant as an all-points bulletin. The only atonement I could think of was to practice the same technique on Terry Wiley and see what I could learn. Unless, of course, his tongue-tied habits were so ingrained that he could sit in silence without any discomfort. I smiled, lifted my eyebrows slightly, and kept my lips sealed.

"Who on earth could have done it?" Terry finally said,

wrinkling his brow in a great show of sorrow and confusion.

I shook my head. And waited some more.

"Of course, I don't know much about Lyle's . . ." He left the idea dangling, shook his head, ending the unarticulated idea. I waited some more. "We've been out of touch a long time."

I nodded and widened my expectant smile.

"Since," he added as the silence persisted, "since Lyle's first wife—Cindy—died. Terrible thing happened to her."

The timing of his split with Lyle surprised me, or at least the way he'd marked it historically. If Cindy had been the old high school friend, the emotional link, I could understand it, but that wasn't the case.

I'd had it with silent passivity. "You were good friends with Cindy, then?"

He nodded.

"What was she like?" It was an honest question. Through some alchemy, this woman whose existence I hadn't suspected two days earlier now felt like someone I'd lost and needed to reclaim.

Terry looked thoughtful. "Wonderful," he finally said. "Kind. Beautiful. Cared about people. About what was right." It is odd to see a blush on the cheeks of a man with a graying mustache. Particularly if the blush is provoked by mention of someone dead for many years. Someone wonderful.

He'd been in love with her. With his buddy's wife.

He cleared his throat and spoke in a hoarse whisper. "She was a good friend," he said. "To both of us." Janine. Of course. He'd been married since high school. "Cute baby, too. Janine pretended . . ." His glance flicked to the doorway again, then around the room, anywhere but near mine. "We, um . . . don't have children. When Janine saw that red-haired baby, she wanted . . . even looked a little like her."

Did that mean that under Janine's borscht dye job there was authentic, if faded, red hair? Would mysteries and surprises never cease?

"Wanted to adopt her. She . . . it wasn't her fault. Babies don't know about guns. Couldn't . . ." His voice and attention both drifted away.

Couldn't know what a gun was or couldn't adopt? He meant both, most likely. In either case, he didn't seem likely to elaborate.

So Cindy died, Wiley and Janine couldn't adopt Betsy, and the friendship ended. Odd timing. Odder still how, no matter to whom I spoke, everything seemed to have happened at the same time. The career break with *Ace of Hearts*, the end of the partnership with Richard Quinn, the accidental shooting of Cindy, the split with the Wileys—too much converged at the same historical moment to be simple random coincidence.

I felt as if the present were the loose ends of a skein that had been knotted together two decades earlier.

How had things really worked? Had Lyle known that his buddy was in love with his wife? Had, perhaps, their break come before Cindy died? Had she loved Wiley back?

Obviously, Terry Wiley, still staring into private space, considered the issue closed. After all, he had carried his secrets for two decades, and there was no reason to suddenly spill them in the middle of a journalism conference. Besides, it was time to go to our meeting. We bussed our empty coffee cups to the trash can. Terry Wiley looked more like a man carrying a corpse than one holding a used plastic cup. And maybe he was.

I DUCKED INTO THE LADIES' ROOM BEFORE I WENT INTO THE meeting, and was shocked to see who was washing her hands one sink over.

"I'm here with my husband." Janine made her words sound like a dare. "Didn't he tell you? I know you had coffee with him. My stomach's a mess. Can't handle the acid in coffee. You look surprised to see me."

"I— Yes. I am. You aren't a newspaper advisor, are you?"

Her nasty laugh was more like a bark. "Nope. But I'm not stupid, either."

"I'm sorry, I don't follow."

"I'm here to protect my interests. Do you follow now? I told him I wanted to know what he did. He thinks I meant what he does with the paper, but I didn't. I meant with you. Keep your hands off my husband."

"Me? My what? *Your* what?"

She carefully dried her own hands. Her nails were an iridescent purple. "I saw the way he looked at you Sunday night. And I heard you coming on to him about when you'd see him again. Don't think my poor health keeps me from seeing what's going on in front of me."

Now I understood Terry Wiley's repeated glances at the doorway, his acute nervousness upon seeing me. I was mildly entranced by her honest belief that I coveted her husband. Terry Wiley, of all people. "I can assure you—" I stopped myself. How do you tell a possessive wife that even if you were stupid enough to mess with married men, her husband would be close to the last possibility on the list? I stopped trying to assure her of anything.

"It's not my fault that your biological clock is running down!" Veins on the side of her neck looked in danger of rupturing.

I couldn't believe I was standing in a bathroom being verbally abused by a woman with beet soup hair and a chartreuse pants suit, and being too polite to tell her that I didn't, no matter how desperate my biological clock, want her husband to reset it.

"And it's not my problem that your chance of getting a man at your age is practically nil! I read that stuff about how you're more likely to be killed by a terrorist than to get married."

"How about if I marry the terrorist?" She was not amused. "Then how about if I tell you that it's been proven that was an inaccurate statistic?" She really had very little intellectual curiosity. "Then how about if I leave?" But she blocked my exit with one screaming green polyester arm.

"I don't care what you do or how desperate you are!" she screeched. "You can't take advantage of a man's mid-life—any middle-aged man would be flattered by a young woman's advances, but that doesn't make it right!"

Okay, it was time to be honest, no matter how insulting it might be. "Listen up," I said, "even if your husband were the last man on earth, I wouldn't want him."

"You chose a *career*, not marriage—now live with that choice! You women think you can have it all, but that doesn't include *my husband*!"

I stood there, flabbergasted, and she took the opportunity to open the restroom door and hold it for her exit line. She took a deep breath. When she spoke, it was in a deliberate, patronizing voice, as if she had to teach me something I should already know.

"He has a certain weakness," she said. "For redheads." She patted her purple hair. "Redheads. Plural. It wouldn't be the first time."

"I'm not even—it's chestnut. Brown, actually. With highlights."

"Stay away from him!" she snapped, her patience and her little lesson both over. "Stay away—or so help me, I'll kill you."

I believed her.

Sixteen

We won a prize. Actually, a single twelfth grader won it for headline writing, but we generalized it into a group triumph.

Next morning, Maurice Havermeyer, my principal, carried on as if it had been the Pulitzer. The headline-writer was congratulated in assembly and named the Philly Prep Student of the Week, and our staff was repeatedly referred to as *award-winning journalists*. Nobody, not even the staff, sniggered.

Dr. Havermeyer, never one to miss a trend, has become high on self-esteem—ours, because his is already up to maximum capacity. It appears that self-esteem, its name notwithstanding, requires enormous outside-of-self esteem. Hence, Philly Prep's RAA! Team, as Havermeyer has clumsily dubbed it. RAA! as in Respect, Appreciation, Acknowledgment!

Respect, appreciation, and acknowledgment, hokey or not, felt good, particularly while sitting in assembly, wondering which of the adolescent souls in the room wished me ill. I scanned the auditorium to see if somebody was directing a less than respectful or appreciative eye in my direction. The sort of eye that imagines gravestones with teachers' names on them.

Eyes—and a few hands—were directed many ways, but

not mine, except for some blank stares and another goofy smile from Raffi Trulock many seats to my left.

He saw me see him and ducked his head. His buddy punched his shoulder playfully, then leaned forward and looked over at me.

And I got it. A bit belatedly. Raffi's slightly dazed grins and overcasual greetings. My cheeks heated up, an annoying trait I can't seem to outgrow. I had become a love object. An awkward but not unusual adolescent rite of passage, and not dangerous when kept in check, just always surprising—and discreetly flattering.

How odd, I thought. I am simultaneously adored and loathed by students. Given my druthers, I would have chosen to keep the fond one anonymous and to have known the face of the latter.

But perhaps he who had me targeted as the next abused teacher had changed his mind. Maybe, influenced by Dr. Havermeyer, he, too, now esteemed me.

More likely, though, he was cutting assembly, lurking somewhere, readying a push or a jab or a poke that would make me a statistic.

I was dismayed that my thoughts had so swiftly reverted to the lurker, the threatener. My pulse was elevated and my hackles up. Raffi had been an ego-boosting intermission in a dark play, that was all. Whatever ultimate act the letter-writer had in mind, he—or she—had already killed any easy pleasure I might enjoy during the workday.

The assembly was the highlight of the academic day. From then on it was all downhill. My ninth graders continued play practice, but Lord Henry had the hiccups straight through rehearsal. We tried every known cure: breath-holding and sugar-eating and paper-bag-breathing and scaring him and whistling. But when the bell rang, Lord Henry was telling Dorian that, "The only way to get rid of a *hic!*—temptation—*hic!*—is to yield to it."

The tenth graders had a mini-lesson on punctuation. This, along with most of the teaching of grammar, is part of the HSE Curriculum, as in hope springs eternal. One more go-round, one more gimmick, one more clever presentation and they'll get it, teachers whisper to themselves like a mantra. And then we whisper it again, the next time we have to teach the same lesson to the same people.

"Punctuation matters," I said.

The tenth graders' eyeballs rolled up into their skulls. The morning of the living dead.

It's not flattering to know your audience is counting the nanoseconds until they can escape. Bravely, stupidly, in need of a paycheck, I plowed on and tried to win them over by writing two sentences on the board.

We're hungry. Let's eat children.

I waited for a response. The journal article from which I'd cribbed it ("A Dozen Ways to Liven Up Mechanics") had promised outrage, shock, delight. At least a pulse.

"Yes?" I said. "Anybody?" My class looked suspicious, but mostly of me, of my expectant air. A waiting teacher is an anxiety-provoking thing. And, ultimately, an anxious thing. "Any ideas?" I asked with some desperation. "Do you see anything that needs changing?"

It was as if they were all on the wrong side of one-way glass. I could see them, but they could only see a reflection of their own bored selves.

"Clue," I said. "The change has something to do with punctuation."

"Wow," several of them muttered.

Finally. A timid hand, half raised, pulled itself down, then fluttered uncertainly in front of a blue and white sweater. I smiled encouragingly. "I think it should have a question mark at the end?" That particular girl thought every sentence had a question mark at its end, but she was so timorous, I kept my response as gentle as possible.

"Let's see. Then it would read: 'Let's eat children?' As if the speaker's not sure that it's a good idea. Is that what you mean?" She looked around the room, signaling that it was somebody else's turn to dare to answer.

I had a sudden flash. Perhaps I'd misread the note-writer's intention. Maybe all we had was a failure to punctuate. Yes! I looked at my class idling, their brains in neutral, waiting for this nonsense to end. The only person with a smile on his face also had a plug in his ear. I could hear the shhh-shhh of the bass beat all the way across the room.

I couldn't wait any longer to check my theory, and the students weren't exactly caught up in the spirit of the quest. "We aren't cannibals, are we?" I asked.

They looked at me, then at each other, then up to the heavens for help with their incomprehensible teacher.

"Do we eat children, no matter how hungry we are?" I inserted a comma after *eat*. This was supposed to have been a lot more fun.

They got it. Finally. They even giggled. That didn't mean they would transfer the concept of the comma to any other sentence, ever, but all the same, I was content. I gave them a punctuation exercise, and while they moaned over it, I pulled out the manila envelope and checked the note.

R.I.P. Teach. Makes you wonder who's next, doesn't it?

Exquisitely punctuated, given the message. I couldn't find a whole lot of interpretational scope in it. No matter where I moved the commas and question marks, the message was the same.

I was being threatened by the one student who understood how to clearly express his or her thoughts.

After lunch my prize-winning journalism team squeezed their newly inflated self-esteem into my classroom. Watching them slap hands and congratulate each other, I had a small epiphany followed by enormous relief. Of *course*. The clippings I'd received were research for an article, an attempt to upgrade the paper's general level of content. Why hadn't I realized the obvious sooner?

"By the way," I said after we'd had another round of self-congratulations and were getting down to work. "Which one of you is preparing the story on teacher violence?"

"I'm doing the fire," Raffi said. "At the Cavanaugh. I figure it's the first time I'm writing, like, actual news. Like a *story*, you know? A real one."

"Great," I said, and he rewarded me with that beatific, weird smile of his. He had too many elbows and knees and

Adam's apples, but you could tell he was evolving into something seriously cute. I did not, however, acknowledge even his potential adorableness in any way. Better to appear chilly than be even an unintentional letch. "But what about the article on teacher violence?"

They glanced at me to verify that I'd asked the question, then swiveled their heads, looking for the answer along with me.

"Nobody'd let us print that," Hal said.

"Violent teachers?" Kelly Cleary asked. "Wow." She was a waiflike creature whose fashionably oversized clothing had gulped her down. All that was left were two wide gray eyes and a lot of surplus material.

"Violence *against* teachers," Hal corrected her. "But would the school really let us print that kind of a story?"

"Who assigned it, anyway?" the editor-in-chief demanded. "I didn't." It was amazing what a title did to a person, even at seventeen. Since being named editor-in-chief, Winkie Mueller had discovered the thrill of power. He had, in fact, dropped his Winkie and was now the more dignified Walter Mueller, Jr. "People can't simply decide to do any story they choose," the former Winkie said. "That produces *chaos*. This paper has a *philosophy*. An editorial outlook."

There was much hooting, although less than there'd have been had we not won a prize.

"The point is, nobody'd let us print it, anyway," Hal insisted.

This led to an encouragingly heated debate about censorship. Normally, such intellectual enthusiasm would cheer me, but not when I'd been hoping for a plain and simple explanation for the threatening note.

Actually, I'd gotten what I'd hoped for. The fact was, nobody was writing an article about violence. My message was from a player, not somebody reporting on the game.

CARPOOLING SUPERSEDES EVEN MURDER AND DEATH THREATS. Three days ago, before I'd trundled off to Lyle's fatal birthday party, I'd promised to be part of my mother's help-your-sister-Beth program. The surprises and shocks of the intervening days did not cancel out my pledge.

Karen's class had visited Betsy Ross's house today. I find it a singularly dull destination for anyone, but particularly an innocent child. You know you're in trouble, attractions-wise, when one of the advertised specials is a peek at Betsy's third husband's family Bible.

The truth is, nobody is really sure if that was the woman's actual house. Furthermore, nobody is certain that she truly made the original American flag. So what you visit is the house of somebody unknown passing as the house of somebody who probably didn't do what she's famous for. The only justification for trucking in class after class of students who are too young to appreciate the nuances of a Colonial woman's life is that the stairwell is so low, only wee ones can get through it without risking concussions.

My mother had subbed for Beth as one of the parents who worked on mob control. But my mother hadn't returned to the Main Line on the school bus. Instead, she and Karen had stayed in town and I had been designated as their homebound chauffeur. I was to meet them at One Liberty Place.

It's shallow of me, but I find this new building a much more satisfying bit of architecture than old Betsy's theoretical digs. It lacks two hundred years of history, but it makes up for it in the sleek brightness of marble and color and brass, almost to the point of overkill. I felt underdressed and out of style in my pudgy down coat over the unglamorous brown slacks and rust sweater I'd worn all day.

I sat on a bench in the balconied rotunda admiring the colorful march of people moving in and out of two stories' worth of glass-fronted shops. Across from me a black grand piano sat under a brass-railed staircase. It was unoccupied and unopened—although classical music was being piped in from somewhere—but the piano stood majestically as the new litmus test for upscale retail. People shopping on the cheap had Muzak to ignore. High-enders were given genuine concert pianists as musical wallpaper.

I abruptly realized I was no longer alone on my bench.

Although I like to think of myself as having a wide tolerance for adolescent and postadolescent diversity, the fellow next to me set off all my mental alarms. I was surprised he hadn't activated sensors on his way in here.

He was very tall and deliberately fierce. He had four earrings in the ear I could see, a heavily studded black leather jacket, black leather boots that should have been declared weapons, and jeans that were terminally ripped at the knees and crotch. Red long johns showed through the tattered denim.

He was out of place in this glitter dome, and even more so next to me.

I wondered if his arrival and placement were pure accident. He felt too much for happenstance, particularly today. He was too extreme and too close.

I wondered how well he punctuated. Assigning the note and the tombstone drawing to him didn't seem a stretch of the imagination.

This was the sort of situation my self-defense instructor had said was best handled by avoidance. In fact, "Git!" is what she had said. I looked around. The other benches were occupied. Surely, he wouldn't harm me here, in the rotunda, with all those witnesses. Nonetheless, I clutched my bag and stood up, but as I scooped up my books, he bent over and reached into a filthy satchel. A gun? A knife? A burning cross?

I stepped back, out of range.

He pulled a book out of the bag, sighed with audible contentment, and settled back to read, a hot pink highlighter in one hand.

I sidled closer and checked the cover. *Cognitive Theories of Personality Differences and Treatments.*

I was really losing it. Seeing devils instead of students. I didn't want him to witness my mortified blush, so I turned away—and saw real peril barreling across the rotunda.

"Wouldn't this be a beautiful place to have a wedding?" she said from halfway across the expanse.

Back to reality. The scary guy seemed preferable. "Mom, it's a mall," I said, teeth gritted.

She pivoted, a shopping bag in each hand, checking how many tables would fit in this rotunda. Actually, it wouldn't be a bad place for the prom if, say, Richard Quinn couldn't open The Scene because he couldn't get that final backing or, say, because he turned out to be a murderer. And of course, here, if dancing became too boring, the kids would be able to buy a little chocolate, or jewelry, or new party clothes between sets, to liven things up.

"How was Betsy Ross's house?" I asked Karen, who was occupied with a pretzel with mustard I hoped she'd want to share.

"*Elizabeth* Ross's house." The child had a little mustard mustache. "That's her real name, like Miss Penelope says."

I had no idea who Miss Penelope was or why my niece suddenly hunched her small shoulders and tried to click the fingers of her left hand. But then she started chanting, a tiny white bepretzeled Main Line girl-child, rapping Mother Goose. Don't try to tell me the U.S. isn't a melting pot.

> "Elizabeth, Elspeth, Betsy, and Bess,
> They all went together to seek a bird's nest.
> They found a bird's nest with five eggs in,
> They all took one, and left four in."

"Grandma explained," she said. "They're all the same girl. It's just nicknames, so she's Elizabeth Ross, isn't she?"

"Absolutely right." My mother flashed a beam at her granddaughter, then aimed a when-are-you-going-to-create-a-genius-like-this? look in my direction. We had progressed, without speaking a single word, from having my wedding in a shopping center to proudly enjoying the fruit of the union.

"We went upstairs for a snack first," my mother said.

"Time to go, then." I offered to hoist the shopping bags. They were pretty solidly packed. My mother looked embarrassed. "We found a wonderful sale. Besides, Beth doesn't have time to shop for Karen right now."

My mother is extremely frugal, but money spent on grandchildren doesn't count, the same way calories ingested while standing up don't count. Some things are off-the-record, free points.

Karen chanted Mother Goose as molested by Miss Penelope all the way home.

> "Great A, little a,
> Bouncing B!
> The cat's in the cupboard,
> And can't see me!"

A Mustang is too intimate a car for such torture. I toyed with the idea of hailing Karen a cab, but that seemed cruel, as did putting her on the Paoli Local and hoping for the best. Instead, we drove on, making conversation and trying to ignore the backseat.

"Your father and I have decided to stay up here until after Lyle's funeral," my mother said. "Whenever that is. It's the right thing to do. I feel so sorry for Hattie. Besides, it'll give Daddy a few more days to heal. I just hope we're not too much of a burden for Beth."

I didn't know whether to tell her to get out of town while the getting was good, or what.

> "If I'd as much money as I could spend,
> I never would cry old chairs to men—"

"Why give men chairs?" I asked my niece. Maybe the kid knew something new about the opposite sex. There was all that talk about wisdom from the mouths of babes, wasn't there?

"Aunt Mandy!" Karen sounded amused and incredulous. "Not *men. Mend.*

> "Old chairs to *mend*, old chairs to *mend*,
> I never would cry old chairs to *mend*."

Damn. For a moment Mother Goose had seemed code for a new furniture-oriented courtship ploy. Instead it turns out I had a hearing problem.

* * *

BETH'S LIVING ROOM WOULD HAVE LOOKED LIKE A WHAT'S Wrong With This Picture? game except that I knew what was wrong with it. Mackenzie.

Last night he'd said he'd see me today, but I certainly didn't think he meant here, now, or for this reason.

Worried as I was about his presence, I still felt a momentary reflexive flutter. He's a looker, after all. Also, I had the threatening note in my briefcase. I couldn't wait to turn it over to him, to have him take care of it and make it all right.

A trick of the light, or of my mind. I was confusing him with a knight, even if one in slightly tarnished armor. But he was a cop, not Sir Galahad. Maybe he'd find out who was threatening me, but only on the side. Mostly, he'd still be a cop on a case. And in this case, one involving my parents.

I shouldn't have told him about my father and Cindy. If I was sure he was going to find out about it anyway, why hadn't I let him do so on his own? Charm and ease and sweet southern mush-mouthing notwithstanding, he'd just been grilling my old, wounded dad. He'd cast Dad as villain, Mom as dupe, both as killers. A more ridiculous duo had never been suspected.

The third degree ceased at our arrival.

"I saw Elizabeth Ross's house and got new shoes and a coat!" Karen skidded across the living room floor, raced across the carpet, and hurled herself at my father.

"Careful!" my mother called out. Then she quickly added: "Everything was on sale." It wasn't her husband who was upset about her buying spree; it was her daughter, Beth.

"You mean Betsy Ross's house," my father said before we could warn him. Karen, delighted at the continued ignorance of adults, smugly, loudly began an encore of her routine.

> "Elizabeth, Elspeth, Betsy, and Bess,
> They all went together to seek a bird's nest.

They found a bird's nest with five eggs in,
They all took one, and left four in."

"Get it?" she demanded. "They're all the same person.
Just nicknames! Like I'm Kari and Pumpkin-face!"

My father did the grandparent admiration bit, then recovered enough to speak again. "There's even more nicknames for Elizabeth," he said. "There could have been ten names at that bird's nest and only one egg would be gone, I'll bet. There's Betty and Libby and Elsie and Elissa."

"And Lissa and Lisa and Lizzie and Lisbeth," my mother added.

Karen had long since lost interest, but my parents were really into it. As for me, I suddenly heard them from a distance. My ears clogged, as if the atmosphere had abruptly changed, as if I were making a too-rapid descent. A crash landing.

"Not just Lisbeth, but Beth herself as well," Mackenzie said from far away, and through a haze I saw him bow, gallantly, at my sister.

My heart palpitated. I didn't want to pursue the path opening in my mind, but words nonetheless had been dropped like a little crumb path to follow. Name words. Elizabeth, Elspeth, Betsy, and Bess . . . Betsy. Cindy's toddler, Cindy's murderer.

Around me real conversation had gone on hold and all was chitchat and pleasantries set to the drumming, finger-snapping—or at least finger-rubbing—enormously annoying sounds of my niece, the rapper.

"The Queen of Hearts,
She made some tarts,
All on a summer's day . . ."

Nobody asked her to stop. My family is pathologically tolerant.

I thought back to Sunday. It seemed ancient times, years, not days, ago; but I nonetheless tried to replay a mental tape in slow motion and listen carefully to every word that had been said in this room. I knew that my mother and father had squabbled trying to date the length of time since they'd seen Lyle, a span that began with Cindy's death. I tried to remember. Nearly two decades ago, isn't that what my father had said, rather testily? Twenty years, give or take one. And Betsy had been three, so she'd be twenty-three or twenty-two now.

> "The Knave of Hearts,
> He stole those tarts,
> And took them clean away."

The kid and her jingles were making me crazy. If I was in this mood when my biological clock sounded alarms, I'd unplug it.

> "The King of Hearts,
> Called for the tarts,
> And beat the Knave full sore—"

How did anybody with small children ever think? I couldn't keep my head on course. My thoughts skidded sideways, sticking on the repetitive rhyme, until, with difficulty, I pulled them free and tuned out Karen's jingles and the conversation of the other adults and concentrated.

I had to think about Elizabeth/Betsy of the changeable name. I had to remember everything I knew before I went off on a wild Mother Goose chase.

A cute redheaded baby, Wiley had said. Janine had wanted to adopt her.

A cute redheaded girl-child whose natural father was in Vietnam. Whose natural father eventually raised her.

Whose mother, of course, was dead.

A cute little redheaded Betsy, Bess, Elizabeth, Lizzie.

I felt sick. When my sister offered cookies all around, I took three, maximum nervous munching in action. As I chewed, not tasting much, more random fragments surfaced in my memory pool, joining to create a picture I didn't want to see.

Hattie's strange reaction when she learned Lizzie's father's name—Lizzie's original name, of course. Hattie saying it was Lizzie's fault the night of Lyle's death and then again when my mother and I visited. I'd thought she'd meant that Lizzie had been guilty of inadvertent food poisoning, but now her real meaning was clear.

Mackenzie was watching me quizzically.

He wasn't going to be surprised. He was forever pulling me out of my webs of speculation, lecturing me on the fact that the odds always favored the most logical suspect. Unexciting, but true. Lizzie, with complete access to the tarts all day and evening, Lizzie, who knew who was coming to dinner, made depressingly obvious sense, particularly when her history was factored in.

But why now? Why this Sunday?

Just because, perhaps. Because, as Dorian Gray said, life wasn't governed by will or invention. Instead, the cells held old passions, and then, when something happened by chance to reactivate the memories—the sound of music, a scent, whatever—everything came back. *And* as he said, "It is on things like this that our lives depend."

Because, by chance, Lizzie and her father had converted a dilapidated boardinghouse into a chic bed and breakfast, and by chance, it was located across the street from where Lyle Z. grew up. And because by chance, Lyle Zacharias was turning fifty and having an acute attack of nostalgia and needed to believe you could go home again, that was the birthday party site.

And because Hattie Zacharias made the arrangements while Lizzie's father was out of the country and spoke to a woman named Chapman, a name with no associations.

So just because. Because something had been waiting to happen for a long, long time. Who knew what poems and passions had simmered and brewed in Lizzie for twenty long years since her nightmarish accident? Who knew how stable or skewed Lizzie had been then—or since, having caused her mother's death. Who could say what the weight of carrying that around every day of her life had done to her spirit and even her sanity?

I wanted to cry. But in private, not here. "I'm sorry to have to leave so soon," I said, "but Mackenzie—Chuck—and I have an appointment."

Mackenzie was too good a cop to ask me what the devil I was talking about, but I could hear the whir as his mental gears kicked in.

"Then you'll come to dinner tomorrow, all right?" my mother said. "I'm cooking. And the invitation is for both of you."

We definitely had to have that talk. Or perhaps now that her name was about to be replaced on the suspect list, I could convince her to jump on the red-eye home. Tonight.

"Much obliged, ma'am," Mackenzie said. I wanted to kick him. Doing his ma'am routine and charming the woman was only going to accelerate and make more desperate her matchmaking. "But I'm afraid I'm on duty tomorrow evenin'," he said. "Real sorry about that."

"Say good night, Gracie," I muttered.

He did so, laying on the accent until he was unintelligible. Everybody else said good-bye in crisp Philadelphese, except for Karen, who was in the middle of something idiotic about a misty, moisty morning and a man dressed all in leather.

> "I said, 'How do you do, and how do you do,
> And how do you do again!' "

"What's this about? This appointment we seem to have acquired?" Mackenzie asked when we were outside.

"About Elizabeth, Elsbeth, Betsy, and Bess."

"You're the first case of post-traumatic Mother Goose syndrome I ever saw," Mackenzie said.

"Lizzie is Betsy. The one who shot Lyle Zacharias's first

wife. Her mother." I stifled the strong urge to add that once we reached Lizzie, we'd say what did you do, and what did you do, and what did you do again?

Seventeen

I FOLLOWED MACKENZIE'S CAR IN MY MUSTANG AND FOUND A parking space not too far from his. Both were in the spots reserved for The Boarding House. Business was obviously not booming.

When we knocked and opened the door, Roy and Lizzie both came into the front hall looking expectant, almost excited. Then, when they saw who it was, their smiles faded.

"I'm sorry," Lizzie whispered. "We must seem rude, but we thought hotel guests, maybe . . ." She looked drawn and puffy-eyed.

She was so pitiable already, I hated knowing that Mackenzie and I were going to make her feel still worse. But perhaps acknowledging what she'd done would ease her distress.

"Two more parties canceled today," Roy said. "It's ripping both of us up. Worked so hard to get this place off the ground, and we got such great reviews, and now . . ." He shook his head.

Despite his words and professed unhappiness, he looked strong and hale after his near poisoning. Made me wonder. "We've interrupted your dinner," I said.

"Need to clear a few things up," Mackenzie said.

"Maybe we should come back later," I suggested.

"We could talk while you eat," Mackenzie said. We were

not exactly synchronized. I didn't think our conversation was going to be acceptable table talk or helpful for the digestion, but I stood corrected and kept silent and wound up, along with the rest of the group, in the kitchen, on high stools around the butcher block, now set for two.

I don't know what I'd expected, but not Roy's take-out hamburger and french fries. Was he, too, afraid to eat his daughter's cooking? He saw my lifted eyebrows and grinned. "Lizzie hates this stuff. I can't get enough of it, so while she's eating rabbit food, I indulge."

Lizzie picked at greens, which she offered to share. I declined. "You're afraid to eat anything I prepared," she said morosely. "But this is only vegetables, and I'm eating them, too."

"No—it isn't that at all," I lied. "It's just that we have a dinner appointment later."

Once again Mackenzie didn't show any surprise as I improvised about his daily schedule. "Mr. Beecher, sir," he said. "You are a widower, am I correct?"

Roy Beecher put down his half-eaten hamburger and looked appraisingly at Mackenzie. "What does my marital status have to do with what happened Sunday?" His eyes slit.

"Well, sir, I was thinkin' it might be relevant. Might shed a little light on the recent unfortunate happenin' here, which is why I asked."

"Everybody knows my dad's a widower," Lizzie said.

Roy took a deep breath and stood up. "Afraid not, Lizard," he said. "Not if you're into legalistic haggling. A policeman asks a question like that, in that way, it means he already knows the answer. Should we go into another room?" he asked Mackenzie.

"No!" Lizzie said. "I want to hear. I *should* hear. What's going on?"

Roy sat down again on one of the kitchen stools. He put his hand on his daughter's freckled forearm. "Sorry to tell you this way, but what the man is getting to is that I never was married to your mother, Lizard."

"Why didn't you ever tell me before?"

"Thought it was for the best. I'll explain," he said. "I promise."

Lizzie looked pensive. "Did you think I'd get upset? It doesn't matter if you weren't married. You could have told me. It's not like it's the Victorian age, or like I'm royalty and I can't inherit the throne now. It's not like a piece of paper making me legal means anything." She turned to face Mackenzie. "Why ask a question like that? Are you some kind of morality patrol, or what?"

Mackenzie didn't answer. Instead, he looked at Roy Beecher. "Are you sure we shouldn't talk someplace else?" he asked.

Roy took a bite of his hamburger, chewed, then put the bun down on the plate again and looked at his daughter. "This Sunday business really rattled Lizzie. She's having weird dreams and feelings she can't understand. She's like I was after the war, but at least I knew what made my flashbacks happen. So I've been thinking that maybe if she understands hers, her mind would be put at ease. Might as well be now." He moved his hand down her arm until it clasped hers. "You feel ready, Lizard?"

She nodded.

"Okay to talk in front of these people?"

She looked at Mackenzie and me, evaluating something, then nodded again.

"Then ask whatever you want," Roy Beecher said. "I got nothing to hide."

I couldn't stop watching Lizzie, whose eyebrows had lowered with concern, whose blue eyes ricocheted between her father and Mackenzie, who looked like a deaf mute trying to lip-read. My theory, so shiny bright and clever in my sister's family room, was rapidly tarnishing in this kitchen. I had been so sure Lizzie had become unbalanced from guilt over her mother's death. But looking at her now, it was difficult—it was, in fact, impossible—to believe that she had known what was going on or what had gone on, or that this father and daughter act was anything but authentic.

"It'll be okay," Roy told his daughter. "Don't be afraid. You know, I went back to Nam to face my devils, get rid of them. You've been seeing yours since Sunday, only nobody ever gave you their name or reasons, so how could you battle them? Always thought I was protecting you, but maybe not."

Lizzie said nothing, her breath high and shallow.

Mackenzie had a real gift for waiting, but not always benignly. Predators are patient, too. He was lolling on his high, uncomfortable stool, making me nervous. Did he see that Lizzie was innocent in many senses of the word?

"I didn't even know your mom was pregnant." Roy Beecher spoke directly to his daughter. "We'd been traveling, staying with people on farms, in communes, doing the typical thing. We were kids, a year out of high school, maybe two. No real plans. But in love, you know? I loved my little Cinderella."

"Cinderella?" I didn't mean to interrupt, but it popped out because I suddenly thought we were talking about two different people.

"She called herself that, said that was long for Cindy. She didn't have parents, just foster families. Little orphan Cinderella. Except she didn't get a prince. She got me, and when I was drafted, I went. I didn't have any way to get out of it, and I didn't want to go to Canada.

"Cindy went crazy. She meant it when she said make love not war. Meant that slogan one hundred percent. Couldn't believe I would go. Called me a pawn and a fool and a dupe and worse, and that was that. She didn't come to wave me off. I didn't even know she was pregnant." He looked intently at his daughter. "It's not like I walked away, you understand?"

Lizzie nodded, eyes wide and solemn.

"I didn't know until after you were born, and then she wrote and told me. Also, that she'd met this older guy and was married to him." Roy shook his head. "That was as weird as my going to Nam. Took me a while to realize that she was just like me. Scared, mostly. Afraid she didn't have any other choice. People didn't raise babies on their own back then. So that was that." He was patting his daughter's hand with his bony fingers. Making nice, we called it when we were children. "The man she married was Lyle Zacharias," he added softly.

Lizzie looked as if someone had sneaked up behind her and slammed her with a two-by-four. I watched as every classical response appeared: jaw dropping, eyes widening, breath holding, head shaking.

I was now one thousand percent convinced that she hadn't known. I had dead-ended with my stupid theory. She simply hadn't known, and any supposition of a poisoning for revenge, or bottled anger at losing her mother, or anything else premeditated was ridiculous.

But there was a less ridiculous corollary. Mackenzie was aware of it, too. I could feel it in the tempo of his hyperrelaxed breathing and in his studied casualness.

Because while Lizzie had known nothing, Roy had known everything. He'd come back from facing his twenty-year-old demons in Vietnam—where the poisonous Barbados nut grew, according to Mackenzie—and found a last, stateside enemy at home. And who would know or suspect him if the enemy were to die?

"He was my stepfather?" Lizzie pressed her fingertips to her temples. "I lived with him? I knew him?"

Her father gave a slight nod. "For almost three years."

"When he walked into the kitchen," she said, "as soon as I saw him, I got so . . ."

Her near faint, her confusion, when Lyle had been talking to my mother and me. What a way for memory to surface—what terrible timing!

Lizzie pushed off her stool and stood, shaking her head. Her normally soft voice was shrill. "I thought I was going crazy. These feelings, these fears, these—I don't know—memories I can't remember, pictures in my head I can't see. Why did you keep it a secret?" She stood, tall and solid, pale skin mottled with emotion.

Her father looked at her, then down at his oversized hands. "I thought it was best," he mumbled. I leaned forward to hear. "I wanted to protect you. You were such a sad little thing. So solemn, so pulled inside yourself when

you came to live with me. I wanted to make you smile, be
happy again."

"Protect me from what? What did she do?"

"Who?"

"My mother! Why did you have to protect me? What did
she do? Walk out when you came back? Where did she go?
Why can't I remember her? You took me away, didn't
you!"

"No—Yes, I took you, but not that way! They—She—
didn't want you anymore. I did."

"My mother didn't *want* me?"

"No." Roy Beecher spoke softly, as if it hurt to say each
word. "That's not who I meant."

"Then what do you mean? What happened to her?
Where is she?"

The question hung above us like a poisoned cloud, but
we sat in silence, each waiting for somebody else to break
the news to Lizzie. I surely couldn't. I wanted, in fact, to
be able to dial the psychiatric equivalent of 911. Nobody
should have a life history so gruesomely revised without
mental paramedics on hand.

Who was going to tell her? The answer was nobody. At
least nobody was going to tell her the complete truth. Roy
was fighting tears, shaking his head back and forth.

"Your mother died," Mackenzie said very softly. "Your
grandmother—your stepfather's mother—was raising you.
She's the woman who, ah, couldn't continue raisin' you."

"My stepfather's . . . that old woman? The one who
screamed at me?"

We all nodded.

"I didn't want you to know." Roy's voice was gruff.
"The whole thing was to get you away from there, let you
forget. Lyle was up in New York, and the old lady said she
wanted to travel, spend time with Lyle, too, and I didn't
think we'd ever see each other again. I thought we'd be
home free, a fresh start. Didn't even want to call you by the
name they used. Betsy was their child. Tried to make you
proper Elizabeth for a while, but it was too much of a

mouthful, so Lizzie it became." He watched his daughter with terrible anxiety.

"Why wasn't he raising me?" Lizzie asked. "How did she die?"

"No," Roy said. "Enough is enough. Don't press, Lizard."

"But I have to know. I have to stop feeling this sick, this afraid, having these nightmares in the daytime, losing pieces of time. Tell me. Whatever there is."

Roy stood up, put his hand on her shoulder and sighed. "There was an accident." His voice was choked. "A terrible accident. You were only a baby . . ."

I STILL FELT SHELL-SHOCKED. MACKENZIE, TOO, LOOKED shaken by our last encounter. "You think she'll be okay?" I asked for perhaps the twenty-seventh time. But each questioning was a variation on the same basic issue of whether we'd done the right thing or simply added to the world's store of pain and problems.

We sat in a restaurant near the Museum of Art with the air of guilty co-conspirators.

"She had to know," Mackenzie said. "Seeing Zacharias triggered her memory and her panic. It's worse to think you're losing your mind, isn't it?"

"I feel so sorry for her. I don't know what good it'll do to have a soda, or a walk with her, but it was all I could think of." We had made plans for after school tomorrow. It felt like a futile gesture, a tiny bandage for a mortal wound. But doing nothing felt worse, like abandonment.

"You'll get her out of that place, away from the crime site. Let her know she's still worthy. Still good. That what happened long ago accidentally doesn't matter to you. That's worth a try. Stop beatin' up on yourself."

He had moments of pure, distilled kindness that stopped me in my cynical tracks. I could pooh-pooh his knightly aura, but in truth, this was the second time during this dinner that I'd looked across the table and seen a curly-haired, blue-shirted, sexy Sir Galahad. The first time had been right after we sat down and I gave him my threatening tombstone drawing and clippings. I was afraid he'd pooh-pooh them, patronize me with stories about pranks vs. the Real World and serious crime. But I had underestimated him—a problem of mine—because he was immediately on alert, and he behaved as if defending me would become not only his number-one concern, but the entire Philadelphia police department's.

Now, I sat and silently appreciated him for a few moments before I returned to the topic at hand. "At least," I finally said, "Lizzie can be eliminated as a suspect. Unless you think she faked the whole thing."

He shook his head. "Unless she's one hell of an actress. Or unless somebody who's that upsettin' to you, like Lyle was to her—even if you don' know why—triggers somethin'. Have to check that out."

We didn't mention Roy Beecher. It was too easy to envision him taking revenge to further protect his daughter. He'd been quite open with his contempt for Lyle Zacharias, who'd put a loaded gun within reach of a baby. Again and again he'd condemned the legal system for lacking the laws to put such a man behind bars.

I picked over the remnants of my pasta and breadsticks and Caesar salad. It felt wrong—heartless, even—to be hungry after such a dreadful, wrenching scene, but the fact was, we had been.

"Take your plate?" a waiter said, whisking away Mackenzie's service before anyone answered.

"Rude," I told his retreating back. "Makes the person who's still eating feel terrible. Makes eating feel like a race. Whatever happened to gracious dining?" But of course the waiter could not hear my oration. On my left, a man barked dictation to someone on the other end of a cellular phone. On my right, a baby cried. Behind me, a beeper cheeped.

"So let's see who we have." Mackenzie pulled a ratty notebook out of his pocket. I had never seen him with a new or unfrayed one. I wondered where he bought predistressed tablets, the stationery equivalent of stone-washed jeans, and why. "Been through the whole guest list. Interestin'. You could split it into thirds: the Pro-Lyles, the

Anti-Lyles and the Lyle Who?s. I've pretty much eliminated the Pros and the Lyle Who?s and the husbands and
wives who were only there for the ride. Eliminated a few
Antis, too. Good-lookin' brunette woman. Remember her?"

I didn't. Nor did I particularly like the relish with which
he did.

"Little tipped-up nose. Dark blue eyes?"

I shook my head more vigorously.

"She works on another soap now. Used to work for Lyle.
Says he harassed her, came to her apartment, touched her—
you know. Then he tried to keep other people from hirin'
her after she threatened a lawsuit. But that was a while ago
and he was about to hire her again and more important, she
is one of the few people who never went near the kitchen.
Power's interestin', isn't it? You and me, we aren't playin'
in that arena."

"Some say that being a cop is all about power."

"Not that way. You and me, would we go to somebody's
birthday party if we hated him? Nothin's at stake for us.
For some of them, reputation, or good old boy status, or
something in the big game was on the line, so they came.
They work for him, or owe him, or fear him."

"I'm not feeling like much of a judge of character," I
said. "When I met Lyle, I thought he was pretty wonderful,
a hyperalive, magnetic, considerate, talented man. But since
then it's been a constant piece-by-piece unmasking. The
Picture of Lyle Zacharias. All the corruption and duplicity
and deception under the skin. At first I wondered who on
earth could have killed a man like that. And then what *a
man like that* meant got really fuzzy, and now, God help
me, I wonder who *didn't* want him dead. It's very depressing."

"Some people should only be viewed from afar,"
Mackenzie said. And then he said something else.

"What's that?" I leaned forward. The ambient din had
mysteriously escalated. Once upon a time, restaurants believed in conversation and encouraged romantic tête-à-têtes
with candles and soft carpets and soft music. Now, we were
surrounded by bare floors, uncovered windows, acoustical

torture chambers. I'd read that people wanted to be where things were happening, and noise, per se, gave the sense of *happening*. I am not one of the people they polled.

Mackenzie also leaned forward. "What?"

"You first!" I projected my voice.

"It comes back to the suspects, then," Mackenzie said, rather briskly. He stood up and relocated himself to the seat at my right, so that we had the possibility of conversation. "I favor Roy Beecher," he said. "He has it all. Motive, opportunity, method. Always intrigues me when the worst of acts—murder—comes out of the best of intentions like protectin' your child."

"Who else?" I didn't want it to be Roy, as logical as he seemed. I didn't want a decent man with too many troubles, but good impulses, to be the one. "Certainly lots more have motives." Even though he was now next to me rather than across from me, I still had to talk loudly. I wondered where spies met to swap secrets these days. Maybe the real reason the cold war ended was that there were no restaurants left in which to secretly inform.

"More? Like who?"

"Whom, I think. Like Tiffany, for starters." Why weren't we paying more attention to her?

"Ah, the dame, like in a Raymond Chandler movie. But she isn't necessarily the villain just because she looks like that."

"Like what?"

He raised one eyebrow. "You've got to be kidding."

"I'm sure all she ever wanted of Lyle was his money—so how would it be when suddenly he decides to change his life, drop his income, maybe even give away assets? Doesn't it make sense?"

Mackenzie shrugged.

"Speaking of Tiffany," I said. "Your name—could the C possibly stand for Cartier?"

"No, it could not possibly."

"And surely the K has nothing to do with a mart of the same letter?"

"Correct again."

"What a relief. Anyway, there is also, of course, Tiffany's lover, Shepard McCoy. There are contracts and money and a love triangle between them, and, I bet, trouble. Maybe Shepard's locked into that doctor role. Maybe he wanted something else, or out. And how about Richard Quinn? His whole life was screwed up by Zacharias, or he thinks so, and that's the same thing. Plus, Tiffany's his step-daughter, for whatever that's worth. If he knew about Lyle and the cute brunette with the tipped-up nose, for example . . . maybe that'd be the final straw."

"Maybe," Mackenzie said. "Maybe not."

From time to time his line of vision dropped to my plate, then quickly rose again. The evil waiter had done his work. Mackenzie was eager for his espresso, and I was standing—or rather, sitting and masticating—in the way of his happiness. I put down my fork, resenting the hell out of that waiter, but more reluctant to look like a pig than to actually finish eating what I'd ordered. "And there's his wife," I said.

"Shepard's?"

"Oh. No. Does he have one? That makes things even worse. I meant Lyle's."

"You already mentioned her."

"Not Tiffany; Sybil."

"The man had a wife glut, didn't he, though?" Mackenzie murmured. "What about her? 'Course she's on my list, too—they all are, but I like hearin' your take on the lineup."

"Sybil? Hell definitely hath no fury. And not only on her own behalf. She thinks her ex and Tiffany ignore and mistreat Reed, and she's like a mother lion about her son. And worst of all, Lyle was about to undergo a lifestyle change, which translates into moving to a farm or a ranch or whatever those people think is the simple life."

"Which translates into less support," he said.

I nodded, first to the question and then to the waiter who must have been lurking like a vulture in search of dead plates. "From now on, his father was going to ignore and mistreat Reed and be cheap about it. Sybil was panicked.

But if Lyle died before he sold off everything, before the show was canceled and so forth, Reed would be better off."

Mackenzie nodded. "She's a real out-front woman, I give her credit for that. She's the only one of 'em told me straight on she was glad the man was dead and better off for it."

"Do you think that means she's innocent?"

"Or real clever," he said.

I am a fairly good reader of upside-down print. It's not a talent that counts for much, but sometimes it gives me an edge. At the moment, I was having trouble deciphering Mackenzie's upside-down scrawl in the frayed notebook. He had divided the pages into three columns. The first had names, relationships to the deceased, and whatever he knew of their whereabouts the night of the poisoning. The second listed possible motives, but I couldn't make out the third, so I asked about it.

"That's how a person might get hold of the poison," he said. "It isn't a household item, somethin' you pick up at the market."

"And Sybil's access?"

"Just what it says. Landscape architect."

It didn't say that at all. It said, I could now see, *lndscparch.*

"She'd know about poisonous ornamentals, 'specially a popular one like that. Could easily get specimens, too."

I spotted the Wileys, Terry and Janine, together in one grouping. "You don't have a whole lot written next to them," I said. They were up top on my list. He, for a motive I could understand, and she, simply because it would be a civic service to have her locked away for a few decades. I ordered an espresso, decaffeinated. Mackenzie took his straight, which had to mean he was working tonight. Through such exquisitely subtle hints did I determine the shape and pace of my love life.

"That business about stealing his idea for *Ace of Hearts*," Mackenzie murmured.

"Lots of people confirmed it."

"Only problem is, those very people are also currently

suspects, isn't that so? How do you decide what part of what they say to believe? How do you decide how much they're tryin' to move the spotlight off their own precious face and motives?"

I had no answer. Instead, I pondered something easier, the question of why I'd ordered espresso, aside from its being culinarily correct. The thimbleful of nuclear-powered coffee didn't allow for much sipping or even hand-warming, which is, by and large, the whole point of after-dinner coffee. "Anyway," I said, "we've named seven people, if I counted correctly. That's a long list."

Mackenzie looked at me, his head slightly tilted. "The count should be a little longer than that, don't you think?"

"You mean Reed? He does seem to know a whole lot about science, and he was nothing if not angry and resentful."

"Didn' mean the boy just at the moment."

"You're the one who had a chance to talk to everybody who was there. I didn't. How would I know who else is on your list?"

"Because."

His expression combined regret and determination. The face of somebody who reluctantly had to inflict pain. By the time his slow southern rhythms moved him on to the next part of his sentence, I understood why he looked that way. All the same, I flinched and felt each word's impact, even though he said them very, very softly and gently.

"You'd know who else is on the list, Mandy, because it's hard to forget your own parents, isn't it?" he said.

Eighteen

"I don' know ..." Mackenzie said. He held his keys, I held mine as we walked to our cars, which sat side by side in separate but equal slots on a trash-filled parking lot on Callowhill Street. Symbolically perfect and just as unsatisfactory as other so-called separate but equal arrangements had proven.

Frankly, I didn't know, either. Not even to what he referred.

But I did know that as of this moment, I couldn't stand all the uncertainties in my life. The week's tension had been steadily building, and I felt as if my central wiring system was about to detonate. I wanted a resolution—of what Mackenzie didn't know about, of who had done what, of what I didn't know about. Of anything.

If the man didn't have to rush off into the night to fight for goodness and right, then there were more amicable ways to reduce the tension. A glass of wine, soft music, and thou.

But he *was* rushing off, he was always rushing off, so I opted for second choice. A fight. About anything.

The problem was, I didn't even know what topic to choose. I was tired of trying to figure out who'd killed Lyle Zacharias—aside from my parents—and tired of worrying

about the kid who wanted me dead, and tired of not knowing what being Mackenzie's you-know meant.

Too tired to fight, frankly. Too cold out on this parking
lot for any extended debate.

"Wish I didn' have to go . . ." he said, touching my
cheek.

His hand was icy. His hair blew in bouncing ringlets.

This March had an attitude. Newspaper fragments puffed
and stuck against the brick building next to the lot. The
wind threatened to cleave my head in two, straight down
between the eyebrows. Thick clouds glowed dull gray and
hid the moon. "Might snow again," I said morosely.

"Don' worry."

"About snow?"

"About this." He waved the threatening envelope with
the letter and clippings. "We'll find the creep." He kissed
the rapidly freezing tip of my nose and then my rapidly
freezing mouth.

When spring arrived, we'd talk, I promised myself. We
honked farewell as we pulled off the lot in opposite direc-
tions. Modern romance.

In the distance, to my right, the Museum of Art loomed,
its columns undefined in the starless gloom. On a night like
this, even Rocky would pass on running up those wide
front steps.

I turned onto the Benjamin Franklin Parkway. America's
Champs Élysées, it has been called. I hoped the Paris version was a little livelier. Tonight ours was almost deserted,
with only uncollected refuse fluttering in the cruel wind.

I felt as if I'd had hundreds of those thimblefuls of espresso, not one. My blood cells did pirouettes.

The trees lining the wide boulevard creaked and shook in
increasingly high winds. I jumped and clutched the wheel
when an unseen trash can toppled with a clang. The night
felt oppressive, low-ceilinged, too dark.

The perfect setting for a horror movie, but too urban. We
needed a deserted road, an owl's hoot. I laughed at my stupid, hyperactive imagination.

Although, truth be told, the road *was* deserted. One or

two cars coming in the opposite direction and only one other car traveling in mine. Creepy.

Nine-twenty P.M. It was streets like this that accounted for the bad joke about going to Philadelphia when it was closed. Wide streets and pretty plantings do not a Champs Élysées make, although in defense of the Champs Benjamin Franklin, it did feel like snow and the wind-chill factor had to be in the single digits. Also, once the museums that lined it closed for the night, the Parkway was not a very logical hangout. As soon as I was around Logan Circle, I headed south on a side street, toward more traffic company.

The car that had been behind me did the same. Too closely.

And honked. Not the short honk that's a semi-irritated notice to get out of the way or get moving, but a long, impatient, hostile honk.

I could see nothing in the rearview mirror except two blinding circles of light. They seemed high. A minivan or a pickup, perhaps. I didn't know anybody with either vehicle.

I accelerated and nearly rear-ended a car waiting for the light at the corner.

I had a momentary sense of relief that had nothing to do with averting a collision and everything to do with no longer being alone with the car behind me. But of course, if I honked at the car ahead, he'd be as confused and nervous as I was about my caboose's honk. And if I jumped out and ran to him, he'd bolt if he had any sense, and I'd be an easy target for the person behind me. My minor moment of elation evaporated.

I had never thought through the loneliness of being in a car.

"I am making this up," I said out loud. I wasn't convinced, so I kept on talking, more and more loudly. "I've spooked myself with dumb stories. Mackenzie waving that envelope of threats. Bad things have been happening lately, but this isn't one of them. This is how people become mentally ill. This is coincidence. A car behind me, not after me. Another impatient driver. Heavy-footed, heavy-handed."

I wasn't completely sure I believed me. The car behind me was dangerously close, and it had been right behind me on the Parkway, too. So to test—to *prove* that I was only imagining danger—I waited until the light was in my favor and the car ahead of me across the intersection, and then, having crept to the middle of the street, I floored the accelerator, twisted the steering wheel to the left and made a sharp, semiwheelie onto Arch Street.

And the car behind me—a pickup, I saw, as I swiveled my head—did the same, complete with squealing tires, its driver honking and speeding until he was once again nearly on my car. And there he stayed.

Okay, I told myself. I'm not paranoid, I'm in trouble. It is happening. *Think.*

All I could think of was doing more of the same. It hadn't worked once, so why not repeat it? I made a second unannounced turn, right this time, onto a one-way street. I immediately regretted the choice. I needed opposing traffic, someone I could wave to, scream to, someone who would miraculously rescue me. But why should traffic patterns be any closer to fulfilling your heart's desire than anything else was?

Don't panic, I told myself, dropping my former, more ambitious advice to think. Stay calm.

It is a real challenge to consider one's options while your car, of its own volition, is violating the speed laws and you are brainless and paralyzed, eyes straight ahead, pulse hammering, hands locked on the wheel like a crash dummy.

I crossed JFK Boulevard and Market in that mode, with all the terrified prisoners in my brain cells screaming *do something!* Easy for them to say.

Do what? Where?

I wasn't about to lead the crazed pickup home. Certainly couldn't go to my parking lot. There was no attendant at this hour, and I wasn't walking the few blocks home from it. The streets had turned more than mean.

And apparently I couldn't even get myself arrested for speeding tonight. Wherever everybody was on this foul night, the traffic cops were among them.

I was afraid the pickup was going to bump my car, push it around, force me off the road, but it didn't. My pursuer seemed only to want to harass and frighten me. He was succeeding, too. He stayed inches away, blaring his horn into the night.

If we were going to play cat and mouse, I would much rather play the cat. I hated this—hated being alone, vulnerable, pursued. I was in a Burgundy '65 Mustang in Center City Philadelphia, but in my mind I wore a cloak, and all around me were desolate moors and howling wind. A woman alone. A victim.

And my epitaph would read: THIS WAS MACKENZIE'S FAULT. HE SHOULD HAVE BEEN THERE.

Damn! I was so shocked by my own thoughts, I stomped so hard on the gas pedal the car nearly broke the sound barrier.

It nonetheless did not lose the pickup.

But all the same—what had provoked that thought? That woman on the moors? Had I become an urbanized damsel in distress, waving my arms, calling for Mackenzie, ripping my bodice and fleeing up the stairs into the haunted house? A whining, puling girlie girl?

The horror of it made my brain kick back in. I made a plan.

"Okay!" I shouted, presumably to the pickup, more honestly to myself. Loud felt good. Much better than the tears that otherwise threatened. "Follow me, if you want to so much!" I accelerated again—over across the Chestnut Street Transitway, which, luckily, was empty of pedestrians. I saw a very startled street person jump back.

"Sorry," I shouted. And the next time it was possible, after Walnut, I made a sharp left and floored it.

The pickup had figured it out and didn't hesitate.

I saw an arm, a gloved hand come out of its window—but the wrong one. The passenger side.

There was more than one of them. I took deep breaths, one for each of my pursuers, two for each. Three. Do not panic.

I looked around for an open store or restaurant. I could

fling open the door, leap out, run, but the ground-level shops were all closed, and brownstone homes and medical offices gave no clue as to whether anyone was in them. An East Coast ghost town.

The street numbers bisecting us dropped. Faster, faster I drove, praying frantically at each intersection. Oncoming cars squealed to a halt, swerved. At least if they hit me, they'd become involved, have to notice what was going on—but they were amazingly fine drivers and they didn't.

And every inch of the way the pickup stayed on my tail.

Cars followed our procession for brief stints, falling back as they observed the speed laws. If they thought anything was odd about the two cars joined at the fender, they kept their opinions and questions to themselves.

I didn't care. I'd be there soon. I'd be safe.

Time for me and my shadow to turn left. It didn't bother me this time. We were on the road to the slaughterhouse—I was leading them to police headquarters. "Tailgate all you want, sucker!" I screamed.

I came to a screeching halt. For once there were cars. Lots of them, all stopped. Somewhere ahead, a red light. A very long red light, it began to feel. I changed my diagnosis. There was an accident or other inconvenience ahead. I had come to a stop in the middle of the block. Again there were no all-night diners or other refuges on the street, only a shuttered children's boutique to my left. To my right, a photogenic and silent old Philadelphia street remarkably like, but unfortunately not, mine, one block long and narrow as a back alley, split the block. It made me acutely homesick.

This waiting wasn't good. The point was to get to headquarters, to snare my pursuers, but now I was the one who felt trapped in a metal cage.

There was nobody on the sidewalks, no gapers nearby. Perhaps they were all ahead, watching whatever was blocking progress. But there was nobody to call to, nobody to answer a cry for help.

Not good, not good. The pickup honked, but so did the whole line of irritated drivers. I was a sitting target. Any moment now the men behind me could decide not to wait for their game to play through. I double-checked that my doors were locked, my windows all the way up, although of course a rock, a gun, any number of things would make those precautions worthless.

Do not panic! I told myself over and over and over. I sounded remarkably panicked as I thought it, however.

My tormentors lost patience. Perhaps they had figured out why I was retracing my path, heading north. Who cared why? The point was: the passenger door of the pickup opened. A long black-jeaned leg emerged.

I wasn't going to lead them anywhere. This was coming to a bad end now. Here.

My girlie-girl impulses kicked in again—my breath grew raggedy and I wanted to scream and I made me so mad I twisted the steering wheel until I thought it would rip off, switched into gear, and pressed on the accelerator as hard as I knew how.

The car shot right, in a wide arc into the alley-thin street, miraculously missing the corner house. *Saved*, I thought. Safe! The pickup, bigger and clumsier and slower, was still on the cross street, its passenger not yet back inside.

The moment was indescribably sweet. I was away, I was safe, I was free. Face it, I was a *genius*!

Maybe not. The moment was interrupted by a sickening crunch of metal. Think of fingernails on a blackboard, then make the nails iron spikes and the board my beloved auto. The effect on the spine and small neck hairs was intense. The effect on the frame and paint and trim of my car was undoubtedly worse.

I had missed the bricks and front steps, but not the wrought-iron fence surrounding a curbside tree.

I drove on, turning furiously again at the end of the street, then again one more block down. Only after four similar maneuvers was I convinced that nobody was behind me any longer.

There was no point heading for the police station now. I had lost the pickup—in every way. I hadn't even ever seen the license plate. I had nothing to report but terror.

And only then, on what felt the very long way home, did I give in to an attack of the girlies and do some serious crying, so in a rather perverse manner I got my wish. After the cry, the tension was almost dissipated.

As they say, be careful what you ask for.

I SLEPT FITFULLY, WAKING FROM A VARIETY OF NIGHTMARES TO check and recheck the locks. By the time I reached school Thursday, I was beyond exhaustion, and at the sight of the school, intensely anxious. What did the pickup driver/ lurker—because I had to believe they were one and the same and that there weren't hordes of people wanting to rid the world of me—have in mind next?

I stood at my mailbox, gingerly extracting what turned out to be innocuous notices. Next to me Harvey Porter snorted and sighed like a proper Type A. "It's one thing if kids forget assignments," he said, almost visibly fuming, "or turn them in late, but it's a whole other issue when they lie. Swear they gave it to me and that I must have lost it." He had a new tic, an involuntary pull at one end of his mouth. During any given academic year, the staff develops enough nervous habits to keep the city's neurologists solvent.

Poor Harvey, teaching all day and running rats at night. "Maybe you should do a unit on the psychology of revenge when lied to?" I suggested. "Kind of a gentle, academic warning."

"I don't know what to do about her."

"Don't cave in," I said as we left the room. Other people's problems were fun. So tidy, so open to solutions, unlike mine. "It's a very familiar ploy. Make her write a new paper."

"It's not a paper that's missing, it's clippings."

I stopped in my tracks. "*Newspaper* clippings?"

"Do you think I ask students for their toenail clippings?"

Perhaps his rats found his wit entertaining. I didn't. "What kind of news stories?" I held my breath.

"That's the point: I've never seen them!"

"Harvey!" He looked startled. I worked to lower my

voice, make it less obviously anxious. "There must have been a topic. What was it?"

"I should have assigned her psychological abuse, because she's a champion at it. Look how she's trying to manipulate me. Bad enough the essay was late—kid said she had the flu—but where's the *evidence*? Can't do research without data. She promised it'd be in my box Monday morning, but here we are at Thursday and there's still nothing, and I am, frankly, furious."

"Teacher violence, am I right?" I could hardly breathe.

"No matter how furious I say I am, I am not out of control." He sounded huffy.

"The report, not you. That's what it was about, am I right?"

"How'd you know?"

I felt light-headed. Giddy. "If kids would only write their names on their work," I said. "I tell them, all the time, but do they remember?"

"Mandy?"

"Your student did hand it in on Monday, but her hand went into my mailbox. Easy mistake. Pepper, Porter . . ."

He looked annoyed that this was a case of stupidity, clumsiness, or poor alphabetizing skills, not of malicious intent. Here was another person who wanted to be angry. I, on the other hand, felt a four-day unintentionally aerobic heartbeat slow down. Almost. There was still the issue of the pickup.

"Could I have it, then?" Harvey said.

"Actually, it's with . . . I, um, took it home by mistake. Tomorrow I'll bring it."

He looked suspicious, as if I perhaps had lied to protect his student, or had not lied but had stolen the clippings. Then he nodded and wandered off toward his homeroom. I climbed the stairs, wishing I could enjoy the moment, experience real relief. After all, nobody had wanted to write my name on that gravestone with the apple for the teacher on it. The articles were only articles. A rose was a rose was a rose, and Wilde was once again proven right. The things one felt absolutely certain about were never true.

Except for the pickup. That had been true, not a case of the wrong mailbox, mistaken identity. The pickup had terrorized me, not Harvey Porter.

Maybe they'd been my statistical terrorists. The ones I had a better chance of being killed by than of getting married. And why didn't that cheer me along with the idea that I might never know what drugged-out stranger had decided to have some malevolent fun with me and my car last night?

I trudged toward my classroom, bothered even by the question of whether I could get the police to release the students' clippings without going through eons of red tape and delay and mortifying confessions to Harvey, Mackenzie, and the entire force.

"Yo, Miss Pepper!" Raffi galumphed up the stairs two at a time and entered the classroom with me. I found myself casing the room, checking for lurking bodies. Pickup trucks. But nobody else was there.

"We booked that place, The Scene?" He smiled excessively. Ah, yes. We had to deal with that, too, in some delicate ego-saving fashion. "It's great, so thanks for finding it. The guy who owns it's weird, though. Like a citified hermit."

Yes. Just so. I could see unsociable Quinn with a long beard, hiding inside the restaurant office.

Raffi looked up at the ceiling. It wasn't all that much above his head and there was no need, except to avoid me. Then he looked down, uncomfortably. If he'd had a cap, he'd have been clutching it in his hands. His expression was suddenly solemn.

Dear God, a confession of undying crushhood. I wasn't up to this. Not today.

"Miss Pepper," he said, in a voice that lacked all his usual buoyancy and charm. "This is really hard to say, but, um, there's something I . . ." He shook his head. "Oh, God," he whispered. "I don't know how to . . . I'm so . . ."

"No need," I assured him. "Besides, the other students will be here any minute. It will keep, won't it?" I thought that had the proper brisk and oblivious quality to it.

Maybe so, but it didn't stop him. "I couldn't sleep all last night," he said. "I kept thinking about you, about—"

"Raffi, I really . . . so much to do. This isn't a . . ." I busied myself erasing already clean boards. I could not face an early morning declaration of love from a boy who was made mostly of knees. I didn't have the psychic energy to coddle his ego, protect him, the way I knew I would have to. Should do. I couldn't spare time to save his face while I was still trying to save my life.

Some other time, please, I silently begged.

"Couldn't stop thinking of what we'd done," he said.

"Come again?" I stopped erasing. "We? You and I?" This was no longer innocent, was it? What fantasies was he entertaining?

He shook his head. "Me and Bart and Les."

I didn't correct his pronoun placement. I was too busy trying to follow what he'd said and where he was leading.

"Last night. On our way back from The Scene, we saw you. Honestly, we were trying to say hello, that was all."

"You?" My formerly clenched bottom jaw went slack. *"You?"*

"Bart really. He was driving. He has a pickup."

"You?"

"Bart. We thought you'd turn around, see us. I waved a few times, too, Miss Pepper." He rubbed at his forehead and looked as if he might faint. "And then, well, I don't like to say this—it's not that I'm criticizing you or anything, but your driving is kind of . . . you're lucky you're not a teenager, or the cops would be on your case. We thought maybe you were, well, maybe you'd been out and had one too many, or . . . so we followed. Thought to stop you. Help."

I could only shake my head.

"So anyway, then I thought maybe Bart was scaring you with the honking and all, and I kept saying it, but he didn't stop. So when we were stopped, I got out of the car, so I could *tell* you, and, well, we saw. That was pretty fast to take a corner, and no offense, but it was a one-way street. The other way. You're really lucky no cop was around." He bit at his bottom lip. "Well, anyway, me and Bart and Les, we want to help pay for the repairs because we think maybe we scared you. Accidentally, of course."

"Scared me?" I hoped the squeak in my voice would be mistaken for incredulity. This was going to cost me, but all of a sudden it wasn't Raffi's face that needed saving. "I'm just a horrible driver, that's all. You had nothing to do with it."

He rewarded me with the goofy smile. It was all I could do to refrain from hugging him and dancing him around the room in a waltz to blissful relief, but the one thing I didn't need at the moment was a further complication.

Nineteen

MACKENZIE HAD FOUND HIMSELF WITH TWO FREE HOURS AND was at my door like a minor miracle when I arrived home. "I am so glad to be alive!" I said. "So glad to see you!"

He seemed startled, but only mildly so. Perhaps it was the norm for females to greet him with hysterical glee. We sat in my living room sipping cinnamon-spiked tea, and I blathered about the student, the psychology project, and my pursuers last night.

He shook his head and had to be talked out of finding some obscure crime—unintentional terrorism was his suggestion—Raffi et al could be charged with. As for the packet of clippings, "That manila envelope is goin' through maybe every known test on earth," he said. "An' if not, then it's already been filed as potential evidence."

I envisioned the poor child's homework entombed in a warehouse amongst thousands of crates, right next to Indiana Jones's Ark of the Covenant.

The doorbell rang. "Tell whoever to go away," Mackenzie muttered. "We need time. Alone."

I agreed. "One sec." But I'd forgotten the invitation I'd issued. "Lizzie!" I said when I opened the door. "Ah, Lizzie."

"You said I should come over." Her red hair was too curly and full of life to seriously sag, but it looked as if it were wilting, and her face resembled inadequately baked puff pastry.

"I thought that once I knew, the fear, the pictures, would stop, or clear up," she responded when I asked how she felt. "Instead, it's like an itch, an almost thing in my brain, a bad, hurting tickle, but when I try to see, it goes to fog. I nearly, nearly remember—and even that scares me."

"Well, then"—Mackenzie slowly extracted himself from the sofa—"sounds like we could all use some fresh air. Nothin's as scary in daylight, is it? Let's find a place and have an ice cream soda, maybe."

"No ice cream for me!" she said. I was amazed. She could do TV spots, become the guru, the idol, of the waist watchers. Make a fortune. "Hi, my name is Lizzie and I'm a dieter. Last night I found out I murdered my mother when I was a preschooler, and I'm having headaches and confusion about the past, and problems about the present, too—a man died Sunday of food that came out of my kitchen. The police suspect me of murder (again!) and business, need I say, is distinctly off. But friends, none of this stops me from dieting."

On second thought, nobody would believe it. Neither did I. I felt myself mentally back off from her before I spoke. "Then coffee, maybe. And a change of scene, definitely. A brisk walk." She still looked fuddled. "Or are you tired? Did you walk all the way here?"

She shook her head. "Took the bus. Two buses. I hate to drive in town."

The three of us ambled out. Talk about ambivalence. I honestly wanted to ease this young woman's discomfort, but I had gotten the distinct feeling last night in the restaurant that the finalists in the Great Culprit Search were the Pepper team and the Beecher team. Them or us. My mother, possibly acting on the behest of my father, vs. Roy, on behalf of or with Lizzie. And when you got right down to Mackenzie's beloved triad—method, opportunity, and motive—they spelled, literally and figuratively, MOM.

So most of me wanted to comfort Lizzie, but some of me simultaneously hoped that en route she would have a revelation and acknowledge that even without knowing the facts of her life, she had been so upset by the sight of Lyle Zacharias that she had taken poisonous seeds her father brought home from Vietnam and put them in his tarts. It would provide such an efficient finality to this unhappy string of events.

And, with the cloud of suspicion removed from their heads—and this was of major importance—the senior Peppers would go home to Florida. Soon.

But of course I felt oppressively guilty about even having those impulses. The only other hope seemed a chance encounter with Sybil or Richard Quinn or Tiffany or Shep McCoy or Terry and/or Janine Wiley, during which some one of them felt an overwhelming need to confess the deed. All of this, of course, had to happen on this walk, while Mackenzie was in tow, because I was sick and tired of tossing theories his way only to have him disbelieve or undermine. He had to be an eyewitness.

We passed a group of Mennonite women in white mesh caps. They wore thick dark capes below which calico hems and black stockings showed. They sang hymns through chattering teeth in front of a newspaper box with an ad for 1-900—HOT—HOT—SEX. The tableau seemed no stranger or more incongruous than anything else lately.

We made small talk, interrupted now and then by Lizzie's need to poke at her new history, like a tongue at the raw socket of a newly extracted tooth. "The old lady— Harriet Zacharias—she knew who I was at the party, didn't she?" she said at one point. "When I said my father's name. I thought she was crazy, but now I understand and I feel so ashamed."

Mackenzie and I said the obvious, feel-better things, knowing full well they couldn't make a dent in her pain.

"Nice day, isn't it?" I said, attempting with absolutely no grace to change gears. Truth was, the air was cold and damp, with only the steely light of a distant sun. "No rain, snow, clouds, or wind," I explained.

"Good weather by default," Mackenzie said. I smiled at him for trying. Lizzie remained preoccupied.

We looked for a new distraction and found it in the store windows, with which we busied ourselves, overpraising, overexcited about everything, from old junk now called Americana to an electric can opener to the ugliest pair of shoes I've ever seen.

And while Mackenzie and I did our back and forth, Lizzie seemed lost on a distant planet. She, too, stared into windows, but seemed not to comprehend what she saw or what we said. Everything had to be carefully repeated and translated for her.

We walked for perhaps a half hour in this curious and unsatisfactory way. "There's a sandwich place over there," I finally said, pointing catercorner across the street. I didn't know what Lizzie wanted, but I was increasingly tense about her, and food is my automatic tranquilizer. "That okay?"

She didn't respond. I turned and saw, first, Mackenzie, watching her, and then Lizzie, who stood in front of a video rental store, staring up at a movie poster in the window. It was placed high, so that cassettes and daily rates could be displayed below it. Lizzie's normally pale skin was ashen, bloodless. Her mouth was slightly open, as if paralyzed halfway to a scream; her unblinking eyes were fixed on the poster, and her breath came in frightened-sounding gasps.

I looked at what held her in thrall. It was the variety of poster my eyes skitter across. Most of the space was taken up by the great overdeveloped back of a man whose white shirt strained across him. His shoulders were enormous, stretching almost all the way across the poster. The angle was from below, so that he loomed and towered and intimidated. The one hand of his that we could see held a gun aimed at the head of a whimpering, cowering woman at his feet. She was, I assumed, begging for mercy. Another woman, in the distance and quite small in the odd perspective, stood with her hands in the air, screaming.

Precisely the sort of movie I run from, no matter how the antifemale sadism and brutality is justified, no matter how Justice triumphs in the end. I don't want those images and ideas transferred into my brain.

Even the poster, designed to titillate and attract, was sickening. It made me feel small and helpless and impotent, like the infantilized women it depicted. Like a child, a baby, a victim.

It was having an even more dramatic effect on Lizzie. Her breathing had become still more uneven and rapid, and she herself more agitated. She shook her head and her hands moved aimlessly in small half circles, tiny motions of holding something at bay.

"I think," Mackenzie whispered, "some of that fog of hers is maybe liftin' for real."

From a movie poster? From *that* movie poster? And then I thought about how insignificant it made me feel.

"I saw," she said in a low, frightened voice. "I saw."

"Saw what?" I asked softly. Mackenzie and I, without consciously planning it, had stationed ourselves one on either side of her. If she toppled, she was safe.

"Him." Her eyes were still on the enormous back and forearm of the murderous man.

I saw him. She had said the same words, over and over, the night Lyle Zacharias died.

"He did it." She lifted her right arm to point directly at the poster.

I thought we'd been talking about Lyle's death. I'd thought wrong.

"Ah." Mackenzie's voice was a purr. "And you saw, didn' you? An' somewhere, y'always knew you'd seen, isn't that so?"

Lizzie nodded, listlessly. "I *saw*." Her voice shrunk, became higher, whinier, more childish. She was down to the diminutive size and ground-level perspective of the invisible viewer in the poster. "He *hurt* her. She *cried*. Gratty cried, too."

Gratty? But Mackenzie skimmed right over that. "Who is she?" he asked in that soft voice that allowed for and accepted anything whatsoever. "Who was hurt? Who cried?"

"Mommy!" she called out. *"My mommy cried!"* She put her hands to her face, covering her eyes, shaking. "I saw!" she cried from between her fingers. "He killed Mommy—

Mother. My mother. I didn't do it, the way my father said!
I didn't, but he told everybody! He lied! Lyle lied. And she
lied!"

"She? Mommy?"

"Oh, God—" Lizzie was wild-eyed, dizzy from her
brain's back-and-forth time travel across two decades,
across the entire span of her life. "I did know her. I called
her Gratty," she said, sounding adult again. "Hattie plus
Grandma, I guess."

"Hattie was there? She saw, too?"

Lizzie nodded. Her eyes welled over. "I feel sick, but not
surprised. When he told me last night, some part of me felt
like it already knew. Knew there were lies. Knew that I
didn't shoot her."

"Maybe you always knew more than you realize even
now," Mackenzie said. "Sunday night, you said that you'd
seen him and that you didn't do it. Several times you said
it. An' that was three days before your daddy told you what
had happened years ago."

"Yes," she whispered. "I don't understand, because I
didn't know I knew. Maybe that little bit came out all by
itself." She shook her head, her features pensive again.

Mackenzie's face had set, and I feared his brain had done
the same. "She doesn't mean she *knew*," I said. "Not consciously. Not the way you're implying. Do you, Lizzie?"

"I don't know. Why'd I say those things if I didn't?"

"You once knew, long ago, but then you blocked it out.
That's the same as not knowing." Mackenzie glared at me,
but I shook my head in annoyance. She didn't realize where
he was leading her.

"But now," she said, "I wonder if I always, on some
level . . . as soon as he walked into the kitchen, I felt sick."
I remembered, too, how she'd been when Lyle put his finger up in a mock pistol position. He'd been trying to remember my mother's name and cocked his hand like a gun.
And Lizzie had become nearly catatonic.

"I had nightmares for years," she said. "A bald, bearded
man and a gigantic noise and screams and redness."

"Dreams are one thing, but you didn't *consciously know*, because if you did—"

"Appreciate it if you'd cease tellin' her what she remembers or knew," Mackenzie said to me.

His summons to cease and desist shut me up long enough to let my central nervous system absorb the shock of what Lizzie had said. Because while revelation via movie poster is not quite orthodox, I believed her the instant the words were out. And I knew Mackenzie had, too. Our only differences were about what to make of its nuances.

Lyle Zacharias had killed his wife, and Hattie had witnessed it. An accident he could have explained, should have owned up to. Instead he took the easy way by lying and soiling a child's life. Sickening. Lyle Zacharias was one enormous lie. He had stolen a lot of lives, cheated and rearranged and destroyed, unconcerned with the damage he left in his wake. What was it to burden an orphaned little girl with—whether or not she consciously knew it—a matricide she hadn't committed?

"Lizzie," Mackenzie murmured, "Mandy here has to head elsewhere, and I'm not of a mind to leave you alone, so why don't you come along with me? I think maybe coffee and food would help. Plus a good long talk."

"Only coffee?" I said softly. "You promise?"

Lizzie was still mesmerized by the poster. I didn't think she could hear us.

Mackenzie nodded, all blue-eyed innocence. "Coffee," he said. "What are you insinuatin'?"

I couldn't tell if I was looking at Mackenzie the compassionate friend or Mackenzie the complete cop. I reminded the man, whichever one was facing me, of Lizzie's right to a lawyer and due process, should the need arise.

"Well," he said, drawling the word out into multisyllables, "I was plannin' to skip the lawyer and rely on the rack. It's real good for confessions, 'specially when you add a good lashin', and the fingernail-puller-outer gizmo, too. Just love to hear them scream, you know."

"I'm sorry," I said. "I didn't mean it that way."

He shook his head. "I try real hard to find out the truth, and I try real hard to do it legally. Thought you knew me by now. Oh, boy, do we need time alone."

It was the badge. Wherever it was, in his wallet or home in a drawer, it had the power to blind me. I apologized again.

"Accepted," he said. "What I think we all do now is move on."

So we did. He and Lizzie across the street to the coffee shop, and I off for dinner with the folks.

I went in pursuit of my battle-scarred car and tried to puzzle out the day. Once again I'd gotten what I'd requested. Something akin to a confession, witnessed by Mackenzie.

Why, then, did I feel so rotten about it?

WHAT AN ANTICLIMAX! FROM THE HIGH DRAMA OF REVELATION to . . . dinner in the suburbs. Ah well, perhaps I could cut short my mother's inevitable nuptial nagging by telling her, finally, how close her neck had been to the noose all week. And for the family at large, I'd have the painfully dramatic story of Lizzie and the movie ad.

That would have to wait until Karen was in bed.

Karen. Damn. I had to return to my house. My niece had been feeling overlooked and miffed since the appearance of her sibling. Assuming that the interloper in question, Alexander, was too new to notice inequities, I'd been bringing Karen special treats when I could. For today I'd bought a superdeluxe minisuitcaseful of felt-tipped pens. And I'd left it home.

The gift-wrapped box was on the kitchen counter. I grabbed it and glanced at the clock. Seconds to go till five, when traffic moved toward critical mass.

Macavity welcomed me with an anxious trot to his empty food dish, but he couldn't hold my attention. My clock-glance had swept on and caught the blinking semaphor of the phone answering machine. I will consider myself fully adult when my pulse no longer quickens at the sight of a waiting message, when I actually learn from the sheer force of experience that the message will not be news that I've won the lottery or been granted the MacArthur Genius Award for undeveloped, unsuspected potential. Or anything else very exciting, to be honest.

But as of now, rationally or not, my heart still flutters at the possibilities in that winking message light.

This possibility turned out to be my sister. My heart de-fluttered. It appeared that my mother had taken the train into town that morning, planning to spend an entire day at the Philadelphia Flower and Garden Show and be back at Beth's by five. "But she called to say she wanted to visit Hattie Zacharias afterward, and that maybe you could pick her up on your way out here. Could you? Call me so I'll know you heard this message."

I called. I agreed. It wasn't relevant that Society Hill was the opposite direction from the Main Line and Beth's Gladwyne house, or that now, for certain, the downtown streets would be impassably clogged.

I had some time, and my mother was notoriously slow at closure, anyway. Her leave-taking speed record had been clocked at twenty-nine minutes from the first good-bye to her actual exit. Might as well feed the beast who was still methodically, nervously, rubbing against my ankles. "Calm down," I told him. "This is not the day you starve to death. And why don't you eat kibble if you're so hungry?" Useless rhetoric on my part. Macavity considers dry food an occasional hobby, not a meal.

I plopped the remnants of today's canned delight onto his plate and felt a misplaced maternal rush as his purr reached all the way up to my ears.

My sympathy for Hattie Zacharias had dissipated given what Lizzie said. I mentally ran and reran the scene with the gun discharging and killing Cindy Zacharias while both her daughter and Lyle's stepmother watched in horror. I pit-ied everyone at the grisly scene. But I could not forgive Hattie for collusion and lies, for sparing Lyle embarrass-ment by burdening a near-baby, already traumatized by loss, with matricide. And I didn't care if Lizzie did or didn't know the facts until recently. They were there, buried in her brain. She was expending valuable energy in keeping them buried. Besides, other people believed the deception and thought of her in the wrong way. She had carried the burden even if she hadn't known what was weighing her down.

I picked up my bag and pulled out my car keys, but the fatal scene played nonstop in my mind. Only the faces weren't the smiling ones that might precede a pure accident. They were upset, strained, and I had a sense that somebody had told me they were that way, but who?

It couldn't be anything Sybil had said, because she'd never known Cindy. Janine had only alluded to Cindy by mentioning her husband's attraction to redheads. And all I could remember from Terry Wiley was praise of Cindy's kindness and goodness. Maybe I was making the whole thing up, rewriting the script to suit me as I liked. I erased the phone message, reset the machine, and said adieu to the cat.

Then I remembered. Richard Quinn had said it. He wasn't a man I'd think of when dealing with words, so I was nearly at the door before it came back. He'd thought she was too emphatic about being holier than thou. Argued the last time Quinn was with them, right before he left the partnership.

Right before . . . the inside of my brain felt like a pinball machine, small hard pellets pinging against the skull, spinning off in new trajectories. Right before Quinn left the partnership, meant . . .

I rushed back to the kitchen divider. "Excuse me," I told Macavity, who was washing up after dinner. I opened the cabinet behind him and pulled out the telephone directory. U-V-W. Wiley. Too many altogether. Wiley, T. Wiley, T.B. Good Lord! Why would anybody want to be known by those initials? Tessa—Telford—Thea—I knew he taught at South Philly, but did he live in the city? Was his number listed? Theodore—Terrence—Eureka!

"Please," I whispered into the receiver. "Be the right Terry. Please."

It was. Or almost. "May I speak with Terry?" I asked after I heard Janine's whine even in her *hello*.

The whine metastasized after I identified myself. "What do you want with him?" she demanded. Her voice threatened to short-circuit the phone wires. "I thought I told you—"

"I need to ask one quick question."

"About what?"

"About—About something that came up on Junior Journalism Day."

"Look, lady." Her voice, like her skin, was muddy.

"It's important."

She inhaled loudly, as if steeling herself for a repulsive and difficult task. "Terrrrrr*eee*!" she screamed, so close to the receiver that it was deafening. Did she think the man was here, with me, on the other end of the line? *"Phone!"*

Sometimes you get quick peeks into other people's lives. Just a word or two, like those she was shrieking, and you know too much about the anger that dusted every surface of their life.

Another phone lifted somewhere in their house. Janine made no effort to pretend she was hanging up. Her aggrieved breaths were quite audible. "Hello?" Terry Wiley's anxious voice said. "Who is this?"

"Mandy Pepper. Remember me from Junior Journalism Day?" That was for her benefit, not his.

"Of course. Nice to . . ." And then, maybe, he decided it wasn't all that nice hearing from me again, after all.

"Remember you were talking about . . . um . . ." The hell with it. Let Janine have a fit. There was no way around the name. "Remember how you said that Cindy Zacharias—" I heard an angry gasp from the second receiver. So did Terry. Before he could say anything, I plowed ahead. "—was a good friend of Janine and yours?" I hoped that placated her. "And that she was the kind of person who cared about people and about what was right? Isn't that what you told me?"

"Maybe. I don't remember what words I said. But sure, she was like that."

A person who cared about what was right. He had said

that. And Quinn had said she was self-righteous about it. And that Lyle and she had been fighting right before he left. Before Lyle terminated the partnership. On the eve of *Ace of Hearts*, which Terry Wiley had written back in high school.

"Why?" Terry asked. "What does it matter?"

"What I need to know is this. Did Cindy—" Another ridiculous gasp from Janine. Twenty years after the object of her husband's infatuation was dead, she was still in a state of perpetual outrage. "Did Cindy Zacharias know that you were the real author of *Ace of Hearts*?"

Heavy two-receiver silence before he spoke. "She'd seen the original, yes. My version. Found it on Lyle's desk. She saw the resemblance, even if the jury couldn't, later. But of course, by then, the original was missing."

"Thank you. Thank you both." After I hung up I put my elbows on the kitchen counter and held my heavy head with both hands to avoid having it fall off.

Cindy knew Lyle had plagiarized, and Lyle knew that she knew. And he also knew that given his lack of talent and ideas, the pilfered work was his one chance. He'd managed to get out of his partnership, to keep his stolen jewel all for himself, except that Cindy knew and was going to ruin his one chance with her ethics. And they fought about it. Quinn said so. And so had Lizzie, who'd said that her mommy had cried and cried.

And nothing at all had been an accident, particularly Cindy Zacharias's death, which had been murder, impure and not at all simple.

I FOUND MYSELF RIDING UP THE ELEVATOR IN HATTIE ZACHARI-as's building without any memory of the drive to Society Hill or the process of parking my car. I had been on automatic pilot while my mind coped with questions, poorly sorted facts, and unreadable meanings. If Cindy had been murdered, then . . . why couldn't I follow the logical string to its end, to Lyle's murder?

One thing was for sure: if Cindy had been murdered, then Hattie's complicity was even more detestable.

The old woman was evil. As for Lyle, the thought of him revolted me.

Lizzie, poor child victim, knowingly or not, had evened the scales. An eye for an eye, a poisoned son for a murdered mother.

Lyle Zacharias had been tried and found guilty and already executed, and the case was, for all intents and purposes, closed. All that was left was to help Lizzie legally and emotionally.

The elevator stopped on every floor. The building seemed exclusively tenanted by elderly and slightly infirm people who entered and exited with measured movements. I tried not to be impatient, but I was eager to get up to the apartment and out of there. Hattie now felt like pollution.

But I wouldn't be satisfied until she told the truth. I wanted her to publicly clear Lizzie of the burden of guilt. Nobody could make up for what had already been done, but somebody had to start undoing its long-term effects, and Hattie was the only somebody left who could.

My problem was deciding how I was going to convince a woman whose entire life had been dedicated to protecting, to pathologically overprotecting, the boy and man she'd mothered, to discard a twenty-year-old lie and to posthumously tarnish forever that same man's memory and name.

And I had to do it quickly, too, or my mother and I would be late for dinner, which would mean real trouble.

Twenty

MARIA, THE HOUSEKEEPER, OPENED THE DOOR. SHE STOOD AT the entryway looking as impassively sullen as she had earlier in the week.

"I'm here to pick up my mother," I said.

Nothing.

"Mrs. Pepper. Bea?"

More nothing.

"In there."

She didn't care, and eloquently but wordlessly conveyed that while she moved aside to let me in.

At least friend Alice didn't appear to be in residence.

My mother was on an easy chair at right angles to the sofa, where Hattie was again swathed in her foamy soft afghan. She looked different than she had on Monday. Not better, but more relaxed. Resigned, perhaps. Accepting.

Maria silently entered and stared at me. "Coat." It was almost a grunt.

"I'm only staying a moment," I said.

My mother raised her eyebrows. "Five minutes, perhaps, Mandy?"

We were disappointing each other. I was not behaving politely by her lights, nor she by mine. Nonetheless, I conceded. I pulled off my coat and handed it to Maria.

Both Hattie and my mother sipped from teacups. At Hattie's urging, I settled onto the armchair across from my mother's, at the other end of the love seat. Within seconds the silent Maria returned, put a teacup in front of me and filled it with an aromatic liquid.

"It's a blend," Hattie said. "My favorite herbs and spices. Lyle had it made up for me." She blinked rapidly several times, then took a deep breath and nodded, as if to reassure herself that she was once again composed.

My mother and she seemed in the middle of some inconsequential collective memory. Something about a picnic twenty-two years ago. I only half heard them. My mind still seethed with accusations I wanted to hurl at the old woman.

Tell her, my brain would flash so heatedly I could feel myself flush. Then I'd almost shiver and ask myself, Why? To what purpose? She's old and she's already lost him. Besides, it would be best to tape the confession or have a witness present. And then again, the banshee howl of: because I want to tell her right now that I *know*. Because I want to stop the lies!

Lyle, lies. Not much difference between the words.

"And how was your day?" my mother suddenly asked me with a wide, social smile. "Everything okay?"

She wanted to include me in this stupid happy chat. Maybe I should ruin it by honestly telling Hattie in particular how my day had been.

My mother looked worried about me, vaguely hurt. Tea talk was required, so she, who found silence not only rude, but unnatural, rushed in with words to hide my social failings.

Across the room the mask grimaced at me. Balinese, I thought she'd said. Powerful, but unsettling. The Queen of Hearts, Hattie had called it.

There were an awful lot of hearts involved, weren't there? *Ace of Hearts*, and this mask, the Queen of Hearts. The queen of hearts who made the tarts, perhaps. Ah, no. My mother was the one who made the tarts.

The jingle stuck in my brain again, and worse, I heard the rhyme in my niece's revolting rap-style Mother Goose.

The queen of hearts she made some tarts all on a summer's day.

Not summer, though. The dregs of winter. Out, out, damned rhyme. Why wouldn't it cease and desist?

The knave of hearts he stole those tarts . . .

The mental prickling became nearly unbearable.

The things one feels absolutely certain about are never true.

Okay. I needed help. I was on overload, bogged down with unrelated quotes and infantile rhymes. I needed the human equivalent of downloading.

"Mandy, is everything okay?" my mother asked.

That was her social equivalent of Final Warning. "Just tired," I said. I gave in. I would actively converse. "Actually, something funny happened to me. Funny in retrospect only. You know my class is making a play out of *The Picture of Dorian Gray*, and there's this line in it about how whatever you are absolutely certain about is never true. So I've been absolutely certain lately that an unknown kid was out to hurt me."

My mother gasped. She is a good audience and a superior parent. Being annoying does not cancel the other traits out.

"I'd gotten these papers, see. And then last night, a pickup truck followed me and I was really scared, but it turns out . . ." I felt inappropriately agitated, a sensation somewhere between annoyance and apprehension. My foot fidgeted and I was momentarily confused. "But you see," I rushed on, "none of it meant what it seemed to mean. Nobody wanted to hurt me—it was all a mistake!"

I knew that I'd missed the point, told the story badly, but too many electrical impulses were fighting for space in my brain. Nothing was coming through clearly, except the agitation.

Hattie looked at me oddly, as did my mother.

"Well, see," I said, "the boy who'd been following me didn't want to hurt me. In fact, he thought I was in trouble with my driving and he was trying to protect me. Isn't that funny? None of it was what it appeared to be!"

The words echoed. Hattie pulled back more deeply into the sofa pillows. My mother continued to study me, her forehead wrinkled.

"I told it wrong, didn't I? Don't worry. The point is, nobody wanted to hurt me even though the one thing I was absolutely certain of was that somebody *was* after me. But Oscar Wilde was right—it wasn't true." I shivered. The words hung in the air between us, like cobwebs.

Impolite, I belatedly realized, to joke about my paranoid fantasies in the house of a man somebody had truly wanted to hurt. "Sorry," I said softly.

But. The images, the poems, the knave, the play, the tarts and Lyle, Lizzie and the movie poster, all still spun in flinty tracks in my brain.

I felt on the verge of hysteria, afraid I might topple with the smallest push, and the anxiety that had been pulsing through me since I began my story manifested itself the way it usually does, with awesome, cavernous hunger. There was a large crystal candy dish on the coffee table in front of us. It held a pyramid of what looked like bourbon balls—dates and nuts and other yummies soaked in liqueur and rolled in confectioner's sugar. A pop in the mouth, a quick energy rush, perhaps even serenity. "May I?" I asked Hattie.

"Of course," she said. "Have two."

My mother looked surprised. I expected warnings about spoiled dinners and sweets before meals.

But even better than forbidden fruit is a forbidden rum ball.

I thought of Lizzie—falling to pieces, but managing to keep those pieces fat-free. Unlike her, I gave lip service to dieting and lip action to ingesting. In that, I was kin to the dead Lyle. If he hadn't added gluttony to his list of sins, if he hadn't broken his diet resolve and gobbled that tart, he'd still be around. But who cared? He was a louse. He'd gotten his just desserts. Literally.

I defiantly popped the candy in my mouth. "Delicious," I said.

My mother looked relieved. "I've been trying to contain

myself, but if you're having one, then I'll indulge, too." There is nothing a woman likes better than another woman with less self-control than she has.

I watched my mother choose her candy, but I did so from a peculiar distance. Everything around me had receded and miniaturized and grown dim, and all I could hear clearly was the deafening echo of my thought a few seconds back.

Lyle had been dieting. He'd been loud, insistent, adamant about it.

Why would anyone *expect* to get to him through an extra dessert when he'd said he wouldn't touch it?

Because he was a chronic liar, that's why.

No. A chronic liar would be too hard to anticipate. That knave of hearts had stolen that tart, all on a winter's day. It and its poisoned mate had been meant for someone else, just like the collection of clippings in my mailbox had been.

Oh, God, was I going crazy? Basing a theory on Mother Goose and a high school student's misplaced assignment?

"Mandy?" my mother said, but I shook my head. I had to think. Had to.

Assume, then, that nobody intended the poison for Lyle. That answered the question of why the killer hadn't waited until Lyle went home with his tin of tarts and ate the poisoned one at random.

It also made me disoriented and light-headed.

"Marvelous candies," my mother said. "Taste home-made, too."

"They are. I've had quite a few myself. That little cook from the place we had the party—The Boarding House, Lizzie? She made them. Brought them over to me minutes before you got here, Bea. A condolence gift, she said." Hattie spoke mildly.

The room pulsed, colors and textures bursting from the walls then sinking into them. Lizzie couldn't have brought candies or anything else here one or even two hours ago, because she'd been with Mackenzie and me since right after school.

And there it was. Simple once I stopped looking at it from a fixed position.

Nobody had wanted to kill Lyle Zacharias, but somebody—Hattie Zacharias—had wanted to kill Lizzie.

Completely identifying with Lyle, Hattie had just as much to lose as he if and when Lizzie Beecher Chapman unearthed her buried memories. Hattie had found out who the girl was early on, as soon as Lizzie said Roy Beecher's name. Hattie had known, and had seen the girl's bizarre reaction to the sight of Lyle. Had recognized the danger in that dawning recognition and had determined to squelch it.

"She's a good little cook," Hattie now said in that same bemused and distant voice. "That's probably why she's so plump. Frankly, a fat girl is a bad ad for a restaurant. Like a warning, don't you think? She should get another job." She laughed, wheezing over her nasty humor.

And that was the last part of the puzzle. Hattie had no way of comprehending how resolute Lizzie was about shedding pounds. Hattie must have been sure that, left alone with the tarts, Lizzie—in just the way Roy had—would at least nibble at them. So she packed them so full of poison, there was no surviving a tart.

How odd that she'd been sure Lizzie would cheat, but had believed her pride and joy when he insisted that he was counting calories and wouldn't touch the tarts until the next day. He'd been a liar and conniver in every corner of his life, but he'd kept his promises to her—the travel and the luxuries—and that was all she chose to notice. "If he says he'll do something, he does it," she'd told us. She'd believed it. And in the end her own blindness and dishonesty about him did her in, because after all his enormous crimes, one tiny infraction, and one large sweet tooth, killed the only thing she loved.

I felt no pity or sympathy. "Mom," I said, "we have to—"

Hattie looked at her watch.

My mother surprised me by standing up without protest. "I apologize," she told Hattie. "I barged in without a warning, and I've taken up too much of your time. You take care now."

"Glad you came," Hattie said. "I've been lonely. Alone all day, except of course for Lizzie, but she only stayed awhile. Mostly was here to drop off the—"

"That isn't true. Lizzie wasn't here at all," I said. "Get up, Mom. We're leaving right now."

"Mandy!" my mother said.

Hattie seemed more amused than insulted. She checked her watch again. "Of course she was here. While Maria was at the store. Look." She pointed, rather vaguely, toward the table. The Boarding House's business card was tucked into the bottom of the pyramid of candies.

"You're making it all up. You probably have lots of those cards from planning the party. It means nothing. Besides, why are you even saying this? What's the point?"

"Now, Mandy," my mother said gently, "why would Aunt Hattie make up something silly like that?" She was treating me like a child who had misbehaved, chiding my bad manners. Soon I'd be sent to my room for rudeness to my elders. My hackles went up.

"Hattie knows the point, which is that Lizzie knows things Hattie doesn't want anyone else to know."

"An awful lot of *knows* in there, Mandy. Could you explain again?" my mother said plaintively.

I looked instead at Hattie. "Lizzie remembered it all. You must have read about adults suddenly remembering buried childhood traumas. Something triggers it, and like that—" I snapped my fingers.

Hattie made a choking sound, fluttered her hands and breathed in raggedly.

"You've upset her," my mother said. "Poor dear. Hattie, please excuse Mandy, she's cranky and—"

"Mother!"

"I have to—" Hattie sounded winded, exhausted, frighteningly so, and there was a terrible sense of familiarity about her behavior. Déjà death.

"Have to make call," Hattie said, struggling to shape the words. "Explain."

"Mother, whatever this is about—we have to get out of here."

"But if she's *ill*—"

Hattie winced as she lifted a portable telephone from the end table and punched three numbers.

She might be calling information, but I doubted it, and the only other three-digit code I knew was 911, Emergency. Hattie winced, half closed her eyes, put her hand to her throat and shuddered. "Help," she said into the receiver. Her voice was hoarse. "I'm poisoned. Poison candy. Help." She hung up.

I hadn't been getting it. Not well enough. *Poison candy.*

My mother's mouth was half open, and slowly her eyes moved to the candy dish and then to me.

The feeling of impending death is by and large indescribable, probably for logical, Darwinian reasons. After all, why get verbal when you won't live to use the words? I stood gape-mouthed and wordless, straining to hear an approaching siren outside, many floors below. I heard nothing.

I was going to die. Killed by candy, my weapon of choice. By a nervous habit of stuffing my mouth when anxious. In fact, if the terrible truth be known, I was now so overwhelmed with near-hysteria that the temptation to grab another poisonous bonbon was close to irresistible.

"Don't want to live," Hattie gasped. "Won't."

I was finally galvanized into action. I grabbed the portable phone and dialled 911 again. "Three stretchers," I said. "Two more of us ate the poison." After I hung up, I panicked—they wouldn't come, would write it off as a crank call from the terminally insane. Maybe they'd be right.

I felt fine, I reminded myself. I was still alive. It had taken Lyle a solid half hour or more to die. Within the hour, I thought Mackenzie had told me. There was time. Hattie had a long head start on us.

"Lizzie's fault," Hattie whispered hoarsely.

"Yours." The mind boggled. She was calmly murdering

my mother and me, not to mention herself, while framing somebody else.

"Loved him." Her eyes welled over. "He saved me. Gave me everything."

I bent over and pulled Lizzie's card out from the candies. "They aren't going to find this. Even if we all die, I won't let you do this to an innocent person."

She shook her head and looked as smug as a woman in obvious pain could. "Don't need card. Told Maria and called Alice. Said how nice Lizzie was. Alice such a gossip. Police believe them."

Alice would adore being the official bearer of bad tidings. "She told me how *kind* that dreadful Lizzie was to her," she'd say. "Snake in the grass, if you ask me. Poor old dear. I was Hattie's bosom pal, you know."

Mackenzie was already predisposed to believe Lizzie was the murderer. Would he readily accept a second murder from her?

Would he ask Maria and Alice precisely at what time the rum balls had arrived so that he'd spot the lie? Or would he be too overcome by my death to think rationally? I wasn't sure which scenario I preferred.

My mother appeared to have worked it through in slow motion. "We're poisoned, too," she said dully. "Like Lyle. The same thing."

Hattie nodded.

"How did you do it?" I demanded. "Where did you get the seeds?" What to say while waiting for your paramedic.

"Guate . . . ma . . . la . . ." Hattie was having trouble with her syllables. She gasped and put her head back on the pillows. "Collect . . . interesting . . . wanted to be . . ."

Wanted to be a naturalist. I remembered, but her desires, realized or squelched were at the bottom of my current priorities. What I wanted was information. "I mean that night," I said. "Where did you get the seeds? You wouldn't have brought them with you."

"Home."

Home? And then I remembered. My mother had wanted to fix Hattie up with somebody, but she had gone home—to

rest, we were told. Her apartment, full of pods and specimens, was only minutes from Queen Village. Maybe, less
of a purist than Lizzie, she believed in canned whipped
cream, and even had one on hand to stick in her purse. If
not, it was no big problem stopping the taxi at a conve-
nience store. "After the paramedics get here and save you,"
I shouted, "I'll make sure you go to jail!"

She shook her head. "Can't save me. Heart too old."

"You—" I sputtered. "You are the most—" There were
no words.

"Then Mandy," my mother said in that same, nearly par-
alytic voice, "Mandy—you ate the candy, too." Her voice
took on more color and energy and she glared at Hattie.
"You let *my daughter* eat poison!" She stood up. I thought
she was going to strangle the old lady, but instead she simply stood there, looking as stunned as if someone had just
clubbed her. And in a way, someone named Hattie had.
"My *child*!" she said. "My *child*! You gave her poison!"

"Mom, be careful. Take it easy." I had this theory that
you shouldn't do anything physical, as if by sitting like
lumps we could slow the flow of poisonous blood through
our veins. I thought I had seen a Western where that was
recommended for snakebite, but maybe not. Still, I couldn't
think of what else to do. "Sit back down. Don't forget," I
said, "you ate it, too."

She gasped, and I wasn't sure if it was terror or the beginnings of the poison's deadly course. "I can't believe it!"
she said, blinking back tears. "You hurt my *daughter*!"

How long did it take paramedics to arrive? I thought of
all the hostile drivers I'd seen blocking ambulances, making
their path even more difficult. And it was maximum rush
hour. And then there was the impossibly slow elevator.

We were dead meat.

"*Spock!*" my mother screamed while rushing to a door
off the living room.

The poison had gone directly to her mind.

"*Spock!*" my mother shouted again as the door swung
behind her. Forget the still-blood theory. I bolted across the
living room, duplicating her exit.

"Mom!" I said when I was in the kitchen. "Please. Don't panic. The ambulance will be here any second."

But she was busy, running water at the sink, shaking something. And then she turned around, holding two glasses of murky water. *"Drink!"* she shouted.

"Shhhh. Calm down. The paramedics will be—"

"Drink! Right now. Immediately! This is your mother speaking!"

"It looks awful. What is it?"

"Emetics! First aid, poisons." She spoke rapidly, doubletime. " 'Vomiting is the best first-aid treatment for suspected poisoning with most substances but not the following: kerosene, gasoline, benzene, cleaning fluids—' "

"That's the Spock you meant? Doctor? You *memorized* it?" Beth and I had often privately joked about that possibility, but we'd never meant it seriously.

" 'If your child is old enough or cooperative enough to do something unpleasant, have him drink a glassful of water to which has been added a tablespoonful of salt—' Mandy, you are definitely old enough to do something unpleasant. Are you cooperative enough?"

"You did! You memorized him!"

"Memorized everything in the emergency sections." She handed me a glass. "Drink. Emergencies happen away from home. Drink more. That's why they call them emergencies. Wanted to protect you girls wherever we—so afraid I wouldn't know— *Drink all of it!"*

And I did. Disgustingly salty water. An entire eight ounces. She watched me down it, then handed me the second glass. "Just in case," she said. We were now beyond Spock. This one was sudsy with dish detergent. "He mentions both methods," she explained.

"One *or* the other, maybe?"

"Drink! Can't be too safe!"

After she was convinced that I'd done my bit, my mother chugalugged her share. I had known she wouldn't begin till I finished. In a crash, she would ignore the airline's warnings about putting on your oxygen mask before your child's. It would go against her basic fiber. Children first, and nothing else a close second.

Maria's impassivity gave around the mouth as she curled a lip in scorn. She did not approve of our drinking habits. "Oh, Maria," I said, "you ain't seen nothing yet." And to clarify my meaning, I then had to rush to the sink and be sick, to be joined within moments by my mother, who said "Sorry" between each retch.

Long after we'd first bent over, we heard a bell and pounding on the door. The medics had finally made it through the congested streets and up the sluggish elevator.

Our heroes. And to think I'd spent a portion of my childhood and perhaps adulthood believing that rescue meant Prince Charming on a white steed, not panting paramedics with purgatives.

However, I didn't need either version's services. Dr. Spock had done the trick for the Peppers.

I staggered rather woozily into the living room, where Hattie was being hooked to wires and tubes.

"Hey!" I shouted at her. Even my mother didn't squelch my rudeness at this stage.

Hattie's eyes fluttered open.

"Look! We're alive," I said. "No thanks to you."

She closed her eyes. It didn't matter to her one way or the other. We had wandered into her plan. We weren't a part of it.

One of the paramedics turned and faced me. "Lady," he said, "give us a break."

"Your trap for Lizzie isn't going to work, Hattie!"

Despite all its preexisting wrinkles, the old woman's forehead creased noticeably. At some level, I knew, she heard me. I also knew this was cruel and unusual punishment, because all she had left was the illusion that she had set matters right, but she wasn't entitled to that satisfaction. "The police won't believe Maria or Alice or you, because Lizzie was with them the whole time! Do you hear? She has the one perfect alibi on earth. The game is over, Hattie, and you *lose*."

"Lady!" the paramedic said. "Have some respect. This woman's in bad shape."

It was obvious. Her skin was parchment dry and pale, and her breath, no matter what they did, raspy and sparse. She'd been right about her heart not being able to take the strain of the poison. "I'm finished," I said. But not out of respect. Respect is earned, and she had forfeited her share long ago.

On the other hand, my mother had won and rewon her share countless times. I hugged her. Overprotective, definitely. Annoying, absolutely. Interfering, most positively. But there were worse arrangements between people.

The paramedics insisted that we be observed at the hospital. After showing no symptoms, we were discharged, but not before my mother lectured the entire staff on how much time and energy Dr. Spock, salt water, and soap could save them.

"Were you telling the truth when you said that Lizzie was with the police?" my mother asked as we made our way back to where I'd parked.

"Didn't you teach me never to lie? She's with Mackenzie. He's been involved with this case from the beginning." I rooted for my car keys in my purse.

"The case is solved now, sweetie."

I unlocked the car doors. "We're a good team."

My mother slipped into the passenger side and looked at me. "Why don't we detour to the station, then?" she said.

I started the car. "Fine. It might be nice, you know, to have Lizzie meet Dad after all these years. Nice for both of them."

She nodded. "That, too."

"Too?"

She sighed. "As I said, darling, the point is that the case is solved, so your young man—"

"Mother, he's absolutely not my—"

"—now has the evening free, and I'll bet he can come to dinner after all."

Now I understood the meaning of my recent existence. It had been no more than Bea Pepper's unique, hair-raising method of getting me a dinner date. Motherhood to the nth degree, but who was I to knock it?

"Which is lovely," she continued, "because—"

There was a further agenda. I held my breath.

"—I was afraid we wouldn't have the chance to spend real time with him—"

"But Mom—"

"—before we leave tomorrow."

"Tomorrow? Florida?"

She nodded.

"No problem." I put the car into gear and we were off. I just love happy endings.

Available now in
bookstores everywhere.

HOW I SPENT
MY SUMMER
VACATION
by Gillian Roberts

Published in hardcover by Ballantine Books.

Read on for the intriguing
opening pages from
HOW I SPENT MY SUMMER VACATION . . .

One

THE SCHOOL YEAR IS MONTHS SHORTER THAN THE CALEN-dar's, which makes people think a teacher's job is easy, cushy. Actually, summer vacation is a public safety requirement. Rising temperatures bring the unstable mix of teachers and pupils to a near-lethal boil and necessitate a cool-down period. Otherwise, there'd be no survivors with whom to start future endurance experiments.

Two days into my vacation, I was still on the critical list—battle-scarred and shell-shocked—and afraid the condition might be chronic.

I felt so miserable I knew I needed to do a lot of thinking about my life—lives, professional and personal—and what I was doing wrong with them. The trouble was, whenever I so much as thought about the need to think, my brain developed hives and I was filled with a sense of futility and dread.

"You look horrible," my friend Sasha said. We were taking what I had hoped would be a restorative, old-fashioned Sunday stroll through Ye Olde Colonial

Philadelphia. "Why don't you get a real job, with real people?" she asked. "What is the point of growing up if you then revisit adolescence over and over for the rest of your life? Get a job with adults!" Sasha waved her arms for emphasis.

I tried to imagine a worklife with peers. People who saw me as an equal, not as an obstacle to be outwitted. People who weren't always testing me or preparing defenses, excuses, or requests. Partners. Team players.

Power lunches. Networking. Ladder-climbing.

Give me a break.

We reached Head House Square, former meat and produce market, current star of camera-ready Colorful Colonial Philadelphia. A table under a cappuccino sign was available. This wasn't a stroke of luck, but indication that summer weather—even real spring weather—had not yet staggered into Philadelphia. Still, we sat down.

It was chilly for early June, and lounging outside was purely symbolic, but I was on my summer vacation and I was going to behave as such. I shivered, ordered, and looked around. The wide cobbled street in front of us was bisected by the former marketplace. Where Colonial chickens and pigs were once hawked there now were objets d'craft: silver bangles, nouveau-native earrings, tooled leather backpacks, and recidivist tie-dyed garments. Whole cycles of fashions and fads had died and been resuscitated while I tried in vain to convince teenagers to punctuate.

I wondered if some day our current markets—say, 7-Elevens—would be converted into craft-laden tourist destinations, with yet more tie-dyed shirts filling shelves now holding Ding Dongs.

250

"I'll be fine," I told Sasha, who was urging vocational counseling. "I need to decompress. I guess I just want to be *alone*. Present company and present moment excluded, of course."

The waitress brought us cappuccinos and a plate of biscotti.

"You *vant* to be a *lawn*," Sasha drawled. "Forgotten your Garbo clichés?"

"But I vouldn't *vant* to be a *lawn*. Given my druthers, I'd *vant* to be a *beach*."

"There are those who think you are one already, Mandy. Present company not necessarily excluded."

A beach. The image shimmered in front of me. The ocean. Nothing was more restorative than the primal soup. Saltwater slapping onto sand while seabirds shrieked and circled . . . Even imagining it made me feel better. I saw myself alone, tall dunes behind me, a book on my lap, salt air and solitude rejuvenating me.

"On the other hand," Sasha said, "the plus of your job is the humongous vacation. Tomorrow, I'm back to work, while you—"

"As if ninety percent of your daily life weren't a variation on playtime, while mine—"

"Beach, beach, beach," she said softly.

"Sorry. But the trick is, we're paid too little to enjoy that humongous vacation. I have two weeks," I explained, "before I have to teach summer school."

"I forgot. Too bad. So what are you doing with them?"

I shook my head. "Nothing. Cleaning closets." I wouldn't be teaching summer school if I'd had the funds to do anything else. The seabirds circling my imaginary beach turned into winged dollar signs and fluttered out of reach. What economically advantaged sadist started the myth that the best things in life were free?

"Maybe the fuzz'll take you somewhere for R and R."

"Very funny." C. K. Mackenzie, aforementioned fuzz and one of the issues that made my brain itch, was a part of the problem, not its solution. One of the bits of wisdom I would have appreciated from those rolling waves concerned matters of my rapidly hardening heart. I know it's au courant to love the process and not the goal. And even a more old-fashioned philosopher, Kahlil Gibran, had long ago urged that there be spaces in a man and woman's togetherness. As I recall, the winds of heaven were supposed to dance between them.

But Kahlil never deigned to measure those spaces, and in my case, they sometimes felt larger than an airplane hangar, the better to let the winds of heaven howl. Much as I have enjoyed our spaces and our togetherness, much as I have focused on the process of being with Mackenzie for the past year—when his detecting duties didn't interrupt, disrupt, and postpone that process—I would have also enjoyed the prospect of closure. Smaller spaces.

I don't like dangling threads and unfinished stories. I am comforted knowing that a suspenseful novel will have a resolution. Why should I ask less of my own life?

Except, to really make matters impossible, I didn't know what variety of closure I wanted. Maybe the cavernous spaces between us were my best option—or even my choice. My call. Thinking of that, admitting that, brought back the now-familiar agitated dread.

Three steps away from where we sat, a mother who looked almost as frayed as I felt shouted at a squatty kid in a hat with earflaps. "Stop eating! You'll ruin your dinner!" she shrieked. "I said no more snacks! I said it over and over!"

Whatever the kid snuffled back was obscured by the bus on the corner, which emitted a flatulent sound and matching stench as it pulled away.

I willed myself away to a beach, and allowed myself to hear only the wonderful white noise of the waves. And Sasha.

"Your parents would send you a plane ticket," she said.

"You have to be kidding. Don't I look sufficiently stressed out?" Granted, Boca Raton had a fine Floridian beach—but all the same, time with my parents could not by any stretch of the imagination be equated with a rest. Since I'd turned thrity-one, my mother's horror at my unmarried state had escalated beyond direct speech, as if singleness were the dirtiest or most classified of secrets. She used to worry about my sex life—mostly she worried that I managed to have one. Now, the euphemism for unmarried was *financial security*. She mailed clippings about long-term investments and, much more depressingly, about trophy wives. Nothing subtle about her message. My mission was to snag a doddering millionaire and live securely ever after.

The horrible truth was that every so often—as today, lost in my unattainable beach fantasies and not at all entranced with the teacherly lifestyle of making do—the idea didn't sound half bad. Well, maybe not quarter bad. Although where in my daily rounds I was supposed to meet the tycoon instead of his adolescent great-grandson, I didn't know.

"So maybe you don't really want a beach," Sasha said.

"Not enough to put up with my mother's nagging. I'm thinking of installing voice mail to save her breath and long-distance charges. You know, 'Press one to nag about my economic security. Press two to remind me that I haven't yet produced grandchildren.' You're lucky your parents let you lead your own life."

"They're afraid I *will* get married. Again. That I'll be like them." Sasha's parents had been in the divorce avant-garde. Long before it was commonplace, they split, reassembled, remarried, and redivorced unto the point of utter confusion—theirs and everyone who knew them. An inability to choose wisely or maintain relationships seemed a genetic inheritance. Sasha herself had already had two kamikaze hitchings, and her quality control, when it came to men, hadn't improved appreciably since. "Every time I mention a man, they shudder. I told my mother about this fellow I'm going to see tomorrow—" She stopped short. "That's it! Cinderella Pepper, you're looking at your fairy godmother!"

I would have thought fairy godmothers were more petite. Six feet tall, with wild black hair, wearing multicolored layers of gauze and high-topped sneakers, Sasha didn't fit the storybook image, but I listened.

"You have just won yourself an almost all-expenses paid trip to the edge of an authentic, genuine ocean! Sand included free of charge."

"How?"

"I have a seaside shoot complete with room and meals. What's the diff if I share my room with you? All you'll have to spring for is what you eat, and you'd have to do that here, too."

254

"Are you serious?" A genuine getaway, a beach vacation for free? The seabirds struck up the chorus in my head again.

"What are friends for?"

Sasha might bemoan the lack of a regular salary or a predictable income, but she did get to take her photographs in exotic locales now and then. I thought about shoots on the Mediterranean, or the Caribbean, or even the cold waters off Maine. Anywhere would be splendid. I'd pay for the plane tickets somehow.

The boy in the earflaps had snagged a bag of chips, and his mother, face red and puffed, shouted, "Not more *snacks*! What did I tell you? They're *bad* for you!" She grabbed the bag from the boy and pushed a handful of chips into her own mouth. Talk about mixed messages, no wonder the kid covered his ears. By the time he'd wind up in my classroom in a few years, those leather sound barriers would have become internalized and unremovable. And I'd be expected to teach him something.

Sasha ate the last of the biscotti. I couldn't protest or complain, given that she was offering a vacation in exchange.

An imagined sun warmed my head—but I willingly accepted a bleak beach as well. Deserted and overcast, heavy with clouds or fog—it sounded wonderful. The silence, the waves, the chance to think and breath deeply . . . bliss. "Thank you," I said. "I gratefully accept."

"Thank the saltwater taffy consortium."

"Saltwater taffy? Where is this job?"

"Where else?"

Atlantic City. Of all the beaches in all the world. My good fairy had arrived with a whole lot of small print. Sand and water, yes, but Atlantic City! Casinos and slums and junk food and all-night lights and noise. More high rollers than breakers. More pigeons than sea gulls. Not the point at all.

"Atlantic City is America's Number One Vacation Destination," Sasha said. "Pure adventure, one hour away. Would you honestly rather clean closets? And by the way, my car's acting weird. I don't need it—I hired an assistant in A.C. and she's renting all the equipment there. So could you drive?"

AND THAT'S WHY ON MONDAY MORNING, WHILE IN search of the soothing touch of nature, I instead wound up parking my Mustang in a labyrinth below several stories of steel, concrete, and glitz.

Sasha and I walked through a lobby done in Eclectic Excess, a potpourri of design history. Greek columns separated Renaissance-style murals beside equatorial waterfalls near an Ozlike yellow-brick walkway. Everything was highlighted with tiny white lights. Our bellman's outfit was Mittel European Operetta. A neo-something marble statue in a toga pointed the way to the registration area. I tried in vain to find a theme, a connecting thread—aside from blatant expensiveness.

Outside, the sky had been tight and sallow, but now we were hermetically sealed in eternal, nuclear day lit by a thousand suns. The eye-tearing indoor season had nothing to do with the existence of the clock or the solar system.

"Why a casino, Sash? Atlantic City has normal hotels. Why'd the saltwater people put you here?"

"I asked them to. I thought I'd be alone, and a place like this is more alive. No matter what hour. I was

256

here once . . . " We passed the entrance to a cavelike side room called the Hideaway. Sasha dropped her suitcase, said, "Just a sec," and ducked in.

I was close to the casino entrance. I waited for Sasha, listening to the siren sounds of silvery music and money.

"He's still working here," she said when she returned a minute or so later. "The bartender, Frankie. One of the good guys."

Which probably meant she had no interest in him. It's women like Sasha who—unintentionally but just as lethally—make men think they have to be rotten with the rest of us. Nice guys do not finish last with me—unless you're being semantically sloppy and equating *nice* with bland or dull. But Sasha's different. Her dials are set for challenge, which often translates into danger or misery.

However, at this point in our long friendship, I was trying not to editorialize about Sasha's fondness for losers. As she was overly fond of pointing out, my own off-again, on-again relationship with the detective was no shining example of brilliant selection.

"I was here before," she now said. "Couple of years ago."

"With Frankie the bartender?"

"No, no. This other guy. Dimples. A genuine louse. Frankie the bartender saved the day, and maybe me—from jail. I didn't think he'd still be here."

"From jail? Why? Or do I want to know?"

"Because Dimples was a little bit of a criminal, and the police thought I was his accomplice." She laughed at the thought. I found it less humorous.

We had reached our destination, the registration

257

desk, decorated in the style of medieval French palaces. I wondered which era, theme, and climatological zone our room would feature. Art Deco Romanesque? Tropical French? Greek Chalet?

It turned out to be Basic Brothel. The room was small, its walls covered with silver foil. The bedspread, drapes, and carpeting were as silvery as fabric can get, shot through with metallic threads. Where there wasn't foil or silver cloth, there were mirrors. Including the ceiling. Cigarettes still sealed in their foil-lined boxes must feel the way I did.

"A money motif, do you think?" Sasha asked.

"I'd prefer the greenbacks room, then."

"The room I had with Dimples was nothing like this. But then, we had an ocean view."

We viewed neither ocean nor bay. Instead, we faced the rooftops and fire escapes of yellow-brick buildings that clashed with our color scheme. I closed the drapes. "I'll take the right-hand drawers, right side of the closet."

Sasha nodded, but before either of us began to unpack, our phone rang and she picked it up. "Sasha *Berg*," she said midway through the conversation. "The photographer. Are you talking to the right person?" And: "The saltwater taffy association isn't going to pay for any—" Then she just listened.

She hung up. "They're moving us to a suite." She sounded bemused. "No extra charge. I thought they only did that for really high rollers."

"It isn't possible that this upgrade is in honor of the guy you were here with, is it? The criminal? That maybe they think you're still involved with him?"

"They didn't comp him a suite then, so why now,
258

when he's dead? And it's not like they don't know. It was in all the papers."

"Tell me the man died of natural causes. Please."

"The man died of natural causes."

I sighed with relief.

"After all," Sasha continued, "it's pretty natural to die when there's a bullet in the back of your skull."

I've often wondered why Sasha's incredible bad luck with men doesn't deter or sour her—or leave her with the sightest trace of post-traumatic shock. She's no dummy or masochist. Maybe it's because she has so much fun until each adventure sours. Maybe she's the world's last great optimist.

"We're not supposed to look a gift horse in the mouth," she now said.

I hoped that neither the horse nor his teeth nor the walls were capped in silver. One ounce more and I'd start mining it.

THE SUITE WAS EXQUISITE, LEAVING ME WONDERING. Were nickel-and-dime gamblers mirrored-ceiling types, while the major players—a group I wouldn't expect to be particularly elegant—connoisseurs of all that was fine?

The living and bedrooms were decorated with Asian tansu chests, porcelain, jade carvings, Chinese rugs in soft pastels, and cushiony contemporary furniture. Shoji screens covered the windows. A six-paneled gilded screen filled the wall behind two oversized beds.

"A Jacuzzi!" Sasha called from the bathroom. "What a shame to be here with *you*!"

Understated and quiet, the rooms were the antithesis of the world downstairs. Things were definitely looking up. This in itself could be my retreat. I unpacked in record time, like a creature nervously establishing her turf.

Sasha dawdled. She arranged her cameras and equipment. She switched to another pocketbook and slowly decided what she'd need. She emptied half her suitcase onto the bed, then worried over the condition of her travel kit. She decided her nails needed polishing and wondered whether she could include a manicure on her expense account. "Did I tell you I'm going out tonight?" she asked.

I didn't mind. This was a place in which to vacate, to luxuriate. This was a style to which I wanted to become accustomed.

I had a four-day vacation and a choice of three books. *War and Peace*, which has been on every summer reading list of my life, because every autumn has arrived without my having read it. *Gift from the Sea*, one of my all-time favorites. And a threadbare paperback with negative literary value and a title like *Lust and Sleaze*. A student had left it behind when she galloped off to summer vacation. Of course, I was reading it purely as research into adolescent interests. But all the same, it might go well with a Jacuzzi.

"I met this guy three weeks ago, when I was down here. At Trump's, the bar in Trump Plaza. We made a date for when I'd be back on this job. If he remembers, and I hope so. He reminds me of Cary Grant."

In what way, I didn't dare ask. More dimpled chins? An English accent? A face to die for? A gift for comedy—or, more likely, a lot of wives?

"He's elegant. Continental. A gentleman." She examined her hand, first with fingers curled toward her, then held straight, nails up. "But not stuffy, the way that might sound." She stood and tossed the nail file back onto the bed.

She pushed back the shoji screens for a view of a chilly—but inviting-looking—beach and ocean, sighed, and looked likely to stay a while.

I suddenly found the room and the situation less comforting. It was too peaceful, too deliberately serene, too incomprehensible and overrich a setting for the facts of my life.

What am I doing? I don't belong here. This is wrong.

This Asian palace was no place to figure things out. Which I felt incapable of doing, anyway.

What am I doing? What am I going to do?

The angst itch began between my shoulder blades and rose through my spinal column into my brain. At such times, it's hard to sit still and impossible to endure Sasha's glacially slow progress. "How about I meet you somewhere later?" I asked. "Downstairs. Maybe in that bar we passed? I have to . . . I have to move around."

"Going up to the health club?"

"No. The beach, I think. See you." I pulled on a sweater and headed out.

In the living room of the suite there was an odd woodcut. A mythical beast, mostly equine, but rearing on thick bird legs. It had thick-lashed almond eyes that seemed to ask me directly, *Do you have any idea what you're doing?* and its mouth was open wide, revealing not horse teeth, but long and lethal fangs.

I looked at that mouth, those fangs. "Tell me you're not the gift horse," I whispered.